Coastal Lights Legacy – Book Four

REKINDLED LIGHT

Marilyn Turk

Marilyn Turk

Published by Forget Me Not Romances, an imprint of Winged Publications

ISBN-13: 978-1-947523-27-2
ISBN-10: 1-947523-27-9

Acknowledgements

Researching the history of an area can be especially difficult when the landscape has changed. Due to two major fires and at least one hurricane, Pensacola records from 1869 are scarce.

I'd like to thank Jacqueline Wilson, archivist of the University of West Florida Historic Trust, as well as Ross Pristera, historic preservationist of the trust, for all their help. Their information about travel between the fort and the town, the Old Christ Church and the Barkley House, (the house Sarah's house was modeled after), was instrumental to make the story realistic. I'd also like to thank Jess Morgan, curator of the Pensacola Lighthouse for her help with the lighthouse history. In addition, I'd like to thank the National Parks Service for their excellent care of the Fort Barrancas Historic Site.

Thanks to preservationists such as the above, some historic sites have been restored and can be visited today.

I'd especially like to thank my husband Chuck for being my research assistant, my military advisor, my cheerleader, who supports me and travels with me both physically and mentally to the places in my stories.

Above all, I thank God for giving me the stories to write and introducing me to people I never knew before he put them in my head.

"Be strong and take heart, all you who hope in the LORD." Psalm 31:24

Chapter One

Pensacola, Florida, 1869

"Are we there yet?" Five-year-old Anna Grace Turner stood in the rear of the wagon holding onto the back of the seat and scanning her surroundings.

Sarah smiled at her little sister whose honey-colored ringlets bounced in step with the horses' hooves. This wasn't the first time Anna Grace had asked the question, the one Sarah wanted to ask too. When *would* they reach Pensacola? She was even more eager than her sister to get there but didn't let on. Surely, she'd recognize a familiar landmark, even though she'd been gone seven years. Sarah surveyed the area, looking for telltale signs they were getting closer, but so far the only hint was how the road changed from dirt to hard-packed sand as they'd made their way south, a sure indication they were nearing the coast.

"Almost," Father said, holding the reins of the horses and focusing ahead. "Just over the next rise."

They were that close to her former home? Sarah straightened her back to sit up taller hoping to get a glimpse. Her stomach fluttered in anticipation, and she gripped her skirt. Soon, she could point out the places she knew to Anna Grace. Her sister had never lived in Pensacola, having been born while they waited out the war in Alabama. Anna Grace had no idea what Pensacola looked like. She didn't even know what life was like living on the coast. In fact, all she knew about the place was what Sarah had told her about the town and the home by the bay.

Sarah adjusted her bonnet to shade her eyes, watching for the town to come into view. But as they reached the crest of the hill, her heart sank. Where was she? The scene spread out before her was not the neatly laid-out town she remembered, with rows of houses and businesses lining the street. In this strange place, houses appeared to be built at random with empty gaps between them. This couldn't be Pensacola. Unless the years of being gone had clouded her memory of what it was actually like.

"Father, what town is this?" She studied his face for an answer.

He halted the horses and faced her. "Sarah, this is Pensacola. I'm sure it looks quite different from the way you remember."

She nodded, unable to comprehend. Ever since they left town when she was sixteen years old, she'd pictured Pensacola the way it was the last time she saw it. She'd dreamed of the day she'd return and find everything just as she remembered. They'd come back home, and life would resume the way it had been before. But the scene that stretched before her was nothing like her vision. And the cold shock of reality hit her that life would not be the same either.

"I know it's a surprise to you, but it looks a lot better than it did when I came back two years ago." Father shook his head. "It truly was a sore sight back then, what with so many buildings burned and destroyed. But a lot has been rebuilt now, including our mill and our pier."

Mother, sitting on the other side of Sarah, patted her hand. "Your father has worked hard to get things ready for us. Be thankful we can live in our same house again. Many of our friends aren't able to do so."

"Yes, thank God our home wasn't one of those burned." Father frowned. "It did have some damage, though, from unwelcome guests who took advantage of our absence." Father muttered "unwelcome guests," his name for the Union soldiers who had occupied the town, who still did, in fact.

"Where is our house? Can we go there now?" Anna Grace whined. "I need to use the privy."

Father clucked his tongue and the horses resumed their trek.

"Hold on, Anna Grace. We'll be home soon, and you can use our new outhouse."

"I'll try," she said.

"Why don't you sit down until we get there?" Mother said, looking over her shoulder.

"But I can't see anything if I sit down." She waved behind them where Uncle Harold and Aunt Betty rode in another wagon piled with household goods. "We're in Pensercoa!" she called out.

Sarah scanned the buildings looking for familiar ones as they entered the town. Where was Stafford's Mercantile? Wasn't it supposed to be over there? She looked from side to side. Where was the Watkins' house? She eyed an empty, dilapidated structure on the corner.

"Was that Klout's Bakery?" She pointed to the abandoned shop.

"Yes, used to be," Father said. "The Klouts haven't come back."

"Will they?" Sarah asked.

"I don't know. Not sure where they went."

"They used to make delicious bread," Mother said.

"And sweet pastries too," Father added.

A couple of blocks ahead rose a whitewashed building, about three stories high. "Is that the Customs' Building?" Sarah asked.

"Yes, it is. You see, you do recognize something. It's one of the few businesses that survived." The road led downhill to the intersection near the Customs' House, where they turned east, going down a broad street that Sarah remembered as Government Street. At the second intersection, Father, pointed down the crossing street. "If you follow this street and cross Main Street, you'll be on the road that runs out between the docks where my warehouse is. It's a two-story brick building on the right. My town office is there."

Sarah shook her head at the strange landscape of old and new buildings. The contrast between the two created an unsettling combination. As they entered a more residential area, she silently counted the number of houses, arriving at the conclusion that there were only half as many as had been there previously. Where were all the people that had lived there before? Many like her own family had headed for Alabama when the Confederate troops left town, but would they all come back?

"Look!" Mother pointed. "There's the steeple of Christ Church."

Sarah glanced to her right and breathed a sigh of relief to see the white spire rising above the trees. "That's one sight I'm happy to see. Was it damaged?"

Father pursed his lips and gritted a reply. "Not terribly, however, our unwelcome guests did not honor the church as they should have. Seems they used it for a hospital as well as a prison."

Sarah gasped, and her mother's eyes widened as her hand covered her heart. "The church?" Mother asked. "Why on earth would they do such a thing?"

Father shook his head. "People's actions can be hard to understand. Surely, some of those men knew better than to desecrate a church." He faced them. "But the good thing is, they only stayed in town a short while before they moved to Fort Barrancas."

The church faced a public green that had existed since the time of Spanish rule and had always been one of Sarah's favorite places. "Seville Square isn't as pretty as I remember it. It's not green anymore." She looked over her shoulder at her sister. "Anna Grace, we used to play there and have picnics."

"There?" Anna Grace pointed.

"Yes." Father nodded. "But years of horses' hooves and soldiers' camping out has taken its toll on the grass. But it'll come back eventually. Thank God, some of the oak trees survived the fires and all the mistreatment." Father turned the horses at the corner. "Things aren't the same as before, that's for sure. But we're definitely making progress rebuilding our town, slowly but surely."

A cool, tropical breeze blew across the square, drawing Sarah's attention to her right, where a short distance away, she glimpsed the water in the bay. Her pulse quickened, knowing she'd soon see her home. Would it still look as she remembered, or had it changed too? She lifted her chin and inhaled the refreshing salt air. How she had missed it.

Father paused at the next intersection and nodded to his left. "This is Alcaniz Street. Down the block there is Quinn's Apothecary. Remember it?"

Sarah nodded, remembering the little drug store beside the owner's house. "Is the doctor still here?"

"Yes, Dr. Quinn and his family returned a while back. Good to have our doctor back in town."

Thank God, she spoke under her breath. "Anna Grace, we're almost home," Sarah said to her sister. "Just a little while longer."

"Where?" Anna Grace twisted her head from one side to the other, eyes wide with excitement.

"One more block," Father said, looking at Sarah. "Once we get settled, we'll have Eben over for dinner, so you can get to know him."

Sarah glanced at her father, then her mother. Why did he want her to meet the man that managed the mill?

The horses must've slowed their gait, because it took far too long to reach the end of the block where the scattered row of houses ended, and the landscape opened up to reveal the broad expanse of the bay. Sure enough, there it stood. Her home, the large white house that sat prominently on an oversized city lot was still there, just as she'd remembered it. With its location directly facing the water, the raised home with its wide front porch beckoned Sarah to return. Sarah's spirit lifted seeing the familiar sight, and her hope was rekindled that her former life might be possible.

Father pulled the wagon up to the back of the house as Uncle Harold followed with the other wagon, drawing alongside Father's wagon.

"I have a surprise for you, Virginia," Father said as he climbed out and helped Mother from the wagon.

"You do? What, pray tell?" Mother glanced around, searching.

After he assisted Sarah from the wagon, Father went to unhitch the horses.

"You'll see soon enough," he said with a subtle grin.

Sarah reached over the side to lift Anna Grace out of the back. What sort of surprise did Father have?

A woman's voice called out from the second-floor porch of the smaller raised building beside the main house. "It's 'bout time y'all got here. I'see been waitin' all day!"

A plump Negro woman wearing a white apron over her plain cotton dress stood on the steps with her hands on her hips. She wore a red turban wrapped around hair whose gray strands peeked out.

"Della!" Mother cried out, hurrying to meet the woman coming down the steps. "I've missed you so! I never expected to see you again."

Sarah's heart leaped in recognition of their former cook, and she, too, ran over to hug the woman. "Della! I'm so happy to see you!"

Della held her at arms' length and studied her. "Who is this fine young lady? Can't be my Sarah! Lawd, chile, you has turned out so fine."

"Della, I thought…" Mother began.

"I knows, I knows. When we be free, we left. But I don't mind workin', and Mr. Charles, he don't mind payin' me, so we're doin' just fine, and both of us got food on the table!" She looked toward the barn where a Negro man waved. "Doc's here too."

"Sissie?"

Sarah spun to see Anna Grace limping her way toward them. Sarah hurried to take her sister's hand and help her over. "Della, meet my little sister, Anna Grace."

Della leaned down and gave Anna Grace a big hug. "Ain't you a pretty little thing?" Glancing at Mother, she said, "Miz Virginia, she looks just like you when you was little."

Sarah jerked her head toward her mother. She'd never heard that before. Surely Mother was aware, but Sarah had never seen any pictures of her mother as a child, so she didn't know. Mother's smile was barely there, as if she'd been keeping a secret all this time. But any smile from Mother was a welcome sight and not a common one.

"How old is you, Miss Anna Grace? Four?"

"I'm five!" Anna Grace said proudly, holding up five fingers.

"Well, I never." Straightening, Della said, "I'see got some chicken n dumplins, greens and cornbread for you all when you ready to eat."

Sarah's stomach growled her response.

"Sounds delicious," Mother said. "I know we're all hungry after such a long journey."

"Yes, ma'am, and I know that's your favorite, so I wanted to welcome you home right."

"Thank you so much, Della," Mother said. "We'll be ready to eat as soon as we get everything unloaded."

"Sissie, I've got to go!" Anna Grace crossed her legs to avoid an accident.

"Oh, I'm sorry, I forgot."

Spotting the tiny frame building at the rear of the property, Sarah said, "There's the privy."

She took Anna Grace's tiny hand and headed toward the little white clapboard building that matched the main house. The men led the horses to the barn, while Mother and Aunt Betty began taking things out of the wagons. Sarah glanced over at the Pensacola Bay where her old friend, the water, greeted her with gentle waves and sparkling water. She could hardly wait to sit on the veranda and count the boats that passed by, just as she'd done when she was a child. Perhaps Anna Grace would enjoy counting the boats with her. Her little sister was learning her numbers quickly, a sign that she shared Sarah's love for figures. Would there be as many boats to count now as there had been before the war?

Anna Grace stumbled, and Sarah gripped her hand more tightly to keep her from falling, casting a look of concern at her sister. "Be careful," she said as she'd repeated many times before. Her little sister's weak leg often caused her to fall.

"I try, Sissie." Anna Grace gave Sarah an apologetic pout.

"I know you do," Sarah said to her sister who did try very hard to walk normally like other people did. But sometimes intentions were eclipsed by limitations.

When Anna Grace was finished at the privy, she spotted the bay, apparently noticing it for the first time.

"Sissie! Look at all the water! Just like you told me! Can we go see it?"

"Of course, we can. Let's go." The two made their way across the expansive lawn to the front of the yard where the road ran between the house and the bay. "You'll get to see it every day now."

Anna Grace looked up at Sarah, her eyes wide with awe. "It's so big. Is this the ocean?"

"Well, not quite. It's a bay, which is much smaller than an ocean."

The two stood together, taking in the sight, their heads following boats that passed. Sarah pointed toward town to one of the wharves where several ships were tied up. "I think that very long pier over there is Father's. See the boats beside it? They either brought things to Pensacola to unload or are going to be loaded with things to take away to other places."

"Can we go over there sometime and watch?"

"I'll ask Father. Maybe he'll allow us to if we promise not to get in the way." Sarah scanned the waterfront, seeing more docks toward town, most which appeared to be newly-built. Tall masts lined every dock as far as she could see, just as they had been before they left seven years ago. She sighed as the ache in her heart returned. So many things about her former life looked the same, but one thing, the most important thing, or person, was missing.

Her gaze traveled to the people standing near one of the docks and her breath caught. Two men in Union uniforms stood watching the boats unload. She studied the men, looking for familiar characteristics, then realized what she was doing—looking for Josiah. Why did she think he might still be in Pensacola? He could be anywhere now, especially since the war sent him elsewhere. Her eyes misted as she remembered the last time she'd seen him, the day her father had sent him away, calling him a traitor.

Why did she continue to hope to see him again? He had probably forgotten all about her, perhaps even married. But if it hadn't been for the war, she and Josiah would be husband and wife now. Her heart squeezed, and she wiped her eyes. How could she keep from thinking of him every time she saw another soldier? She gave a start. What if he had been killed in the war? How would she know unless his parents still lived in town?

She glanced around, feeling she was being watched, but saw no one looking her way. No one waited and watched for her anymore. Even though some things were the same as before, her life never would be.

Chapter Two

Josiah disembarked from the steamship that ran between town and Fort Barrancas, then headed down the dock. When he reached the main street, he paused to take in the area, and drew a deep breath. Pensacola looked so different than the last time he'd been there. He shouldn't be surprised, though, because everything else had changed since he'd left to join the Union side. When war was declared, friends and neighbors were suddenly enemies on opposing sides. As a West Point cadet, he'd considered no other choice but to support the Union, even though some of his classmates had chosen the Confederate side.

But for some reason, he'd expected his hometown to be the same as he'd left it. How foolish of him to entertain such expectations. He proceeded down the street and could tell by the way people looked at him whether they'd been on the side of the North or the South. Still wearing his dark-blue uniform, he presented his side clearly. But he wasn't here to fight, nor was he here to maintain order as the occupying troops were. As a civil engineer with the US Army, he was here to help get the Pensacola lighthouse back in good working order and supervise the building of the new keepers' house.

However one of his first assignments was to find the first order Fresnel lens that had been in the lighthouse before the Confederates removed and hid it. How they managed to do that was no small feat. Chances were slim the lens was still intact and not broken into pieces, but if it was still together, the government would be spared the cost of buying a new one from France and having it shipped over. In the meantime, the lighthouse was operating with a replacement lens, a smaller one that didn't have the range as that of the larger, first order lens. Where on earth they hid that huge lens was a mystery, but he'd heard about someone in the area who might have information about it. If he could find the person. And if they'd be willing to share that information with him.

Josiah took in his surroundings, trying to identify places he knew from growing up in Pensacola. Charred ruins lay scattered throughout, victims of the Confederates' goal to destroy what they left behind so the approaching Union troops would not enjoy the fruit of their victory. Thankfully, new homes and businesses had cropped up in a few places where others had been. Had his own family home survived the destruction? He had to find out. Not that they would ever return to it. Bitter memories remained after his parents were forced to move north when animosities between them and their fellow townspeople became too difficult to bear. His father and mother had returned to the place of their ancestors in Pennsylvania and had no plans to come back south.

Josiah sought familiar landmarks to guide him, hoping his memory served him right. He traveled a block, then he turned down another street and went two more blocks, finding his way through town until he finally spotted the place where he had once lived. His heart was heavy as he stopped in front of the empty two-story shell of a house that looked like a hollowed-out pumpkin. Thank God, Mother and Father couldn't see the house now in its pitiful state. They'd be dismayed to see the condition of the once-impressive home they'd kept so well-maintained for years. Perhaps it could be restored, but who would care enough to bring the house back to its former charm?

Would he ever want to live in it again? Alone? He shook his head. The home was too large for one person. And he didn't even know how long he would be stationed in Pensacola. Besides, the army provided him a decent house at Fort Barrancas. After moving around so much the last few years, he wasn't sure where home really was anymore.

Before the war, he had planned to marry Sarah Turner and settle down here, but her father put an end to that dream. How his arms had ached to hold her ever since they were forced to separate and end their plans. He could still remember the hurt mixed with love in her soft brown eyes, the tears that had fallen when they said goodbye. Even after he'd reported to his regiment, he had sent her letters, hoping she'd get them, to know he still loved her. When a friend told him her family had moved to a cousin's home in Alabama, he'd sent his letters there for over a year. But he never heard back from her. He didn't know if she'd received the letters or had given up any shred of hope for their future.

Where was she now? Had she married? He wouldn't be surprised. In the years that had passed, another man had more than likely won her affection and claimed her for his wife. Yet the emptiness in Josiah's heart still yearned to see her again, if even from a distance, just to know she was well and that whoever her husband was, took good care of her. He turned away from his old house and headed back to the waterfront, making a wide circle from where he'd started. He had some business to take care of while he was in town, but first, he couldn't resist the urge to go by her former home. What kind of condition was it in? Had it also been destroyed or damaged as his had?

When he reached the end of the intersection with Main Street, the harbor facing him, he turned in the direction of her home. There at the end of the block was the house, still standing just as it always had. A fresh coat of paint and a new fence around it told him someone lived there. Could it be her family or someone else? Just as he reached the corner where the Turner property used to begin, a woman and a little girl came around the house, walking toward the bay.

His heart skipped a beat. It was Sarah. She was as beautiful as ever, her long brown hair escaping from the bonnet she wore and flowing behind her in the breeze. He backed away and stood in the shadow of a tree to keep from being seen. The little girl walked with a limp, and Sarah held her hand. Was this Sarah's daughter? No doubt it was. So, his suspicions were true. She'd married since he last saw her. Why had he hoped there was still a chance for them? Reason told him there wouldn't be, but his heart still longed for the only woman he'd ever loved.

He glanced toward the house, hoping to catch a glimpse of her husband. Two men carried items up the front porch steps and into the house, and Josiah recognized one as Sarah's father. Surely the other man wasn't her husband. He looked a lot like Mr. Turner and about the same age. When Mrs. Turner came out onto the porch with another woman, Josiah figured she must be with the other man and he hadn't seen Sarah's husband yet. Wonder where he was? Mrs. Turner still wore black, reminding him of the death of her two young sons to yellow fever when the disease swept through town before the war. Either she was still in mourning, or she'd lost someone recently. But who?

The four older adults stood on the elevated porch carrying on a conversation as they gazed out at the bay. Mr. Turner leaned against the railing and pointed to the pier near their property, the one that Josiah remembered as belonging to Turner Companies. Josiah backed even further out of sight. He wasn't up to a confrontation with Mr. Turner again, not now. At present, Josiah only wanted to look at Sarah. He'd waited so long to see her again, to talk to her, possibly embrace her. But it was too late. She had a new life. And he needed to accept that fact and get on with his.

"Fire!" Voices rang out behind him.

Josiah turned back toward town. Flames and black smoke raged from a building down the street. He ran as fast as he could and arrived at the scene of a small building engulfed in fire. Two lines of people had formed from the building stretching across the street and out to the bay. Buckets of water were being passed quickly down to the last man who tossed it onto the fire. Shouts rang out. "Over here!"

Josiah hurried to join the water brigade while bystanders gathered in the street to watch. As he passed a bucket of water along, he eyed the surrounding buildings, then cast a glance at the overcast sky. Thanks to last night's rain and the separation between the building and its neighbor, the fire didn't spread. But what if it had been dry and windy? Most of the town was built of wood, and it wouldn't be hard for fire to jump from one building to another. Thank goodness this one hadn't yet.

For over an hour, men worked to pass buckets as fast as possible to extinguish the flames. Was there no fire department to handle these situations? Surely, the town needed one. Josiah's arms ached when the fire was finally extinguished and only the smoldering ruins remained. He shook hands with the men on either side of him, one a Negro and the other a tall, pale fellow.

The latter didn't seem too interested in shaking hands, but indulged, then turned away quickly afterward. No doubt he was a former Confederate still bitter toward the federal government and resented the soldiers still in town. When would they accept the fact that even though they had been on opposite sides during the war, they were fellow citizens now, working together to save the town? Josiah straightened his jacket and wondered if he looked as sweaty and disheveled as the others around him who had participated in the brigade.

"Josiah Hamilton." He introduced himself to the Negro man. Josiah motioned to the burned building. "What place was this?"

"Hosea Jones," the man replied. "Nice to meet you. This was Mr. Crawford's office. He owns the Crawford sawmill. That's Mr. Crawford over there." Mr. Jones motioned to a soot-covered man beside the charred rubble shaking his head as he surveyed the damage.

Crawford? That was one of the sawmills he was going to speak to about providing lumber for the construction projects he supervised.

"Any idea how the fire got started?"

"No, suh. Somebody smokin' a pipe or sumthin'?"

"I hardly think pipe ash would start a fire, especially in these damp conditions."

Jones shrugged. "Whatever started it don't matter, I guess. The building is pretty much gone."

Josiah nodded. Mr. Crawford's office was a total loss. Would the man be able to resume his business any time soon? Even though this was only an office, the man more than likely kept important records and perhaps even money stored in the building. Mr. Crawford was fortunate that the sawmill was located elsewhere, or no doubt it would've caught fire too. Sawmills could be prime tinder for fires, quickly growing out of control.

Across the street, a young woman caught his attention. She glanced at him and offered a shy smile as she turned to another young woman and said something that made both of them giggle. Josiah straightened his shoulders, feeling his ears warm from the attention. Had he seen her before? He'd met the other officers' wives, so she obviously wasn't one of them.

He looked away lest the women thought him staring. Sarah's father and the other man he'd seen at the Turner house stood off to the side. They were speaking with the unfriendly man who had been next to him in the bucket line. The three were engrossed in conversation, while each one stole glances over at the burned-out building. Josiah turned his back to the group. Had Mr. Turner recognize Josiah as well? Or did the man simply see another blue uniform?

~~~

When Father and Uncle Harold came back to the house, a third man accompanied them. Sarah restrained herself from running up to Father and peppering him with questions after she saw the stranger. Who was he? She didn't think she'd ever seen him before. He was tall and thin and walked with his shoulders stooped, reminding her of one of the blue herons that she and Anna Grace had seen strolling along the water's edge. His face was similar as well, with a pointed nose and an unsmiling face. Although he didn't appear to be as old as Father, his mannerisms were more like an old man than a young one.

She and Anna Grace had waited on the front porch with her mother and aunt, eager to find out what had happened ever since Father and Uncle Harold raced off to the fire. Aunt Betty called out to the men as they crossed the lawn below.

"What's on fire?"

The men looked up at the porch. "Fire's under control," Uncle Harold responded.

The men climbed the steps and reaching the top, Father said, "Look who I ran into downtown."

Mother offered a smile and a nod, looking as though she wasn't sure she recognized the man, but being polite, nonetheless.

"This is Eben, Eben White. You remember him, don't you?" Father turned toward Eben. "Eben, you know my wife Virginia."

Eben White removed his hat and bowed. "Mrs. Turner, you are looking well. It has been several years."

"It has," Mother said.

"And Eben, do you remember my daughter Sarah? She's grown up quite a bit since you last saw her." Father extended his
~~~

arm, motioning for Sarah to come closer. "Sarah, this is Mr. White. He runs the sawmill up in Milltown for me."

Eben bowed to Sarah, smiling with stained tobacco teeth. "You certainly have grown up, Miss Sarah."

Sarah forced a smile, but couldn't fight the discomfort than crept down her spine as the man surveyed her. "Nice to meet you, Mr. White."

"Oh, we've met before, but I guess you don't remember."

Sarah shook her head. "I'm afraid I don't." Anna Grace bumped against Sarah's skirt. "But I'm sure you haven't met my little sister, Anna Grace."

Anna Grace curtsied and smiled. "Nice to meet you, Mr. White."

Eben White stared at the little girl with no expression, then said to Father, "I forgot you said you had another child."

Mother paled at the comment, no doubt remembering the children she'd lost.

"Yes, Anna Grace was born since we left Pensacola."

Uncle Harold, who apparently had met Eben earlier that day, introduced Aunt Betty.

Father walked to the door and held it open. "Eben, you'll join us for dinner, won't you? Della has dinner prepared."

"Why if it's no imposition…" Eben hesitated to enter.

"No, no, I'm sure we have plenty. Besides, we have a lot to catch up on."

"Well, then thank you, Charles. I believe I will."

Eben started to walk through the door, but Father cleared his throat and Eben halted. "Ladies, we'll let you enter first."

Eben looked sheepish and backed away. "Yes, please, ladies." He waved his hand toward the door as if that was his plan all along. Clearly, the man was lacking in social graces.

Once everyone was inside, Father started a fire in the fireplace, taking the damp chill from the house. The tufted velvet sofa and arm chairs they'd brought back were already in their familiar places as they'd been years before. Even the hall tree and grandfather clock stood guard over the foyer as Sarah remembered. Only the pictures still leaned against the wall, waiting for Father to hang them.

"Come, lets everyone sit down." Father swept his arm toward

the dining room where a lace tablecloth-covered table waited, the family china set in front of each chair. It hadn't taken long for Mother and Aunt Betty to make the place look like home again.

"I'll tell Della we're ready to eat," Mother said and went out the side door toward the kitchen.

"Eben, you sit here." Father motioned to a chair beside him. "Sarah, you sit there on the other side of Eben."

Sarah frowned, but obeyed, pulling Anna Grace to sit beside her. When Mother returned, she sat at the opposite end of the table from Father, and Aunt Betty sat next to her, while Uncle Harold sat on Father's opposite side, leaving one seat open between him and Aunt Betty.

Della carried in a steaming tureen that smelled heavenly and placed it before Mother. Mother began ladling chicken and dumplings into bowls and passing them down. When Della's gaze landed on Eben, her eyes narrowed. She turned and left the room, returning in a few minutes with a big bowl of collard greens, then brought a tray of cornbread and a small crock of butter on her next trip. Was she avoiding eye contact with Eben, or was that Sarah's imagination? Maybe Sarah was letting her own feelings affect her observations, and Della wasn't intentionally avoiding Eben at all.

When everyone was served, Eben lifted his spoon to eat, but Father said, "Let's say grace." Eben dropped the spoon into his bowl making it splash onto the plate beneath it, then he lowered his head along with the rest of the people at the table.

"Thank you, Lord, for bringing our family together in our home again. We thank you for this bounty we are about to receive. Amen."

Eben picked up his spoon again and dove into his food. The man must be starving. Sarah turned toward Anna Grace. "Do you need any help buttering your biscuit?"

"I can do it by myself." Anna Grace picked up her cornbread and looked for the butter. Seeing it in front of Eben, she glanced at Sarah. "Can I have the butter please?"

"May I," said Mother, giving Anna Grace a stern look.

"May I?" Anna Grace peered up at Eben, waiting for a response.

Eben didn't seem to realize the butter was beside him, so Sarah also asked him to pass it. Before he did so, he grabbed his knife and dipped it into the crock, then buttered his own cornbread. He continued dipping into the crock again until he was satisfied he'd slathered enough onto his bread, as if no one else wanted butter. When he turned his attention to eating, Sarah reached for the butter and passed it to Anna Grace.

"So tell us, where was the fire? Was anyone hurt?" Aunt Betty asked.

"Someone's office burned down, but no one was hurt," Uncle Harvey said. "Whose office did you say it was?" He glanced at Father.

"John Crawford's office." Father said. "He owns the Crawford and Sons sawmill."

"Oh dear, was it lost?" Mother said.

"Yes, I'm afraid it was."

"Guess he'll have a hard time filling orders if they got burnt up," Eben said, his mouth full of cornbread.

"I'm not so sure about that, Eben." Father wiped his mouth with his napkin, then placed it back in his lap. "John has an excellent memory. I bet he can remember what orders he had, even without the documents. And hopefully, there's an office at his mill where orders are kept as well."

"Hmmph." Eben lifted his glass and took a swig of tea. "Well, it's a good thing the fire was in that block and not where ours is."

"Yes, we can be thankful for that."

"Charles, do you expect to gain more business from Mr. Crawford's accident?" Uncle Harold said as he reached for the bowl of greens again.

"Perhaps. But there are other mills. However, it might take Mr. Crawford some time to recoup his loss. His sons manage the mill for him."

Sarah glanced at mother, knowing how the reference to "sons" affected her. She and Father had had sons too, but now all they had was an unmarried daughter and a little girl who'd been a surprise at that time in their lives.

Father reached out and placed a hand on Eben's shoulder. "But I'm glad I have Eben here to manage our mill."

Sarah wanted to cringe. If only Father would allow her to learn more about the business. She could help with the mill too. But she wasn't a man.

"Father, I'd like to ride up to see the mill sometime," she said.

Father rubbed his chin, but Eben laughed. "The sawmill is no place for a lady," Eben said. "It can be dangerous."

Sarah gripped her skirt in frustration of Eben's remark. "But Father," she continued, ignoring Eben, "I shouldn't have anything to fear if I'm with you, should I? Remember when you took me there last? It's been years, and I want to see it again."

"Well, I guess there's no harm in your taking a little trip to see our mill," Father said. "I'll take you up there one day next week."

"Can I go too?" Anna Grace asked.

Eben guffawed. "No children are allowed."

"No, dear, you need to stay home," Father said, with a note of tenderness, noting the little girl's crestfallen face.

"Eben, do you live here in town?" Uncle Harold said.

"No sir, I live up near Milltown. I had to do some business in town today, though."

"Well, you won't be going back now after dark," Father said. "We can put you up in the guest room for the night."

Eben pushed back from the table and glanced at Sarah. "I would appreciate that, sir."

"Fine. You and Sarah will have more time to get acquainted."

Sarah gulped, the food in her stomach turning sour. The last thing she wanted to do was get more acquainted with Eben White. Why was Father so concerned about that?

Chapter Three

Josiah's horse plodded down the hard-packed sand street of Warrington, a town between Pensacola and Fort Barrancas. Built back in the 1820's, the town was mainly occupied by shipbuilders and dock workers and their families. Children played outside the modest houses as women hung their laundry on clotheslines strung between trees in their yards.

Rumor was that a woman in Warrington knew about the missing lighthouse lens, and he hoped to find her. In this area, his presence wasn't met with the wariness he encountered from the former residents of the city. Many of the people of Warrington were freed men and appreciated the military's presence.

So why would anyone from here aid the Confederates in stealing the lens? Josiah glanced at the crudely written note in his hand. *See Mabel Smith, house at end of street with broken gate.* Josiah glanced around, wondering if anyone thought it was unusual for him to be there. Two boys ran past him, playing chase, perhaps. What if he went to the wrong house? What if the resident had been a Confederate sympathizer?

A woman walked past holding a basket, heavy shawl wrapped tightly around her shoulders. He tipped his hat in greeting as she hurried on, giving him a brief glance. He hoped to appear friendly and non-threatening to promote cooperation. As he neared the end of the street, he saw the broken gate hanging ajar. This must be Mabel Smith's house. He sure hoped she was agreeable. He dismounted, tied his horse to the fence, then approached the small frame house with the sagging front porch.

As he lifted his arm to knock, the door creaked open slightly, and a young girl peered out.

"Excuse me, can you tell me where I can find Mabel Smith?"

The girl stared at him and Josiah wasn't sure she could hear. She wore a frock that hung on her thin body and her pale brown hair straggled around her face, escaping the long braid that ran down her spine. He opened his mouth to repeat himself.

"Granny! A soldier's here asking for you," she hollered over her shoulder.

A cough sounded before a scratchy voice answered from inside the house. "Let him in, Hazel."

Hazel stepped back, pulling the door open wide enough for Josiah to enter.

"Thank you." He nodded to the girl, then lifted his gaze to the woman across the room, seated in a rocking chair with a quilt drawn around her. There was no fire in the fireplace and the house was cold. He stepped forward, removing his cap.

"Mrs. Smith?"

"That's me." She pointed to a ladderback chair. "Sit down." He complied, holding his cap over his knee. The woman studied him. "And who might you be, son?"

"Josiah Hamilton, ma'am. I'm an engineer, and I'm here to get the lighthouse back up to its original condition."

"Hmph. I figured one of you would come someday."

The little girl curled up on the barren couch, tucking her feet under her and leaning against the back cushions, shivering.

He rubbed his hands together and glanced toward the empty fireplace. "Ma'am, may I start a fire for you?"

"You could, if I had any wood. We run out, but Hazel's going to go find us some sticks, aren't you girl?"

Hazel bobbed her head and shivered at the same time.

"If you need wood, I can get some for you." How long had they been without? Who was supporting these people?

"That'd be nice, but I don't have any money to pay you for it."

"Oh, don't worry about that. You won't have to pay me."

She raised her eyebrow. "Why not?"

He searched his mind for an answer that wouldn't make her feel obligated. "It's only me in my residence, and I have more than enough wood for myself—government issue, you know. I'd be happy to share it with you. In fact, my house hardly gets cold at all, so I don't even have a fire every day. And you know, here in Florida, it doesn't stay cold very long."

"Long enough."

"Yes, well, I'll bring some back as soon as I can get it."

"That's right nice of you, Mr. or is it Captain or something?"

"Lieutenant, ma'am." He pointed to the silver bar on his epaulet. "You said you expected one of "us" to come someday? Why is that?"

"Cause of what my boy done."

"Your boy?"

"Roy. Roy Smith." She pointed to the little girl. "Her pap."

Hazel drew her knees up to her face and wrapped her arms around them, resting her chin on top as she stared at the floor.

"Did Roy have something to do with the removal and disappearance of the lighthouse lens?"

Mabel nodded and rocked. "He did. He and a bunch of hooligans decided to take the light out of the lighthouse so you Union boys couldn't see where you were going."

"So your son was a soldier for the Confederates?"

"Yep. Joined up as soon as Florida declared its independence."

"Do you know where they put the lens?"

Mabel shook her head. "Nope, but I have my notions about it."

"And they are?"

Mabel started coughing and soon she couldn't stop. Josiah looked around for something to help. "Hazel, can you get your granny a cup of water?"

The child nodded and slid off the couch to grab a cup. Josiah followed her, and she pointed to the pump outside. He took the cup, hurried out and pumped until the cup was full, then carried it back in to Mabel Smith. The woman's eyes were runny, and she had sunk into the chair, weak from coughing, yet she still shook from each cough. Josiah held the cup to her lips and she sipped, then took it from him with her own hands and sipped some more. Finally, the coughing eased, and she nodded her appreciation.

Clearly, he would not be able to get any further information from her today. Right now, he needed to get some warmth in the house and into these two people as well.

"Mrs. Smith, I'm going to get the wood for your fireplace. Do you have anything to eat?"

She shook her head and choked out some words. "My neighbor's been bringing us some of what they have. I haven't been up to cooking much lately."

From the looks of the two of them, neither of them had eaten very much as well.

"I'll bring you some soup when I come back. Our cooks always make plenty for the soldiers, especially in this sort of weather."

"I'm much obliged," she whispered.

Josiah raised his hand to stop her from talking anymore. "If my mother was here, she'd bring it to you herself, but she's not."

Mrs. Smith lifted her eyebrows and choked out, "Sorry you lost your mama."

Realizing she misunderstood him, he said, "Oh, she's fine, but she doesn't live in the south anymore. She and my father moved back to Pennsylvania when the war started."

"Cold there too."

"Colder, actually." He smiled, put his cap back on and turned toward the door, eying the child Hazel. It was a shame she didn't have warmer clothes to wear. A picture of the little girl he'd seen with Sarah stole into his mind. They were close in size, but far apart in privilege. What had happened to the girl's parents? Had Roy Smith been killed in the war? What happened to the mother?

The war had been over for four years, but people on both sides were still suffering its aftermath. And although his mission had been to discover the location of the missing lens, right now he had a different kind of mission, one that was more important.

~~~

"Sissie, I counted fourteen boats!"

"You did? That's all?" Sarah and Anna Grace sat in rocking chairs on the front porch watching ships move in and out of the port. "Are you sure there's not more?"

"I forgot how many fourteens I counted."

Sarah chuckled and poked her little sister in the side. "You silly goose. Did you forget what comes after fourteen?"
~~~

"One?" Anna Grace grinned.

"No, silly. Fifteen!" Sarah never tired of her sister's creativity. "Then sixteen, seventeen, you know the rest."

"But I lose track, so I start back at one."

"Well, there's at least fourteen, and a whole lot more."

Seeing the port so busy was a sign that the city was coming back to life. Father said there were now at least ten sawmills in the area, so he had plenty of competition. Recently, he'd expanded into turpentine too, and his business was doing very well. He'd worked hard to rebuild, living here by himself for the past two years until he had things ready for his family to return. If only he'd let Sarah participate in the business too. She wanted to see how things worked, how goods were bought and sold, how expenses and profits were balanced.

But Father didn't think a woman's place was in business. A woman's place was at home, preferably her own home. But would she ever have her own home? First, she had to have a husband, according to most people. However, she did know of a couple of women who had remained unmarried, "old maids," and both were schoolteachers, an acceptable occupation for women. What if it was her destiny to be one of them? Someday she'd have to be able to support herself, but she didn't care to teach a roomful of boisterous children.

"Sissie, can we do something else now?"

"Of course. Do you want to go visit Della in the kitchen?"

"Okay." They stood and smoothed their skirts. Anna Grace peered up at Sarah. "Did Della know Mother before you were born?"

"Oh yes. She knew Mother when Mother was a child. Della used to work for our grandmother."

"She must be really old."

"Well, older than Mother, that's for sure, but she's not too old." Sarah calculated Della was around sixty.

They climbed the steps to the kitchen and went inside the screen door. "Hello Della. Do you mind if we watch you? Maybe there's something we can do to help."

Della's eyebrows raised. "You knows how to cook?"

"Yes, we all pitched in at Aunt Betty's house. There were always peas to shell or corn to shuck or something."

"Hmm. Well, let's see. First, you two misses put on aprons."

Sarah grabbed one off a wall peg and put it over Anna Grace's head. The adult-size apron swallowed the little girl and they all laughed. Sarah folded the skirt at the waist and tied it up higher so that it went under Anna Grace's arms. "There. That's better." Sarah took the other apron off the wall and tied it around herself.

Scanning the room, Della said, "Why don't you pull that stool over here to the table and let Miss Anna Grace stan' on it?"

Sarah fetched the stool and helped Anna Grace climbed up on it. Della leaned over to the little girl with a twinkle in her eyes. "How'd you like to make some tea cakes?"

Anna Grace's face lit up, and she clapped her hands together. "Tea cakes! I love tea cakes!"

Della put the flour and sugar on the heavy work table, then grabbed a sifter and a large bowl, placing them in front of the little girl. She poured some flour into the sifter, then handed it to Anna Grace. "Here, you can start sifting the flour. Can you do that?"

"Yes, ma'am." Anna Grace used both her hands and started squeezing on the handle while Della brought the other ingredients to the work table. Soon the three of them were stirring, mixing and kneading until the dough was ready. Della handed a rolling pin to Anna Grace who tried to push the dough flat. Sarah's heart warmed at the way Della paid such attention to her little sister, something her mother failed to do.

"Della, you know you've shown three generations of the women in our family how to make tea cakes."

"That's right." Della put her hands over Anna Grace's and helped her press down on the dough to roll it out.

Anna Grace looked up at the woman. "Do you have little girls too?"

Della looked surprised at the question, then chuckled. "Oh, I used to. Had three of them. But they done growed up and moved away. Got families of their own now, so I has some grandchildren."

"Don't you have a son too?" Sarah asked, trying to remember what she'd known about Della's family.

"Yes, I did. Two sons. They left town too, when they got their freedom. But my grandson Zeke, he's still here. He's 'bout your age, I reckon. Got three children hisself."

Sarah winced at yet another reminder of how old she was not to have a family too. "He lives in Pensacola?"

"No, he lives up in Milltown. Works at your father's sawmill."

"Oh, I didn't know."

"I think it's ready to cut now." Della handed a metal cookie cutter to Anna Grace. "Here. Why don't you see how many circles you can make in this dough?"

Della grabbed a cookie sheet and rubbed some lard over it, then set it beside the dough. "Miss Sarah, would you put them on the sheet when she cuts them? I'll check on the oven."

"I've asked Father to take me to see the mill sometime."

Della was bent over the oven. She stood and looked at Sarah, wiping her hands on her apron. "What did he say? Is he goin' to?"

"Yes, he said he would. Even though I know he doesn't think women should be around the mill."

Della shook her head. "I'm not surprised. It's a dang'rous, noisy, dirty place."

"Maybe when I go there, I can meet your grandson."

Della frowned. "I doubt you gonna get close enough to the workers to see him. He's one of the men that rides the logs on the river, keeps 'em floatin' to the sawmill."

"That requires a lot of balance, doesn't it?"

"Yes, it do. You don't wanna fall off and get crushed by all those other logs."

Sarah shuddered at the image Della painted. "You must pray for his safety."

"Every day. All the time."

"I wish Father would at least let me work in the office. I'm good with numbers and could help with the books."

Della eyed Sarah while Anna Grace continued to carefully cut circles in the dough. "I wish you could too."

"You do?" Hadn't the woman agreed that the mill was no place for a woman?

Della glanced down at her apron. "Nevermin' me. I just thought it would be a good idea for your father to have someone good with numbers."

"Father's good with numbers. And you know he has Eben White there to run things. I suppose Eben is as good with numbers as I am."

Della's brow creased. "Hmmph. Maybe he is and maybe he ain't."

What did she mean by that? Della reached for the full cookie sheet, but Sarah stopped her. "Wait. Before you take them, I want to ask Anna Grace how many cookies she cut out."

"Fourteen!"

Sarah shook her head. Why did she bother to ask? Anna Grace hadn't gotten past fourteen yet and still needed help with her numbers. But was Della inferring that Eben did too? Why would she think that?

Chapter Four

"Lieutenant Hamilton, I'd like to introduce you to Mr. Asa Ponder. He'll be taking over as the new lighthouse keeper," Captain Stewart said, nodding to the man beside him in the shadow of the great lighthouse towering above.

"Pleasure to meet you, sir." Josiah extended his hand to the man whose graying beard covered most of the face below his cap.

Mr. Ponder grunted a reply and nodded, taking Josiah's hand in a viselike grip, a grip surprisingly strong for a hand missing two fingers. Good thing the man had a strong hand. He would need it to carry cans of oil up the numerous steps of the Pensacola Lighthouse to the lantern room.

"Mr. Ponder is one of our honorable veterans and served under General Grant."

Ponder nodded, puffing out his chest and rocking on his heels. "Yes, sir. I served under our new president!"

General Grant had won the recent election and would be sworn in as the country's president in March. No doubt that Ponder's affiliation with the general had garnered his position. Favoritism went a long way for such a desirable position as a lighthouse keeper.

"I told Mr. Ponder that you would be in charge of restoring the lighthouse, as well as, overseeing the construction of the new keepers' house."

Ponder crossed his arms, squinting as he studied Josiah, as if sizing him up to see if he was capable of the assignment.

"I'm sure you'll be happy to move into your new house," Josiah said, hoping to ease the tension.

"My wife and daughter will be, and I'll be glad to live at the lighthouse instead of over in Warrington." Ponder glanced over his shoulder at the small building attached to the base of the lighthouse. Currently, there was only one room where the keeper could stay during a night at the lighthouse, alternating with the assistant keeper. "Mr. Madden, my assistant, will be happy about it as well, since I hear he'll be sharing the house."

"We'll try to get the building finished as soon as possible and get you all living there. The new house will be sufficiently sized for each of your families to have your own separate area."

"You do that."

A soldier approached Captain Stewart. When the captain faced him, the soldier saluted. "Excuse me, sir, you're needed at the wharf."

Captain Stewart turned back to Josiah and Mr. Ponder. "Excuse me, gentlemen," he said, then followed the soldier.

"You going to find that first order lens them Rebs stole?"

"I'm gathering information about its possible whereabouts. Of course, even if we find it, we can't be certain it will be usable anymore."

"Hmmph! Guess they thought stealing that lens would win the war for them." Ponder emitted a sound Josiah assumed was a laugh although the man's facial expression didn't change much.

"It certainly didn't help our side." As Ponder frowned, Josiah quickly added, "Of course, replacing the lens with a smaller one put it back in operation."

"Well, a lighthouse that size is supposed to have the biggest lens, not a measly fourth-order one! You find it, you hear?"

The man had no authority over him and no right to give him orders, but Josiah needed to work with Ponder and had to overlook the man's ill manner. Josiah bit back his retort. "I'm going to try my best."

Would Ponder act as demanding if Captain Stewart were still standing there? Just how much did the man know about lighthouses anyway? Josiah could recite the mechanical details of the lighthouse probably beyond the lightkeepers' ability, but what would be the point? He didn't have to prove himself to the man, whether Ponder knew it or not.

Out of the corner of his eye, Josiah saw a familiar young woman walking nearby. She looked at him and twisted coyly, a shy smile on her face.

"That's my daughter, Lizzie," Mr. Ponder said.

The wind blew her bonnet off her head, though it remained tied around her neck, and revealed sallow skin and wispy blonde hair escaping from its restraints.

"I believe I saw her downtown the other day, but I could be mistaken."

Ponder shrugged. "You probably did. She and her mother have been anxious to see the town."

Josiah remembered her as the woman in the crowd that had gathered to watch them put out the fire.

"I'll introduce you." Ponder beckoned the woman, not giving Josiah an opportunity to refuse.

"Lizzie, come over here. I want you to meet someone." Josiah's face heated as the girl strolled over, a grin stretching across her face. "This is Lieutenant Josiah Hamilton. He's going to build us a new home and fix the lighthouse."

Josiah removed his cap as the girl dipped a curtsy. "Pleasure to meet you, miss."

"I saw you in town," the girl said in a childlike voice.

"Ah, I thought you looked familiar too."

She set her bonnet back on her head, then twisted the ends of her shawl as she swayed back and forth. "You put out the fire."

Josiah's collar tightened. "Not by myself, thank goodness. I'm glad so many others joined the water brigade and stopped the fire from spreading."

"Did you say there was a fire?" Asa Ponder lifted an eyebrow. "What burned?"

"A business downtown across from the docks." Josiah replaced his cap. "The office of a sawmill, from what I understand."

"Were you able to save it?"

Josiah shook his head. "No, it was a small frame building and burned like tinder. I'm just glad the weather was damp, and the wind wasn't blowing."

Ponder nodded his head. "Yep, seen entire blocks catch fire

when the wind carries it."

Lizzie stared at him while the men spoke, the way she had when they'd been in town. He was tempted to check a mirror to see if he had food on his face or left a spot when he shaved that morning. He cleared his throat. "Miss Ponder, how do you like it here in the South?"

She brightened and smiled. "I like it so far. It's not as cold as Illinois."

"Not quite, although it can get rather cold here. Like this morning, the temperature was close to freezing, but with this sun, it's warmed up at least twenty degrees."

"Our current house feels damp even with the sun shining though," Mr. Ponder said. "We're looking forward to a new one."

"Yes, I'm sure you are, and hopefully, it'll be ready by the summer. In fact, I'm in the process of procuring supplies for it."

"Don't skimp on the materials," Ponder ordered. "Build a house that will survive the elements here, what with hurricanes and all."

Josiah bristled inside. Why did this man think he needed to tell Josiah what to do? Was it because he thought Josiah too young or inexperienced, or just simple-minded?

"I assure you, I will resource the best quality available. There are plenty of sawmills around here."

"Good." Ponder glanced up at the tall tower looming over them. "Shall we examine the lighthouse?"

Josiah nodded. "Yes. I've assessed its condition, but I welcome your observation."

"Hmmph." Ponder headed toward the tower but cast a glance at his daughter. "Lizzie, doesn't Mother need your help with dinner?"

Lizzie frowned and pursed her lips. "But…yes, Father." She stood in place watching as they walked away. No doubt she wanted to accompany them and was unhappy about being left behind.

Josiah gave her a nod as they walked away, acknowledging her so she didn't feel abandoned. Lizzie wasn't unpleasant to look at, nor was she remarkable in any way. Had she any brothers or sisters? Josiah got the impression she was lonely and wanted company. Perhaps one of the young ladies in the area could befriend her. He could mention his concern to Mr. Ponder, but didn't want his intentions to be misunderstood.

Josiah and Mr. Ponder took their time walking around the tower, examining it for cracks or any signs of weakening. The keeper paused to point to a pock-mark in the building. "Here's a place."

"Yes, I saw that one." Josiah had thoroughly examined the building already, but Ponder apparently needed to do his own investigation, not to mention advise Joshua about what should be handled. After all, it would be the keepers' domain and his responsibility once Josiah was finished with it. "The lighthouse took several direct hits from the cannon at Fort Pickens across the bay during the first year of the war when the Confederates were positioned on the beach here in front of the tower."

"Hmmph. So I heard." Ponder proceeded around the base of the white brick tower, which was sadly in need of new paint. He looked up and pointed. "There's another one."

Josiah had already counted the number of marks, but kept the information to himself, since Ponder wanted to draw attention to them as if Josiah had never seen them. Establishing how many times the lighthouse had been hit was not the main issue. Josiah had to prove whether the building was structurally sound or not. They continued around the building until Josiah was certain they had seen every dent the lighthouse had sustained from the battle.

"Shall we go inside to see if any penetrated?" Ponder asked.

To reach the inside of the lighthouse, they entered the small attached building that housed the kerosene on the first floor and the keepers' room just off the stairwell on the second. Even though Josiah had been in the lighthouse before, he allowed Ponder to take the lead.

The lightkeeper unbolted the latch and pushed the heavy door of the tower which creaked as it opened. They stepped into the cool vestibule and over to the bare brick walls. Josiah had done a thorough examination of the interior already too, but this part was more important, and he didn't mind someone else's scrutiny of the walls inside. Running their hands along the wall, they felt for cracks or missing pieces that might have been knocked out by a cannon ball. When they had walked the inside circumference, searching high and low, they slowly climbed the iron spiral staircase, pausing on each step to search the wall.

All the way to the top, they examined the tower. Ponder thought he saw a couple of places that were damaged, but when Josiah inspected the area, he couldn't find anything that revealed an unstable wall. In fact, there didn't seem to be any place the cannon balls had penetrated.

"We can add some mortar to those places that are missing it, but the building appears sound to me," Josiah said.

"Maybe we need to get someone else to look too," Ponder said.

Once again, the man appeared to doubt Josiah's ability. Of course, other engineers had examined the wall before Ponder got there, but he didn't seem to know that. Clenching his teeth, Josiah refrained from speaking his mind. Whether Ponder realized it or not, Josiah's job was not to satisfy the lightkeeper. He reported to higher authorities, even higher than the military. *Lord, help me seek only your praise, not this man's or any other's.*

"On *our* previous examinations, *we* didn't find any interior damage either. So now, we're agreed, and we can move forward." Josiah hoped Ponder would understand the thoroughness of the army engineers.

They had reached the lantern room at the top of the stairs. Ponder's brow creased as he considered Josiah's words. Josiah stared out the windows, taking in the vast panorama in front of them, the view of the bay, the barrier island across the way where Fort Pickens sat, as well as Fort McRae on a peninsula which jutted out to the west.

"We'll fill in the places that were hit outside, then paint the entire lighthouse," Josiah said, taking charge of the situation. "Meanwhile, I'll keep searching for the missing lens."

Ponder faced him, looking him over. "You do that, son. You do that."

Son? As they headed back down the stairs, Josiah considered the patronizing attitude Mr. Ponder had with him. He wasn't accustomed to being called "son" by any of his commanding officers. But there was little he could do about it. Ponder hadn't insulted him, only his pride. And according to what he'd read in the Bible, God hated pride.

Chapter Five

Della picked up the sheet out of the basket and shook it. Sarah grabbed the other end and together, they draped it over the clothes line.

"She's a sweet child." Della nodded toward Anna Grace.

Sarah put a wooden clothespin on the line to secure the sheet, then glanced at her little sister who was kneeling on the ground in the garden beside Doc, intently watching how he handled the plants.

"She is. I love her dearly."

Della shook her head. "I don't understand why her mama don't like her."

Sarah jerked her head toward Della. "Of course she likes her. Why do you say that?"

"I never sees her payin' any attention to the girl. She act like she don't know her." Della picked up another sheet while the first one flapped in the breeze. "Is she embarrassed because the child is crippled?"

Sarah's heart squeezed. She glanced over her shoulder to see if Mother was within earshot. "No, I don't think embarrassed is what she is. I think she feels guilty."

"Guilty? Why, what she done to that girl to make her crippled?"

Sarah moved a little closer to Della, so she didn't have to raise her voice. "She didn't intentionally do anything. Anna Grace came so fast, the midwife hadn't gotten there yet, and the baby fell on the floor. We weren't sure how much she got hurt until she started to walk and one leg wouldn't hold any weight. I know Mother feels terrible about what happened, like it's her fault, and every time she looks at Anna Grace, she's reminded."

Della clucked her tongue, shaking her head. "But don't she know she's punishin' the child by payin' no attention to her?"

"I don't think she does." Sarah lifted a napkin from the basket and secured it to the line. "I don't think she's ever quit mourning for Benjamin and Zachary since they died of the fever. She was happy again when she discovered she was with child, but then the accident happened and Mother's convinced God's punishing her."

"Good Lord, why would He do that?"

Sarah shook her head as they pulled a tablecloth from the basket. "I don't know. I don't know what Mother ever did so wrong, but I think she blames herself for the boys getting sick. When so many people were getting sick, she didn't keep them inside when they wanted to go out to play, so they got sick."

"Po' woman." Della watched Anna Grace for a moment before resuming the laundry. "Po' little girl. Thank goodness, you'se around to look after her."

"I've been doing it almost since she was born. At first, it was like having a live doll. I didn't mind, because I pretended she was my child." Sarah's eyes misted as she remembered the pain she'd experienced wishing the child had been hers—hers and Josiah's. "And Mother just let me take over. Anna Grace is almost always with me."

Della shook her head again. "It ain't right, no it ain't." She looked at Sarah. "But you'se doing a good job. That little girl, she dotes on you like you was her mother."

"Well, somebody has to be." Sarah wiped her hands on her apron after securing the last napkin to the line.

"Miss Sarah, it's none of my bizness, but I'se surprised you didn't marry some young man back when you was in Alabama."

Sarah flinched as heat rose to her face. "There was no one I cared to marry." She looked away to avoid Della's gaze.

"You still pinin' for that Hamilton boy, ain't you?"

Sarah nodded, biting back tears.

Della put her hand on Sarah's arm. "You'll find somebody else, you will."

But Sarah knew she was wrong. How could she ever love

another man?

Sarah wiped her eyes with the back of her hand and straightened. "Let's go see what Anna Grace and Doc are doing."

Della left the basket on the ground as they walked to the corner of the property where a garden was laid out. Neat hilly rows were lined up side by side. When they reached Anna Grace and Doc, the two looked up at them.

"Ms. Anna Grace is helpin' me, she is," Doc said, smiling his wide toothy grin.

"Is that right? What is she helping you with?" Sarah spotted several green piles lying on a piece of burlap.

"We're getting our dinner!" Anna Grace pointed to the greenery.

Della put her hands on her hips. "Well, what is we havin' for dinner, Miss Anna Grace?"

"Collard greens and onions!" the little girl announced, pointing from one pile to the other.

"That sounds right good, don't it, Miss Sarah?"

"It does indeed. I'm glad you're being a help, Anna Grace."

"Doc is teaching me to be a farmer. He's showing me how to grow things."

"And you want to be a farmer when you grow up?"

Her head bobbed up and down. "Yes, I do. I want to grow all kinds of things."

"What kinds of things?" Della asked.

"Beans, t'maters, corn, pie and cake!"

Doc laughed out loud and Della chuckled, while Sarah smiled at her little sister, her heart warmed by the child's innocence.

She had to ask. "Anna Grace, did you count the rows Doc made here in the garden?"

The little girl nodded. "Yes. There are fourteen."

Sarah shook her head. How was she going to keep her sister from always giving the same answer?

"You'se right, Miss Anna Grace. I got fourteen rows!"

Sarah's mouth fell open. She quickly counted the rows herself and discovered her sister was right this time. "Good counting, Anna Grace!"

"Well, let's get to cleanin' these veg'tables so we can have 'em for dinner." Della brushed her hands together. "Take 'em over there to the pump and we'll wash them off. You'se gotta wash greens a whole lot to get the sand and bugs off."

Sarah helped Anna Grace up. "Can I see the bugs?"

"Oh, all right." Sarah took Anna Grace's hand and they followed Doc carrying the vegetables wrapped in the burlap to the hand-pump, set them down, then began to prime the pump.

"I need to get a bowl to put the greens in," Della said.

"I'll get it," Sarah said. "You go ahead and start washing them."

"Thank you, Miss Sarah. Missy can help me find the bugs."

Sarah returned to pick up the laundry basket then headed for the kitchen stairs. In the kitchen she found a large bowl and returned to the others with it. Anna Grace was thrilled when they found a tiny beetle on the greens.

"Can I keep him? He can be my pet." She watched the little bug crawl over her hand.

"No, he needs to go back home to his family," Doc said. "I'll take him back over yonder." He extended his arm to let the bug crawl onto his hand.

Sarah took over pumping the water on the greens while Della examined and rinsed them off, rubbing her hands across the vegetables. They were rinsed several times before the water ran clear and Della was satisfied they were clean. Sarah was glad too, having bit down on some gritty greens in the past. Once they were finished, Della carried the vegetables back upstairs to the kitchen, calling out to Doc to bring a bucket of clean water. Sarah and Anna Grace followed along behind, Sarah holding one of Anna Grace's hands while the little girl held onto the stair rail.

In the kitchen, Della bent down to turn on the oven, then put the cast iron skillet inside. Next, she took down a big pot from a hook in the low ceiling and set it on the stove where she filled it to the top with the greens. When Doc brought the water up, he poured the pot half full, then set the bucket on the floor. Della poured some salt over the greens and added a big spoonful of lard, then lit the fire.

"Can we help you do something else?" Sarah asked. She hated to stand by while Della did all the work. At her aunt and uncle's, everyone had worked, and they'd had no one like Della to help them.

"You likes to be busy, don't you?" Della dipped into a bin of cornmeal and put it in a bowl.

"I do. I got used to it since we've been gone, and I don't like sitting still and feeling useless."

"I help too!" Anna Grace said, pulling the stool over to watch Della.

"Yes, you do. You'se a good helper," Della said as she broke an egg into the cornmeal. "I know Doc was glad you helped him."

"T'morrow, he's going to teach me how to hoe." Anna Grace crossed her arms, lifting her chin as she proclaimed the next step of her new aspiration to be a farmer. Sarah smiled at her little sister, but her heart cracked inside. What kind of future did she have to hope for? Once she had hoped to marry Josiah and have a family with him, but that hope had died. And Father wouldn't let her work in the business, even though she believed she could be useful handling his books. There must be something worthwhile she could do, but Father wouldn't approve of her working the garden now that they had Doc to handle that chore. But he wouldn't mind Anna Grace "helping" Doc, since he considered her work to be child's play. So what was Sarah left to do? Sit around the house and needlepoint? She couldn't imagine spending the whole day that way.

"He is, is he?" Della said, chuckling while she stirred the cornmeal. "He might have to cut the handle off the hoe so's you can use it."

She straightened her back, wiping her hands on her apron, then grabbed a towel, and leaned over to pull the hot skillet from the oven. Placing it on top of the stove, she took the bowl of batter and poured it into the skillet, scraping the bowl with a wooden spoon. The skillet sizzled as the cornbread hit the surface. When it was full of batter, Della put the skillet back into the oven. The smell of turnips cooking wafted through the air as the water in the pot began to boil. Sarah's stomach rumbled in anticipation.

Della stirred the pot of greens. "I wish I had some fatback to put in here and season 'em up good. I'll see if Doc can get some next time he goes out to his brother's farm."

Sarah looked around the kitchen. "I guess there's nothing else we can do."

"No, not in here. But I bet you two can make sure the table's set. Do you think Miss Anna Grace can help with that?"

"I sure can!" Anna Grace bobbed her head. "And I can fold napkins too."

"Let's go, Anna Grace." Sarah helped her down from the stool, then took her sister's hand.

"Bye, Della!" The little girl waved to the smiling cook as they left the kitchen and went outside.

A cool breeze blew from the bay, a stark contrast to the heat of the kitchen.

"Look how the water sparkles!" Sarah pointed to the water.

"Ooh, it's like Momma's pretty necklace!" Anna Grace clasped her hands.

"It does look like diamonds, doesn't it?" The winter sun was especially bright against the water, and Sarah shielded her eyes against the glare.

"Can we go closer?" Her little sister looked up with imploring eyes.

"First, we better see if Mother wants us to set the table now."

Inside the main house, they found Mother bent over the table where she tenderly touched the hair wreath inside a picture frame.

She looked up as they approached, tears in her eyes. "The wreath got disturbed during the move. I'm repairing it."

Sarah fought back a sigh. Her mother's mood was as gloomy as an overcast sky. The wreath made of her little brothers' hair looked the same to her that it always had. It'd been over eight years since they died, but Mother acted like it was yesterday. Why couldn't she leave the past behind? Instead, her grief kept a shadow over their home and separated her from the rest of the family. Sarah fought back her bitterness, the words she wanted to say, to spare Anna Grace.

"We've been helping Della in the kitchen." Sarah attempted to bring her mother's attention back to the present.

"And I've been helping Doc in the garden!" Anna Grace added.

Mother stared at them, her face blank as if she had no interest in Anna Grace's announcement. "That's nice. I'm sure they appreciated your help."

The light dimmed in the little girl's eyes with her mother's flat, uninterested response.

"I thought perhaps we could set the table, but I suppose that can wait."

When Mother didn't acknowledge, Sarah said, "Anna Grace, let's go outside and look for wildflowers to press."

Anna Grace's face brightened. "Okay, Sissie." She walked toward Sarah, then stopped and looked back over her shoulder. "We'll find you a pretty flower, Mother, so you won't be sad anymore."

Bless her heart for trying. If only there was such a flower, one that would work its magic and take away everyone's sadness, Sarah's included.

Chapter Six

"Here's one!" Anna Grace squatted beside the fence and pointed to a tiny white flower with a yellow center.

Sarah straightened, rubbing her lower back, sore from bending over to look for flowers. She went over to see Anna Grace's discovery. "That's a pretty one." She gently plucked it from the stalk and placed it in her sister's little hand. "Hold it carefully, and let's see if we can find some more like it." She knew the chances were slim that they'd find many wildflowers in January, but any at all would be exciting to Anna Grace.

"How many do we need to make a picture?"

"It depends on the size of the picture."

"Can we make a little bitty picture?"

Sarah laughed. "We can try. But we still need more than one flower. Let's keep looking." Sarah's Aunt Betty had shown her how to press the dried flowers and create pictures. Sarah enjoyed making the colorful framed floral arrangements so much more than the sad hair wreaths Mother had made. Even though some people made hair arrangements from those still living, the one Mother had made was to commemorate her sons who had died. And floral pictures were pleasurable for she and Anna Grace to do together.

"Look, Anna Grace." Sarah pointed to a tiny lavender flower she spotted.

"Ooh. So pretty! Let's find lots and lots!"

They spent the rest of the afternoon finding tiny white flowers, lavender ones and also some yellow ones that had survived the southern frost. "Hold them gently," Sarah said. Anna Grace held the corners of her pinafore folded up to hold the flowers and carefully carried them back to the house. Sarah helped her up the stairs since she couldn't hold the railing with her hands full.

"We'll press them in the Bible, then arrange them after they dry."

Inside, they opened the massive family Bible sitting on the sideboard. Sarah took a flower and spread it flat on the page. Anna Grace followed suit. Once the whole page was covered, Sarah carefully closed the book, knowing it wouldn't be moved. No one ever lifted the book, much less opened it besides Sarah. Had it become part of the furniture, something they carried with them to Alabama and returned to its former place in their dining room? When did Mother and Father quit reading the Bible? Sometimes Sarah opened it to Psalms and read out loud to Anna Grace, just as her mother used to do with her brothers and herself.

"There. We'll have to wait a day or two before we can arrange them. Meanwhile we can ask Doc about a frame. Let's wash up and set the table."

Mother walked into the room with napkins she had been ironing and laid them on the sideboard.

"Mother, we got some pretty flowers to make a picture!" Anna Grace beamed.

"That's nice. I'm sure you and Sarah can make a pretty picture."

"You can make one too. I'll show you how," Anna Grace said.

"Maybe some day I will. I want to see what you and Sarah make first."

Anna Grace's face fell, her disappointment evident.

Sarah wanted to shake her mother and force her to participate, but she couldn't do that. What would it take for the wall Mother had built around herself to come down?

"Would you please help me fold the napkins?" Sarah handed one to her little sister who nodded and proceeded to copy Sarah's motions as she folded a napkin.

As they finished setting the table, Father came in the front door and put his hat on the hall tree. "What have all my young ladies been doing today?"

Anna Grace excitedly filled him in on all the details of their busy day, from helping in the garden to finding flowers to press.

"Well, Anna Grace, you've been busy," Father said, then turned to Mother. "Virginia, have you had a good day?"

Mother nodded. "Yes, dear."

Della brought in their meal and they sat down to eat.

After Father said grace, Mother asked, "Any news about what started the fire?"

Father shook his head. "No, but there was another fire up river at Smith's lumber yard. Not a big one, thank God, but frightening, nonetheless."

Sarah leaned forward. "And no word on how it started?"

"No. Started around dawn before anyone got there." Father rubbed his eyes.

"Do you think there's any connection between the two fires?" Mother asked.

"Doesn't seem likely, with them being so far apart. Just both happened to be lumber companies. Thankfully, some men coming to work saw the smoke and put the fire out before it could spread."

"Thank God." Sarah blew out a breath.

Father placed his palms on the table and gazed at each of them. "Speaking of which, tomorrow is Sunday, and I look forward to having my family with me in church again."

"I can't wait to go to Christ Church," Sarah said. "I wonder if it will look the same." As soon as the words left her mouth, she knew the answer. Even if the building looked the same, the congregation would be different, since Josiah and his family wouldn't be there.

"It's been cleaned up since the unwelcome guests left, but it still needs some work." Father frowned. "But Dr. Scott has returned as the rector, and we're all pitching in to get the church back to its former glory." Father leaned back in his chair. "And … if the weather's warm enough tomorrow, we might go for a sail after church."

"A sail?" Mother's eyebrows lifted.

"Yes, it's been a long time since I've taken my family sailing."

"Can I go too?" Anna Grace asked, wide-eyed.

"Certainly! You've never been sailing, have you, Anna Grace?"

She shook her head. "No, sir." She turned to Sarah. "Is it

scary, Sissie?"

Sarah chuckled and patted her sister's hand. "No, silly goose, it's delightful. I think you'll enjoy it. I know I will."

~~~

Josiah stepped into the small chapel on the post, removed his cap, and glanced around. He headed for an empty seat, then out of the corner of his eye, he spotted Keeper Ponder with his wife and daughter sitting on the other side. He'd intended to sit alone, but before he could take his seat, Lizzie Ponder turned and saw him. She elbowed her father who looked as well and waved him over. How could he refuse without offending the family?

The seat beside Lizzie was open, therefore he was compelled to sit beside her. Even though there was ample room for him, she scooted too close, smiling in a gleeful way. He smiled in return, nodding at her parents before settling back in the seat. Although he tried not to look at Lizzie, he was aware of her eyes on him. His collar grew tighter under her gaze, and he begged for the service to start and divert her attention.

She wasn't repulsive, but her attention was more forward than he was accustomed to. Her thin blonde hair was tucked under her bonnet with several wisps escaping. Her face was round, though not full, and her eyes were brown. Although she wore a shawl, her tight-fitting bodice revealed an ample bosom which seemed unusual for her otherwise thin body. He averted his gaze, embarrassed to have even noticed. However, he got the distinct impression that she wanted him to notice. *Josiah, why are you having these thoughts? You should be ashamed.*

He faced the front of the church to focus his attention elsewhere and observed the other congregants, many in uniform. His gaze traveled to the architecture of the building, simple, compared to other churches he'd attended. It was plain and rather small but served the purpose for which it was built. Yet he couldn't help but think of Christ Church in town, the church he'd attended when he'd lived in Pensacola before the war. He and his family always sat in the pew beside Sarah's family, and when they were courting, he and Sarah sat together. Surely that's where she was today. With her husband and daughter and an approving father.
~~~

Why, she might even have other children he hadn't seen. In seven years, she could have had several children. His heart sank lower at the thought.

Who had she married? A rebel soldier? He thought back to the day of the fire and seeing her father with two other men. Was one of them her husband? The one that looked like her father appeared to be too old for her. And the other one? He wasn't as old, but he was older than Josiah. And Sarah. Josiah shook his head. Surely, she wouldn't have married that man. The very idea made his stomach churn.

The people around him stood up, jolting Josiah back to where he was. He quickly joined them, grabbing hold of a corner of the hymnal that Lizzie shoved in his direction. He glanced down and sang the words on the page, "Immortal, invisible, God only wise, in light inaccessible hid from our eyes." The words hit him as if speaking directly to him, reminding him of the missing lens from the lighthouse. Hidden, was it inaccessible? Was God trying to tell him something?

He'd been so busy the last few days, he'd had no time to think about the lens. Perhaps he could go back to visit Mrs. Smith, and she'd be able to tell him now what she hadn't before. He hoped she was feeling better after receiving food from the kitchen he'd arranged to have delivered each day. A pang of guilt stabbed him. He didn't want Mrs. Smith to feel better just so she could give him information; he truly wanted to help her.

When the service ended, he hoped to go see the woman again. But when they stepped into the aisle, Mr. Ponder addressed him.

"Lieutenant Hamilton, it's nice to see you in church today." His wife stood behind him smiling and nodding.

"It's nice to see you too, sir … and your family." He glanced down at Lizzie to acknowledge her presence.

"Mrs. Ponder and I would like to invite you to join us for Sunday dinner, that is, unless you have other plans?"

He really didn't have other definite plans but couldn't lie and say he did, even though he wished so.

"I wouldn't want to impose on you."

"No bother at all." He glanced at his wife who nodded. "Please."

Lizzie grinned and batted her eyelashes as if a gnat had flown into her eyes.

"All right then. Thank you."

They walked to the rear of the church where the minister stood, shaking hands and thanking people for attending as they exited the building. As Josiah was shaking the minister's hand, he noticed an old woman, hunched over and walking slowly away. Realizing the girl beside her was Hazel, he excused himself and hurried over to them.

"Mrs. Smith."

She stopped and turned toward him. "Ah, Lieutenant Hamilton. I thought I saw you in church."

"How are you doing, ma'am? Are you feeling better? You must be, seeing that you're out."

"I'm doing some better, thanks to this warm, sunny day. And some food that's been brought to us. I s'pose I have you to thank for that?"

"Yes, I requested it, and I'm glad to hear you're getting it." He'd have to thank the cook for getting the food to them. Joy filled Josiah seeing how much healthier the woman looked. Hazel too, looked brighter, although still terribly thin. She was wearing a nicer dress, which must've been her Sunday-go-to-meeting dress, and she wore a straw bonnet tied with a yellow ribbon under her chin. Mrs. Smith was also better dressed than he'd seen her before, wearing her Sunday best as well, he assumed, a brown wool dress.

"I suppose you want to talk to me some more about that missing lighthouse piece." Mrs. Smith peered up at him.

"Yes, ma'am, when you're up to it."

"I'm up to it. Would you like to come by today?"

Josiah glanced over his shoulder where Mr. Ponder and his family stood waiting and watching him.

"I'm sorry, I can't. I have another commitment. But perhaps tomorrow?"

"That will be fine. Come on by when you get the time."

"I'll do that. Thank you."

She smiled and turned around to resume her slow journey home. Josiah wished he had a buggy to take her in, but he had walked too. As he watched her walk away, the words of the hymn came back to him. "Light inaccessible, hid from our eyes." Would the light indeed be inaccessible to him?

Chapter Seven

"Won't you have some more potatoes?" Mrs. Ponder offered the bowl to Josiah. "No, thank you." He raised a hand in protest, then patted his stomach. "I am quite full." The meal had been sufficient—boiled ham, boiled potatoes and bread, more like a New England dinner than the Southern-style meals of the area. Conversation at the table had focused on him, as Mr. Ponder drilled him on his time at West Point and in the war. Josiah endured the interrogation, although he was ready to put the War behind him. Men like Ponder wanted to dwell on the matter though. He regretted that the women had been subjected to their discussion, one he thought too unpleasant for their ears.

His collar felt tight and he couldn't breathe in the tiny house. Their new home should be much more comfortable, but maybe it wasn't the house that was bothering him. At the moment, he needed fresh air. He grabbed the opportunity when there was a break in the conversation.

"It's such a nice day. Who wants to join me for a stroll outside?" Much as he wanted to go talk to Mrs. Smith, it would be rude to leave right after dinner

Lizzie's eyes brightened, and she looked as though she'd jump out of her chair, but a glance at her mother settled her. Mr. Ponder and his wife exchanged looks, then her father said, "Fine. Let's go out." He stood, and Josiah followed suit. Josiah helped Lizzie out of her chair, and Mr. Ponder pulled his wife's chair out for her.

The women donned their bonnets and shawls while the men grabbed their hats. As they stepped outside, Josiah inhaled the fresh air, then glimpsing the bay some distance away between the trees, was drawn to the water. "Would you like to take a stroll down to the water, perhaps to the dock behind the lighthouse?"

"I would," Lizzie said, then glanced at her father as if seeking permission.

"You two young people go on down then. Mrs. Ponder and I will be along shortly."

Josiah felt like a leashed animal, tethered to Lizzie, but he welcomed the freedom from the confines of the house. He looked at Lizzie and offered his elbow to her. "Shall we?" She readily accepted, grinning from ear to ear.

The lighthouse was a little distance from the neighborhood. Lizzie clung to his arm, smiling and nodding at people they passed as if they were a twosome. There was no way for him to change their opinion without being rude to her, so he tipped his hat in passing as well. Josiah wanted to glance back to see how far Mr. and Mrs. Ponder were behind them but had the impression Lizzie's parents intended to give them a chance to be together without close supervision.

When they arrived at the lighthouse, they headed down the sandy hill behind it toward the dock. Craters were still visible from pits Confederate troops had dug for cannon placement while they defended Fort Barrancas from below the lighthouse. It was here that the Union soldiers at Fort Pickens on Santa Rosa Island had fired on them until they were forced to leave. The wide beach was still littered with rifle shells, tent pegs and other evidence of the former occupants. Josiah took Lizzie's hand to help her through the soft, deep sand as they made their way to the water.

As they stepped onto the dock, Josiah took in the scene he never tired of. Pelicans dove into the bay, their huge bills open to scoop up their catch, while mullet leaped out of the water closer to shore as if taunting the pelicans. The azure sky was even more blue during the southern winter, and snow-white clouds were few and far between. Brilliant winter sunshine bounced off the water, almost blinding him with its reflection.

"It's nice here," Lizzie said as she stood beside him, squeezing his arm.

He'd almost forgotten she was there until she spoke, he was so immersed in the scenery.

"Yes, it is. Very nice. I've always enjoyed it here."

"You lived here before the War?" She peered up at him, head cocked.

"All my life. My family's home was in Pensacola."

"But you fought for the Union."

"I did. The town was divided over sides. Many of my childhood friends chose the other side."

"Your family—are they still here?"

Josiah shook his head. "No. Everyone left. My family went back north where they had relatives. They have no plans to return."

"Is your former home still in town?" She twisted an errant strand of hair. "Was it a nice house? I'd like to see it sometime."

Josiah quirked a brow. What an odd request. "There's not much to see. I'm afraid it's been ransacked. Although I supposed it could be salvaged if anyone wanted to take on the job."

"Why don't you want to live in it again?"

He sucked in a breath. "I might not be here long enough. The Army may send me someplace else."

"Oh. Do you have any idea how long you'll be here?" She watched his face with concern etched on her face.

He shrugged. "Not really. But I imagine they'll transfer me after the work is finished here—the lighthouse is repaired, and the keepers' house is built."

The sound of laughter caught their attention as one of the many sailboats out on the water glided by, the people onboard obviously enjoying their outing. "Have you ever been on a boat like that?" Lizzie said.

"Of course. My family and I used to sail quite a bit. It's very pleasurable."

"I've never been on one. Would you take me sometime?"

She was rather brazen with her requests, for a seemingly shy girl. Was he obligated to escort her? He didn't realize that duty was his responsibility. Yet, he didn't want to offend her and possibly her father too, since he would have to work with Mr. Ponder. And she seemed to be rather sensitive.

"Perhaps I'll be able to take you sailing someday when I don't have other commitments. However, I know I'll be pretty tied up for a while. Maybe one of the other soldiers from the fort can take you sometime. I can inquire for you."

She leveled a steely glare at him, sending a message of intense dislike of his suggestion. The change in her demeanor was almost frightening. Apparently, she was accustomed to having her way. Josiah determined to stay very busy as long as possible.

~~~

Sarah held onto her bonnet with a hand on top of her head as their boat floated along, its sails full. With her other hand, she held Anna Grace's. Her little sister was mesmerized by the scene around her with a fascination Sarah remembered having when she was the same age. However, it had been so long since she'd been sailing, she was exhilarated as she inhaled the salt air. The wind blew a mist off the water as their sloop cut through the waves, occasionally sending a spray onto the occupants. Anna Grace squealed with delight.

"How do you like sailing, Anna Grace?" Father called out from his place by the tiller.

"I love it!" She wiped a wet curl from her face. "The water tastes salty."

"It certainly does," Father said.

"Sarah, what about you? You miss sailing?"

Sarah smiled. "There's nothing like being on the water."

"We must have some sailor blood in our veins." Father laughed, more relaxed than usual.

Mother stared off in the distance as if she were far away. Was she remembering when Benjamin and Zachary had been with them? Instead of sadness, the memory of her little brothers fighting over who would help Father hold the tiller was pleasant for Sarah, reminding her of happier days for her family. If only Mother could enjoy the outing too.

"We should have a picnic on the island soon. Virginia, wouldn't that be nice?" Father attempted to pull Mother back into the family.

Anna Grace clapped her hands. "I love picnics! Mother, can we?"

Mother turned and gazed at Father, then Anna Grace. The hint of a smile worked its way onto her face, then she nodded but gave her answer to her husband, not Anna Grace. "Yes, we should,
~~~

Charles. That would be nice."

Father smiled in return, as he savored his small victory.

Sarah squatted down by Anna Grace and pointed to the opposite shore where white sand stretched along the horizon. "That's the island, Anna Grace. It's called Santa Rosa Island."

Anna Grace shielded her eyes to look. "There's lot of birds over there. Can we count them?" Near the water where the sand was wet, little birds ran back and forth as if chasing the waves going in and out. Behind them, some seagulls rested in the sand, while others flew into the air. A line of pelicans glided low over the bay, their bodies almost touching the water.

Sarah's heart warmed at her sister's suggestion. "We can try."

"One, two, three, four … they won't be still!" Anna Grace pouted.

"Well let's try counting just the ones on the beach, not the ones in the air."

"One, two, three, four, five, six …" the little girl began again.

Sarah counted silently, seeing the impossibility of keeping track of all the birds. Nearest she could guess, there were over a hundred birds on the shore.

"So, how many did you count?" Sarah asked, expecting the usual answer of fourteen.

"Thirteen. There was fourteen, but one flew away, so I can't count him anymore."

Sarah laughed and hugged her sister. What a joy she was.

"What is that building over there?" Anna Grace asked.

"That's Fort Pickens, Anna Grace." The intimidating walls of the brick fort on the island, a short distance from the beach, had been the site of many battles before the Confederates left. Sarah knew it was a sore spot for Father, a reminder of the Union's control during the war. She thought it best to refocus his attention to something more pleasant.

"How far are we going, Father?" she asked.

"I thought we'd go as far as the lighthouse before we turn around."

The lighthouse. She recalled her last trip there with Josiah. They had gone sailing in his boat, stopping at the lighthouse where they tied up at the dock. As friends of the keeper and his family, they were welcome to climb the tower. Sarah and Josiah had raced up the 177 stairs which she counted all the way. At the top, they'd climbed outside to stand on the gallery and gaze across the bay beyond the island as far as the Gulf of Mexico.

Josiah had wrapped his arms around her as they viewed the panorama. He had pledged his love to her and asked her to marry him when he graduated from West Point. Sarah had never been happier. Life was perfect, and she thought it always would be.

But that was before Florida seceded from the Union. Before her friends and family took sides. Before Josiah, in her father's eyes, had taken the wrong one.

She didn't think she could look at the lighthouse again. Once it had been a special, magical place for them. But now it was just a symbol of her pain.

Sarah kept her eyes averted to the opposite side of the water, watching other boaters who waved as they passed. She forced a smile and waved back. She wouldn't be like Mother and allow her own unhappiness to affect others. Somehow, she had to focus on the future. Coming back to Pensacola had summoned memories she'd repressed for years. But she couldn't let them make her a miserable person.

"There it is!" Father said, and Sarah turned to see. The tall white tower rose above the trees, appearing so much higher than she remembered. Of course, looking up at the tower from the water to its position at the highest point of the sandy bluff, the lighthouse seemed to have grown in size. But its façade was no longer unflawed as she remembered it being. Instead, it was marred, damaged and badly needing paint.

"What happened to the lighthouse?"

"Cannon shot from Fort Pickens. Our men were here on the beach around the lighthouse, and the Yanks were shooting at them from the island." Father shook his head. "The lighthouse suffered, just as we did."

"But does it still work, still shine its light?" Sarah recalled the huge lens taller than Josiah that had been in it before, and the hard work the keeper did to maintain the lighthouse in good condition. "Is there a keeper there now?"

"The light works, but it's not the same one we had before. Our men took the light out, but the Yanks put another, smaller one in when they took it over. As far as the keeper, I don't know who it is now. But it's not the same keeper we knew before the war. I believe he quit, rather than work for the unwelcome guests."

Movement below the lighthouse caught her attention, and a soldier and young woman made their way down the hill toward the dock. Sarah jerked her head to look away. She couldn't bear to see another couple where she and Josiah had once stood together.

"Sissie! Look!" Anna Grace called out.

Sarah glanced in the direction her sister was pointing. A pod of dolphins frolicked beside the boat, rolling through the water.

"Those are dolphins, Anna Grace." Sarah knelt down and put her arm around her sister to watch the dolphins perform. "Aren't they fun to watch?"

"Yes. They look happy like they're playing with each other!" One of the dolphins leaped out of the water, arched through the air and dove back into the water with a splash. Anna Grace giggled with delight. "I think they like us."

"Maybe they do. Maybe they're performing just for you because they know this is your first boat ride and they want to make sure you enjoy it."

Anna Grace beamed with joy. Eventually, the dolphins moved farther away from the boat, and she waved at them. "Bye dolphins! Thank you for the show!"

"I'm so glad you got to see them," Sarah said.

"Me too." She looked back at her Father. "Father, can you bring me back here again to see the dolphins?"

"Certainly, I can. We'll come see them again when we have our picnic." Father glanced up at the sun. "We better head back now, so we'll get home before it's too late."

He brought the boat around and they proceeded toward home, leaving the dolphins and the lighthouse behind them. Like Anna Grace, Sarah looked forward to seeing the dolphins again the next time they were out. But she didn't care if she ever saw the lighthouse again.

Chapter Eight

Although Josiah intended to visit Mabel Smith first thing the next week, he'd been given other tasks to do that prevented him.

First, he'd met with the Army architect who went over the plans for the new keepers' house and given him specifications about what materials to buy. With an extensive list of items to make the lighthouse repairs, as well as building supplies for the new keepers' home, Josiah was instructed to visit all the available suppliers in the area to find the right materials at the best price.

If he wanted to take his horse to the Pensacola area, the trip was longer since he'd have to take the trail through the piney woods that ran beside the shore and cross two bridges. Getting there by water was faster, and the army had its own steamer to convey travelers to the waterfront in town. However, if he went north or west, he would go by horseback. Josiah laid a map out on his desk and marked the location of each lumber mill he needed to visit. Measuring the distance, he concluded the closest mill was a half-day's ride. Other mills were farther and could take an entire day. He would make these trips alone, giving him plenty of time to think. Maybe too much time.

Several sawmills were scattered along the bay on the other side of Pensacola, built as far north as where the Blackwater and Escambia Rivers flowed into the bay. Many of the mills were new, having been built since the war. Others had been rebuilt, having been burned down during the war. Entrepreneurs from the North had come down to buy up land and start new companies, so he was confident more lumber mills would open eventually. Josiah was encouraged to know new industry was being established in the city. However, he couldn't wait for more mills to be built. For now, he'd have to work with the mills currently available.

If only he could capture the enthusiasm of those who saw a better future. The country was ready for it and so was he. But first, he had to close the door on his own past, when life was so promising, and he looked forward to a future with Sarah. Coming back to Pensacola had awakened his memories of the times they'd spent together.

The first mill he was going to visit was in Molino, north of the fort. He saddled up early one morning after breakfast and headed out on the trail. He forgot how far he had gone as he reminisced his past. When his horse snorted and shook his head, Josiah came out of his reverie. He looked around. Nothing familiar. Where was he going?

He pulled a piece of paper from his pocket that had the directions he'd written. Molino was twenty miles north of the fort. Josiah consulted his pocket watch to see how long he'd been traveling. Already noon. He leaned down and patted the horse on the neck. "You're right, Prince. I need to focus on today, not yesterday." He glanced up at the afternoon sun as grey clouds covered it. "We better move faster if we're going to get there before dark." Hopefully, he wouldn't have to wait long to talk to the mill owner. He'd hate to get caught in a storm on the way back.

The rutted road through the countryside wasn't heavily traveled, and he went miles without seeing another person. An old barn lay back off the road and a small farmhouse was visible near the tree line, but no one appeared to live there anymore. The horse snorted again as if telling him someone or something was near. Josiah glanced around and prepared to draw his gun. The war had been over for four years, but he was trained to handle unpleasant surprises. Some folks in the South hadn't gotten over their animosity toward the Union. Snipers were rare, but occasionally an incident occurred. His ears sharpened for sound of movement while his pulse quickened.

He urged his horse to a faster trot, knowing a moving target would be harder to hit. Once he was past sight of the dwellings, the tension in the atmosphere lessened, and he no longer sensed danger. Josiah blew out a breath. Thank God he hadn't had to shoot anyone, much less get shot. But if someone had been aiming at him, why didn't they try to shoot him when he was going so slowly? Had he been out of range? Maybe the danger hadn't really existed, and he was just too suspicious because of his time in the war. Yet Prince's reactions indicated that it sensed something amiss as well.

Someone had been watching, there was no doubt about that. Someone who preferred not to be seen. Josiah shrugged. Some people just didn't like strangers in their territory and wanted privacy, and he'd be happy to let them have it. At least he wasn't trespassing on someone's land. That could definitely get him shot.

By the time he got to Molino, the sky was black, and a chilly wind began to blow, sign of cold weather arriving. Up north, they'd call those clouds snow clouds, but snow rarely made an appearance this far south. Still, the wind was biting through his uniform already, and it wasn't even nightfall yet. Looked like he'd have to stay in town overnight. There was no hotel, so he'd have to find some place to bed down out of the wind.

Josiah followed the sound of a sawmill and the aroma of fresh-cut trees to the lumber mill, the largest enterprise in town. As he rode onto the property, the workers cut their eyes toward him but went on about their duties. Josiah glanced around and spotted a small building with a window facing the lumber yard. He tied his horse to the post outside and tapped on the door.

"Come in!" A voice called out from inside.

Josiah pushed the door open and entered the one-room building where a man with a long, shaggy, rust-colored beard stewed over a desk covered with papers.

"What yer want?" he asked without glancing up.

"Excuse me, sir," Josiah began. "Are you the proprietor of this mill?"

The head jerked up and the man's eyes squinted. Pushing his chair back, he stood. "I am. Homer Hopkins. I own this place. What kin I do fer ya, Lieutenant, ain't it?"

"Yes, sir." Josiah extended his hand. "Josiah Hamilton, U.S. Army Corps of Engineers. I'm in the market for lumber."

"Well, I got lumber. Tell me what you need."

Josiah noticed no other chair in the room, so he pulled out his pocket journal and began quoting the amount and type of lumber he needed.

Mr. Hopkins pulled on his beard while Josiah spoke. "I think we could help you. When do you need it?"

"How soon could you deliver it? I need your asking price."

"We can get the wood, no problem. But the deliverin' might be. The Army can't come git it?"

"Maybe. And it might depend on the price too. I'm taking quotes from other mills as well."

"Well, let me think on it." He glanced at the clock on the rough wood wall. "Better be getting' home now. It's quittin' time and the wife don't like it when I make the family wait on me at supper." Hopkins grabbed his cap off a nail. "You come all the way from Pensacola?"

"From Fort Barrancas, yes."

"You gonna ride back tonight?" Hopkins peered at him.

"No, I think I'll throw my bedroll somewhere tonight and head back in the morning."

"You can stay in here. 'Least you'll be outta the wind."

Josiah touched the tip of his cap. "Much obliged, sir."

"Go ahead and git comfortable. We'll see you at sunrise."

Josiah nodded, then followed the man to get his bedroll off his horse. The wind was biting cold now, and he was thankful to have a roof over his head for the night. Inside, he stretched out his bedroll, then pulled a small Bible out of his inside breast pocket and settled in the chair to read. He had been reading through the book of Proverbs, appreciating the wisdom they gave. When he reached the last chapter, his eyes fell upon verse ten. "Who can find a virtuous woman?" Who indeed? He'd found one, but she was no longer available to him. Was Lizzie virtuous? He wasn't so sure about that, but guilt pricked his conscience over judging her.

He flipped back to the inscription on the inside cover of the book. "To my darling Josiah. May God's Word provide you comfort until you return. All my love, Sarah."

He stared at Sarah's handwriting, the closest he was to her anymore. He'd kept the Bible in the pocket over his heart throughout the war, feeling its protection over him. And he'd survived unscathed, unlike so many of his fellow soldiers. Sometimes he asked God why, why he'd escaped pain and suffering when others hadn't. But so far, he hadn't gotten an answer.

A knock sounded on the door, startling him, and he instinctively reached for his gun. “Who’s there?” he said, then stood, waiting for an answer.

“Pa tole me to bring you some vittles,” a voice called out.

Josiah relaxed and opened the door where an older boy held a basket containing something wrapped in a cloth.

Josiah’s stomach growled at the aroma of hot food. The boy shoved the basket and a jug of liquid into Josiah’s hands.

“Ma sent some coffee too.” The tall, skinny boy wore baggy trousers that might have been an older brother’s or his father’s, hitched up with a rope belt. His cotton shirt hung on him like a scarecrow’s clothes without the benefit of hay stuffing and his bare feet were larger than Josiah’s.

“Tell your ma and pa I said, ‘thank you.’”

“You a soldier?” The boy tossed a shock of dark hair out of his eyes as he ogled Josiah’s uniform.

Josiah motioned the boy in and closed the door against the cold. “I am, although I prefer to be called an engineer.”

“An engineer, like on a train? Do they fight like soldiers too?”

“I’m the kind of engineer that builds things, like bridges or lighthouses. We only fight when we have to, and thank God, I don’t have to.”

“Ma wouldn’t let me go fight during the war. Said I wasn’t old enough.” He crossed his arms across a chest he tried to puff out.

“You probably weren’t. Be glad you weren’t, and that it’s over now.”

“My friend Jude says it ain’t never gonna be over.”

Josiah grimaced. “Well, it is, officially, over. What is your name?

“Luke. Luke Hopkins. My pa owns this place.”

“Well Luke, I say it’s time to move on and leave the war behind us, so we can rebuild our country together.”

Luke studied him. “So why do you still wear a uniform?”

“I’m still in the Army and I have to. It’s a rule.”

“It’s a right nice uniform. Too bad it’s a Yank uniform.”

Josiah bristled but held his tongue. “Yes, it is, and I’m proud to wear it.” Needing to change the subject, he lifted the basket and sniffed. “This smells wonderful. Thank you for bringing it.”

Luke took the hint and put his hand on the door knob. "Yeah, it's Ma's chitlins and cornbread." He pulled the door open. "I better git home now."

Josiah nodded, then closed the door behind the boy, shaking his head. Why did some people refuse to accept the outcome of the war? If sentiment around him was that strong, maybe there really was someone near that farmhouse willing to shoot him.

He ate the hot tasty food, thankful for something besides the hardtack he carried, and washed it down with water from his canteen. Before he bedded down for the night, he opened his Bible again, this time to Psalms 23, and said a prayer of thanks for the Lord being with him, even in the "valley of the shadow of death," the prayer that had encouraged him throughout the war. No doubt he still needed to remember it.

~~~

"Come here, Miss Anna Grace." Doc stood just outside the barn and motioned her over. "I got somethin' to show you."

Anna Grace paused at the bottom of the kitchen stairs and looked up at Sarah with inquiring eyes.

"Let's go see," Sarah said. "Wonder what it is?"

Her little sister tugged Sarah's hand, pulling her toward the barn.

"Let her come by herself," Doc extended his hand to Anna Grace. "It's a surprise."

Sarah let her sister's hand slip out of hers and so she could limp toward Doc by herself. When she reached him, he pointed inside. "Come on, I'll show you."

They disappeared inside the barn. What on earth was it? Sarah waited a few minutes, then walked over, expecting to hear her sister talking but didn't hear any noise at first. Stepping into the open building, she heard a little voice coming from the loft above.

"Doc? Anna Grace?" She peered up.

Doc looked down and put a finger to his mouth. "Shhh. You don't want to wake the babies."

Babies?

"May I come up?"

Doc nodded and motioned to the ladder.
~~~

Sarah took hold of her long skirt with one hand and grabbed the sides of the ladder. When she reached the top, she saw her sister sitting on her heels in the hay, her attention focused on something in front of her. Doc knelt beside her, and Sarah crept over to see what the object of their interest was.

"Can I pick them up?" Anna Grace asked Doc.

"Not yet. They's still too little. They hasn't even opened their eyes yet."

Sarah kneeled next to the other two who watched tiny kittens nursing the mother cat. "Oh my, kittens!"

"Aren't they sweet, Sarah? I love them!"

"They are precious. And so tiny. Doc, how old do you think they are?"

"Just a couple days, to my thinkin'. I heard the little things this morning."

"I didn't know we had a cat," Sarah said.

"She's been around here a week or so beggin' food. I figure she was lookin' for a place to have those kittens."

"Anna Grace, how many kittens?" Sarah couldn't resist asking.

"Four! I already counted them." Then to prove her answer, she pointed. "One, two, three, four!"

"That's right." Thank goodness there weren't fourteen.

"What's their names?" Anna Grace asked Doc.

"Don't know. I think the Momma cat wanted you to name them."

"Me? Do you know the Momma cat's name?"

"I been calling her Mouser 'cause she's good at catching those varmints."

"Oh. Sarah, do want to name the kittens?"

"No, that's your job."

Anna Grace grinned from ear to ear.

"Well, okay. Let's see, that black and grey striped one that looks like its momma can be Foggy. The gray one is Smoky. Hmm." Anna Grace tapped her chin. "The yellow striped one looked like Sunshine, so that's her name."

"And the white one?" Sarah hoped she wouldn't name it Eben, as in Eben White, for Father's manager.

"I know. The white one is Cottonball, because it looks like the cotton in the fields around Uncle Harold and Aunt Betty's house!"

"So let me see if I can remember them," Sarah said. "Smoky, Cottonball, Sunshine and what's that one?" She pointed to the black and grey-striped kitten.

"Foggy!"

"When can I hold them, Doc?" Anna Grace implored Doc with her expression.

"Wait a week or so. You can touch them very gently 'til then but pet the momma too, so she don't get worried and move 'em."

"She will? I don't want her to do that."

"Momma cats sometimes do that. They get worried 'bout their babies and move 'em somewhere else. Had cats do that before. And sometimes you don't know where she done moved 'em."

"Doc is right, Anna Grace. So don't come visit them too much at first, maybe once a day, and don't be loud and scare the mother." Sarah remembered other cats who got skittish when they had a litter.

"I won't. I want them to like me." Anna Grace pouted.

"Here, pet the momma cat," Doc said, demonstrating how.

Anna Grace laid her hand gently on the big cat. Mouser stretched and purred, then licked the kitten nearest her.

"There, she looks happy now. Let's go and leave them alone now." Sarah stood, ducking her head to keep from hitting the rafters and backed away from the cats.

"Bye, Mouser, Smoky, Foggy, Cottonball and Sunshine!" Anna Grace couldn't take her eyes off the animals as she moved away.

Doc helped her to the ladder where Sarah waited on the second rung.

"Turn around and hold onto the sides, and I'll help you down."

Anna Grace did as she was told and carefully worked her way down the ladder with Sarah just below her in case she slipped.

When they reached the bottom, Anna Grace turned to Sarah. "Can we tell Mother and Father about them?"

"Of course." Sarah hoped her parents would have a favorable response, so they could keep the kittens. Anna Grace was so excited. "But don't be coming out here and climbing the ladder by yourself. Make sure either Doc or I are here to help you up and down."

"All right. But what if y'all are busy? Can Della help me too?"

"Certainly, if she has time."

Sarah was grateful her little sister had something to entertain her. Without any brothers and sisters to play with, Anna Grace was forced to spend time with adults like herself or her aunt and uncle back on the farm. The kittens could be her friends and playmates. Sarah knew what it was like to feel alone, but maybe Anna Grace didn't, since she'd never known anything different. But the war had separated Sarah from her closest friend, Kate McFarlane, who hid on her father's boat when she was supposed to leave with her family. She'd lost touch with her after that night, but Father said she was living with an aunt in Apalachicola.

Not having friends to visit was another reason Sarah wanted to work for Father. She had too much time on her hands and needed to be busy, not just to be occupied but doing something meaningful too. Maybe now that Anna Grace would be entertained with the kittens, Sarah could go with Father. She'd ask him again at dinner.

Chapter Nine

"Where have you been?"

The female voice startled Josiah as he dismounted from his horse. He spun around to see Lizzie Palmer with her mysterious smile that made him think she knew something he didn't.

"All over." He straightened. "It takes quite a while to travel to each sawmill in the area."

She swayed as she spoke. "Where did you go?"

"Well yesterday, I went to Molino. Stayed overnight because it was dark when I got there, and a storm was approaching." He glanced around to see if her parents were nearby. "Unfortunately, I missed getting back in time for church."

"I wondered why you weren't there." Lizzie carried a covered basket over her arm and wore a heavier woolen shawl against the colder temperature, appearing more modest than the last time he'd seen her. What a coincidence that she showed up just as he returned.

"Are you going somewhere?" He motioned to the basket. He was tired and in no mood to socialize but forced himself to be polite. All he wanted now was to bathe and find some food so he could rest from his long trip.

She glanced down at the basket as if she'd forgotten she carried it. "Oh, yes. Father told me to come to the commissary for a few things. He said we had permission to use the government supplies. We're almost out of flour and sugar."

Any other time, he'd offer to accompany her as any well-mannered officer should. But at the present, he wanted to excuse himself. How could he do that?

"So, did you find the suppliers you need?"

"I haven't made a decision yet. There are several choices, and most of them want the government's business."

"I see." She frowned, twisting a piece of her blond hair that hung loose from its confines. Then she brightened. "So, I guess you'll be busy for a long time."

"Yes, although once I select the right suppliers, work should move forward. Aren't you eager to have a new house?"

Lizzie shrugged. "I suppose that will be nice."

Josiah lifted an eyebrow. Why wasn't she excited about having a new house? He thought any woman would be, especially after living in their current home.

"Have you seen the plans for the new house?" Perhaps she didn't realize how much better it would be.

"No. I just heard Mama and Father talk about it. Maybe you could show me the plans sometime?"

Josiah's collar tightened. How did he get into this? "Maybe so, when I have time." He didn't tell her he carried the plans in his satchel when he visited the sawmills. Hopefully, she wouldn't notice it, as he hadn't taken it off his horse yet.

Out of the corner of his eye, he glimpsed a man slouching in the shadow of one of the huge live oaks. Was the man watching them?

He glanced over at the person who wasn't in uniform, then back to Lizzie. "Looks like you have an admirer."

Lizzie jerked her head toward the man and frowned. "Oh, that's an old friend."

Old friend? She hadn't been in town that long. Wonder where she knew him from? Not that it was any of his business.

"Lieutenant Hamilton!" Captain Stewart hailed him from the other direction and headed toward them.

Josiah breathed a sigh of relief for the interruption as he turned to salute his superior. "Captain Stewart."

Captain Stewart tipped his cap to Lizzie, then faced Josiah. "Did you just get back?"

"Yes, sir. I did. Haven't even returned home yet."

"Long trip, heh?"

"Yes, sir."

"Have you eaten lunch?"

"No, sir."

"Then come on to the house with me after you return your horse to the stables. Mrs. Stewart cooked a fine meal, and I'm sure she has plenty left. I'd like to hear about your trip." Even though he was tired, Josiah welcomed the opportunity to be with the captain's family in his comfortable, two-story commanding officer's quarters with a sweeping view of the bay from its shaded veranda. It was much more preferable to Josiah's empty, sparsely-furnished home at the other end of the street. The company was more preferable too, to his own and to the lady's standing beside him.

Josiah turned to Lizzie. "Please excuse me." He touched the brim of his cap.

She nodded, and he turned away to walk alongside Captain Stewart. He welcomed the opportunity to end the conversation with Lizzie. Was it because he was tired or just uncomfortable being around her? He had to admit he was a bit uneasy in her presence. But was it her fault or the fact that he wanted to avoid women altogether? Especially unmarried ones hoping to snag a husband. Perhaps if he wasn't so concerned with his assignment, he'd be more open to social activities. Then again, it might be because there was only one woman he wanted to spend time with and that possibility didn't exist anymore.

~~~

"Look, Sissie! Sunshine has her eyes almost open!" Anna Grace pointed to the yellow kitten with half-open eyes.

"She sure does." Sarah sat cross-legged beside her sister in the hay loft. The sun had barely peeked over the horizon, but Anna Grace couldn't wait to see the kittens first thing in the morning. Anna Grace had to be forced to finish her breakfast which she did at breakneck speed, despite Father's scolding to eat more slowly. "They should all have their eyes open in a couple of days."

Anna Grace reached over and gently picked Sunshine up and cradled the kitten in her pinafore. Stroking the tiny creature, she said, "She's so soft."

Sarah lifted Smoky, putting the grey kitten in her lap. "Yes,
~~~

they all are." The animal rumbled under her fingers as it purred. What contentment. Seeing her little sister so happy warmed Sarah's heart. Anna Grace now had something to occupy her time, something to love. They weren't friends, but they provided good company and perhaps even filled some of the space she missed from her mother's love and affection.

"Miss Sarah!" Doc's voice called from the open barn door. "Miss Sarah, your mother wants to see you now."

"Coming, Doc." Sarah laid Smoky down next to its mother where it soon began nursing. "Anna Grace, you be careful up here. Call Doc when you want to get down, and he'll help you."

"I can get down by myself." Her sister pouted.

Sarah stood and put her hands on her hips. "Maybe you can, but I don't want you to. Promise me you'll call Doc if you want to get down before I get back."

Anna Grace muttered. "Okay."

Sarah climbed down and shook the hay off her skirt before rinsing her hands at the pump and hurrying across the yard to the steps. What could Mother want? When she entered the house, she was surprised to find her father still there.

Glancing at each one, she said, "Father, I thought you had already left for the mill." When Father made his weekly visit to the mill, he usually left by dawn. The rest of the week he worked at his office in town near the waterfront. She sought her mother's face. "Mother, did you need me?"

"Yes, your father was waiting for you to come back in."

"Father, what is it?"

"Would you like to go to the mill with me today? You've been asking, so I thought today would be a good day since the weather is accommodating."

"Today? Why, yes, I'd love to go!" She looked down at her simple blue muslin dress. "Do I need to change?"

"No, I think that dress will be fine. Just get a thick shawl because it's always cooler up in Milltown and the wind off the water can be bitter cold, even on a sunny day."

Sarah hurried to the stairs, anxious to reach her room and fetch her things. But at the bottom of the stairs, she paused and turned back to face her parents. "But what about Anna Grace? Will she come with me?"

Father shook his head. “No, the mill is no place for children.” He glanced at Mother. “There are plenty of people here to take care of Anna Grace. I’ll be waiting for you in the carriage. Let’s make haste. It’s a long ride.”

As she ran upstairs for her shawl and bonnet, she hoped her mother would be one of those people who would take care of Anna Grace. But more than likely, Doc and Della would watch Anna Grace instead. Surely, they would keep her safe. Sarah pushed down her concerns of leaving Anna Grace behind. Her sister wasn’t an infant anymore, and she could do many things for herself, despite being crippled. In fact, she wanted to do more than she was allowed, but Sarah worried about her trying and getting hurt.

Sarah put on her bonnet and tied it under her chin, then pulled on her warmest gloves. She grabbed the heaviest shawl she had, wrapping it around her as she headed back down to the living room. “Bye, Mother. You should go see the kittens. They’re adorable and about to open their eyes.”

“Maybe I will.” Mother’s flat tone indicated she had no such intention. “Here’s something to eat on your trip.” She handed Sarah a basket covered with a cloth.

When Sarah climbed into the carriage, she called out to Doc in the yard who paused and leaned on his rake. “Doc, I have to leave. Please make sure Anna Grace gets down out of the loft safely.”

“Don’t you worry, Miss Sarah. I’ll watch the little girl.”

Father snapped the reins and clicked his tongue. “She’ll be fine, Sarah.” He faced her. “You have to quit treating her like a baby.”

“But Father…”

“I know, she’s crippled, but she can get around all right by herself now.”

As they rode out of the yard, the reality hit her. She’d never left Anna Grace alone before. She’d spent her entire life with her sister by her side. The farther away from the house they got, the more Sarah felt like she was abandoning Anna Grace. What would her sister do when she discovered Sarah was gone? Would she miss her or even notice, now that she was so infatuated with the kittens?

“I don’t know what you expect to see at the mill. It’s not quite the same as it was before the war, but we've built it back just as large. Our business has been very good, and the way things are booming now, I've no doubt we'll do even better this year than last."

"So things are back to normal?"

Father's brow creased. "Not normal, but we're adjusting. We don't have slave labor anymore, so we have to pay the workers. To make a profit, we can't have as many workers as we did before."

"Della told me her grandson Zeke works for you."

"He does, and he's a good worker too. Glad to have him."

The rutted road led out of town and followed the shore along the bluffs that overlooked the Pensacola Bay. Father pointed out some businesses beside the road, including one that had bricks stacked around it with a sign on the building reading Mendoza Brickworks."

As they passed the brickworks, a tall brick chimney loomed ahead standing exposed in its solitude by the water.

"What is that?" Sarah asked.

"All that's left of the Hyers-Knowles Mill. Used to be one of the largest sawmills in the area. They burned it down in the war."

Sarah gaped at the faint remnants scattered around the lone chimney. "Union soldiers burned it down?"

Father shook his head. "No, our men did it. They had orders to destroy any and everything like mills and factories that the Yanks could use, so they did before leaving the area. Burned it all."

"And our mill, Father, was it burned too?"

"Yes, but we came back and rebuilt it. Not many other mill owners wanted to start over, though. Some moved far away from here and have no intention of moving back."

Sarah remembered Josiah's parents and how hurt they had been when they chose the Union side along with their son and were ostracized by people who had once been their friends. Friends like her father. She heard they had moved up north and didn't expect to ever return. Her heart squeezed at the injustice of it all. Mr. and Mrs. Hamilton had been such gracious people, the kind of people who would've made wonderful in-laws. She gave a start. Were they now in-laws to Josiah's new wife?

The long ride would have been boring had they not traveled alongside the water with its flourishing activity. Ships moved through the main channel of the bay as they traveled to pick up lumber from the mills north of Pensacola or returned loaded with their cargo. Numerous fishing boats of various sizes peppered the rest of the wide waterway. The raucous cry of seagulls rang out as they hovered over fisherman, hoping to seize any fish that were rejected.

"There certainly are a lot of fishermen out," Sarah said.

"Fortunately, the fishing business didn't suffer from the war. In fact, it's picked up quite a bit. Between the gulf and the bay, we're supplying fish to other parts of the country. I've even thought of getting into the business myself."

Sarah raised her eyebrows and studied her father's face. "Would you abandon your other businesses?"

"Oh, no. Just like to take advantage of good opportunities." He smiled, then shook his head. "Just can't do everything I want to do. However, if I hear of someone who needs a silent partner, I might take him up on it."

Sarah was amazed that her father who already worked so hard would entertain the thought of adding even more to his obligations.

"Do you need to relieve yourself?" Father asked after they'd been traveling about two hours. "There's a little store up ahead with an outhouse you can use."

Sarah nodded. "I would like to stretch my legs a bit too."

Father drew the horse to a stop in front of a small mercantile where two men sat on a bench on the porch. A crutch rested against the wall beside the bench.

"Good morning," Father said to the men as he climbed out and came around to help Sarah.

"Morning, Turner," one man answered while the other nodded.

"The outhouse is around back," Father said, and Sarah walked briskly to find it. "I'll water the horse meanwhile."

When Sarah returned to find Father carrying a bucket of water to the horses, he motioned to a pump on the side of the building. "There's the well where you can wash your hands.' He placed the bucket on the ground between the two horses. "Are you ready for some lunch?"

Sarah rinsed her hands, then joined him at the wagon. He lifted their basket. "We can't tarry long. We still have a ways to go until we get there, then we have the same trip home. I hope to make it back before dark."

After a short meal of cold biscuits stuffed with a piece of salt pork, they resumed their trip. Father clicked and urged the horses to speed up.

"You know those men back there?"

"Sure do. They're right there in the same place, every day I go to Milltown."

"That's all they do? Just sit there? Seems like they'd get bored."

Father chuckled. "Oh, they eat and drink coffee too. And sell a few things." His face sobered. "They're brothers and both served in the war. I think they appreciate their peace and quiet now, and the fact that they both survived."

Sarah's opinion of the men took a turn, and she wanted to kick herself for judging them.

"Eben should be expecting us," Father said.

Eben? She'd forgotten he would be at the mill. "Does his family live in Milltown?"

Father laughed. "If you mean his parents, no. If you mean his wife and children, he has neither."

"I didn't know. I just assumed, since he is older than I am, that he was married."

"If he ever was, I don't know about it, since he's never mentioned it. All I know is that he's not married now." Father glanced at her and winked. "Which makes him an eligible bachelor."

Sarah's eyes widened at his suggestion. Did Father think she was interested in Eben White? Heaven forbid.

Father saw her reaction and chuckled. "Sarah, you shouldn't scoff at the idea." He grew more serious. "You must admit you're more than old enough for marriage. And Eben would be a good match for you. He's fine and upstanding and has a prominent position at the sawmill."

Sarah's stomach turned, and she didn't think it had anything to do with what she ate. Surely, Father wasn't serious. *More than old enough*. Father's reminder that she was already twenty-three years old and well past marrying age cut like a knife. Did he think she was too old to find a husband now? True, in the four years the war had been over, she could have married one of the men in Greenville who came back home from the battlefield.

Mother and Aunt Ellen had tried their best to match her up but were unsuccessful. They'd said she was too hard to please. Too finicky. Too inhospitable. Too distant. That's why she couldn't get one of the men interested in her, apparently. Truth was, she wasn't interested in those men. Why should she try to make them want to court her? Why should it be such an effort? When two people wanted to be together, it was natural, not forced. Like it had been with Josiah. But maybe that only happened once in a person's life.

She knew many girls who had married for other reasons, for stability, security, or just to be married and have a family. But those girls never used the word "love" when they talked about their intended. Sarah had asked her mother if she'd loved her father when they got married, and her answer was "Of course." But Sarah had always thought her mother had answered her that way because that's what Sarah wanted to hear. Some even said that love came after marriage, that it grew naturally as a result of being married. That arrangement sounded rather awkward, in her estimation, and one that didn't appeal to her.

But was it possible to learn to love someone *after* you married them and not before?

Chapter Ten

The sun was directly above them when they rode into a stretch of shanties. Small, poorly-constructed houses with clotheslines hanging between them dotted the area. Children ran in and around the houses and clothes. Sarah scanned the area and saw only Negroes.

"This is where many of the millworkers live," Father said, as if reading her mind.

"Does Della's grandson Zeke live in one of these houses?"

"I believe he does."

Which house was Zeke's? Were some of those children his? She was a little surprised her father didn't know.

Up ahead, piles of logs at least as high as Sarah's house were visible.

"Here we are," Father said as they rode into the lumber yard.

The loud buzz of a steam-powered saw filled the air while men piled cut logs on wagons in one area. A tall open shed was down the hill near the water and seemed to be the source of the saw. On the opposite side of the shed, logs floated in water as far as she could see coming down the river to the mill. Men stood on the floating logs, moving them along, pushing the sea of logs with a long pole.

"So this is our business." Father surveyed the scene. "We're pretty busy, as you can see."

The lumber yard was filled with activity, but their arrival didn't go unnoticed. Sarah felt the stares as Father slowed the pace to ride through. She pulled her shawl tighter as if she could hide inside it, looking away from the yard and the unwanted attention to the river.

"That looks like such a dangerous job." Sarah motioned to the floating logs. "Does anyone ever fall in?"

"Sometimes, but not often. These men have been doing this for years." Father looked over at the river. "One of them is Zeke."

Sarah jerked, and she squinted for a closer look. "Which one?"

"Hmm. Over there, the one at the far right."

The man Father indicated pushing the logs was broad-shouldered and lean. "He looks pretty strong. What balance that kind of work must take."

"Requirements for the job—strength and balance. You wouldn't want to slip and get trapped between or under all those logs."

A shudder shook her. "If I were Della, I'd be so worried about him."

"She may be, but she's also glad he's gainfully employed." Father pulled the carriage up to a building at the highest part of the property with windows that looked down toward the lumber yard and shed. "This is the office. Let's see if Eben is inside."

Father hopped down, then helped her out. She straightened her skirt, then followed her father as he stepped up on the wooden platform that ran alongside the building. The sign on the front announced "Turner Sawmill and Lumber Co." An inkling of pride coursed through Sarah knowing this company belonged to her father. Yet, did it belong to her as well? Or would it someday?

"Good afternoon, Eben!" Father said as he opened the door.

Eben spun around from his chair facing the window, then jumped up. "Good afternoon, Charles." His gaze shifted to Sarah and his eyes widened. "I didn't know you was bringing company."

"You remember my daughter, Sarah." Father motioned for her to come inside, then pulled the door closed. "She's been wanting to come see the mill."

Eben nodded. "How you doing today, Miss Sarah?"

"Fine, thank you." Sarah nodded back. A curtsy seemed too formal in the situation.

"What are you working on, Eben? Have you looked over that estimate for the Marler Warehouse?"

Eben frowned, then laid his hand on some papers on the desk.

"Not yet. It's kind of complicated, so it's taking longer. I gotta do payroll first."

Sarah's interest was piqued. Just how complicated was the estimate? Despite her fear of a negative reaction, she took a step forward to look at the papers.

"Could I see it?"

The men looked at each other with raised eyebrows, then laughed.

"Now Sarah, what do you know about such things? I know you like figures, but you've never done this kind of work." Father patted her on the shoulder. "Eben knows what he's doing. Let's not interfere."

She bit back her first response. "I wasn't implying that he didn't know what he was doing." Sarah forced a smile at her father's manager. "I'm sure Mr. White is quite efficient. I'm just so curious about the business."

Father chuckled, but Eben seemed uncomfortable, picking up the stack of papers with both hands and tapping them on the desk, truing the edges. It was evident to her she wasn't welcome to look at them. Father seemed to be aware that Eben took umbrage at her request.

"Eben, why don't you give Sarah a tour of the lumber yard?" Father waved toward the window. "Satisfy her curiosity," he said with a broad grin. "I'll just stay in here and look over the other projects we have going on. Sarah, Eben knows everything about the mill. He can tell you all you want to know."

Eben lifted his eyebrows, then straightened and puffed out his chest. "Be glad to show you around, Miss Turner." He strode to the door and opened it, motioning for Sarah to exit.

Sarah longed to stay inside and examine the company paperwork, but she was obligated to follow Father's suggestion. Besides, she really did want to see more of the property while she was there.

Sawdust filled the air amid shouts from the men in the yard and the whining of the saw, making it difficult to hear anything else. Eben raised his voice to yell above the din as they walked toward the shed where the saw was. Sarah tried to ignore the gawks of the men who were obviously unaccustomed to seeing a woman walking in the lumber yard.

Pointing to a huge covered cast-iron kettle, Eben shouted, "This here is the boiler where we burn the scrap wood to make the steam."

"Those pipes carry the steam to the steam engine." He pointed to pipes that left the boiler and traveled to an engine that resembled a smaller version of a train engine, complete with a tall smokestack that went through the roof. A wheel on the side of the engine spun around.

He motioned her to come closer, and when she did, he pointed to some belts that were attached to the other side of the engine. "Those belts are pulleys that make the track move the logs up and through the saw."

Several men under the shed adjusted the logs and pulled levers along the route of the logs. A gust of wind blew through the shed, blowing sawdust all over Sarah. She jumped back, brushing it out of her face and off her clothes while Eben did the same.

"Yep, that's what can happen when you're too close to the saw." He didn't need to encourage her to move away. The noise alone was deafening as the logs ran through the saw.

They strolled between stacks of cut logs piled high as the roof of the shed. "Are these all from pine trees?" Sarah asked.

"Yes, yellow pine."

"Such as the floors in my house?"

He nodded. "The same. Hardy wood. But we have to stack it to dry out before it can be used."

"What if it rains?"

"Then it has to dry out some more."

"Why don't you build sheds for the logs?"

Instead of answering, Eben twisted his lips and looked annoyed, a hint that he was tired of her questions. She'd just ask Father on the way home.

To the south of the piles, boat docks bustled with activity as ships were loaded with cut lumber. Sarah took in the expanse of the lumber yard which stretched as far as she could see on this side of the river, appreciating all her father had done to rebuild his business. Shouldn't it be natural for his daughter to have the same desire for accomplishment?

A worker approached Eben, and he stepped aside to speak with the man privately. Sarah looked away, trying not to eavesdrop but stole some glances at Eben. He wasn't a bad-looking man, and perhaps would have been more attractive if he'd stood up straight and took more pride in his appearance. Why did tall men frequently keep their shoulders stooped? Were they afraid they'd hit their heads on something? Perhaps that was the reason.

His hair was black with a few streaks of gray running through it, which hinted he was older, yet she'd known some people to show gray hair when they were in their twenties. Eben didn't have a beard on his chin but had thick salt and pepper sideburns. He was obviously a loyal employee, exuding an air of confidence as he showed Sarah around the mill and explained how everything functioned.

The worker pointed toward the water and seemed rather agitated. Sarah followed his gaze. An argument appeared to be going on between several men who were waving their hands and pointing at each other. Eben also looked at the scene and frowned, shaking his head. When the conversation ended, the worker nodded and left. Sarah expected an apology for the interruption, but none came. Apparently, *she* was the interruption, not the other man.

Eben glanced up the hill toward the company office where Sarah's father waited on the boardwalk with his hands on his hips. "You better get back," he said. "Your father looks like he's ready to leave, and I need to take care of a problem."

Sarah looked back at the situation by the river. Was that Zeke? What had happened? She wanted to find out but knew it wasn't her place to ask.

"I'll let you walk back by yourself," Eben said and strode away.

Still curious, she returned to her father.

"Where'd Eben go?" Father asked.

Sarah turned and pointed to Eben's retreating back. "There's some problem down by the river. It looks like Zeke is involved. I wonder what happened?"

Father shook his head. "No telling. These things happen." He ushered her toward the carriage. "Don't worry, Eben will take care of it."

But she did worry. About Zeke and about the paperwork Eben didn't want her to see.

~~~

Josiah checked his map and counted the remaining sawmills he had marked to visit. He'd already been to three mills, the last two located several miles west of the fort in the Perdido Bay area near the coast of Alabama. Plus his trip to the mill north in Molino. There were seven more mills to see, all on the east side of the fort, the Pensacola side of the big bayou. News about a future railroad running the eight miles from Pensacola to Fort Barrancas was in the air. Too bad it wasn't built yet. It would certainly make Josiah's job easier. But until then he had to visit each place on horseback, foot or boat, or some combination of all three.

The mills north of the Pensacola Bay were set along the Blackwater River. One of the mills belonged to Mr. Turner, and it was located in Milltown, a town that got its name long before the war due to all the mills in the area. Josiah dreaded going to Turner Mills and face the man who broke off the engagement between Josiah and Sarah. The visit to that mill would be the last one he'd make. Hopefully, the company wouldn't be the final choice when all the bids were in. Dealing with Mr. Turner would be difficult, but what if he ran into Sarah? On the one hand, he wanted to talk to her again, even though so much time had passed. And now she had a family.

Josiah's heart pricked at the memory of seeing Sarah with the little girl. Why did he ever consider she might be at a lumber mill? Women didn't frequent those places. Besides, he should just forget about Sarah. As his grandpa used to say, "Too much water had gone under the bridge at this point."

He folded up the map and tucked it in his saddle bag, then mounted his horse and took the route through Warrington and Woolsey before reaching the bridge he'd take across Grand Bayou. He'd take the trail through the piney woods, then cross the next bridge at Little Bayou. Urging the horse with his heels, he trotted away from the fort. Bright sunlight warmed the winter day and stole the chill away. As ship masts from the water came into view, he neared rows of houses where the ship workers lived. A young girl darted across the street in front of him.

"Whoa!" Josiah pulled back on the reins. The girl looked
~~~

familiar. "Hazel?' he called out.

She stopped and turned around, eyeing him. "You know me?"

"It's Lieutenant Hamilton." He removed his cap to reveal his face. "Remember me? How's your grandma?"

Hazel walked back toward him, shielding her eyes from the sun as she looked up at him. "Granny's fine."

Josiah's mind battled over his plans for the day. "Do you think she'd mind if I come visit now?"

The little girl shook her head, her braid bouncing from side to side. "She don't mind. She's been 'specting you to come back."

"She has? Well, then, let's go." He leaned over and extended his hand to her.

She stared wide-eyed at his hand. "You gonna let me ride on your horse?"

"Sure. Take my hand and I'll pull you up."

She grasped his hand and with one swift move, he hauled her up behind him. He couldn't believe how light she was.

"Hold on to me tightly."

With her skinny arms wrapped around his waist, he urged the horse to a slow gait. Behind his back, she giggled. Josiah smiled, glad to make her happy. They trotted to the road where Hazel lived and stopped in front of the house. Josiah helped her slide down off the horse before he dismounted, then tied his horse to the fencepost. Hazel's face was one big grin as she skipped to the front door. Josiah followed as the girl disappeared inside, leaving the door open a crack. He knocked on the door jamb.

"Come in, lieutenant!" A voice inside called out. "Hazel, where's your manners? Go open the door for the man."

Hazel opened the door to let him in. "I was telling Granny about riding on your horse!"

Josiah removed his hat. "You were, huh?" He touched the end of her nose with his finger, smiling at the girl.

"So that's what she was jabberin' about. I couldn't understand half of what she said." Mabel Smith sat in her rocker near the fireplace, keeping a gentle rhythm.

Hazel skipped around, looking much happier than the last time he'd seen her. A low fire burned in the fireplace warming the room.

"Settle down, girl," her grandmother scolded.

Hazel knelt by the fire, picked up a long piece of kindling and began poking the burning logs, watching the sparks fly up the flue.

"Have a seat, lieutenant."

Josiah obeyed and motioned to the fire. "I see you have some firewood."

"Yessir, strange thing about that. I haven't run out since the last time you was here." She studied him with a crinkle in the corner of her eyes.

"That's good to know. And you look well, too."

"I'm much better and not coughing as much. Food in my stomach and a fire in the fireplace makes anybody feel good." She gave a slight cough.

Smiling, he said, "Yes, ma'am. I agree." He slapped his hands on his knees and leaned forward. "Perhaps we can continue with our conversation from my last visit."

"You wanted to know about Roy and what he done."

"You said he and some of his friends took the lens out of the lighthouse. Did he tell you where they put it?"

"Not 'zackly. But somewhere out in the country." She waved her hand.

"Do you know which direction? How far from here?"

"I don't remember him sayin'. I think someone's farm."

That could be anywhere. Anything outside of the city was farmland. "What about a name? Did he mention the name of the person who owned the farm?"

She shook her head. "Don't remember. You know, that's been 'bout seven years ago. I can barely remember yesterday." She chuckled, which ended in a cough.

"Yes, ma'am. I know it's been a long time. Did he tell you anything else about how they took the lens? Do you know if any of it got broken?"

"No, he said they were real careful so when the Yankees left, we'd get our lighthouse back. But they didn't want the Yanks to use it while they was here." She peered at him. "It still don't work?"

"Oh, it works. We have a different lens in it now that's not as big as the one that was supposed to be there, so the light doesn't extend as far."

"That right?"

"Yes, ma'am. We really need the larger lens to help ships farther out at sea be able to see their way here safely."

"You don't say." Mabel frowned. "You can't build another one?"

Josiah fought back a chuckle but shook his head, less he embarrass her. "No ma'am. That lens was built in France and shipped all the way over here. They're pretty hard to replace."

"Is that so? My, my." Mabel stared at the fire. "I'll think on it real hard. I promise I will. If I can just remember the names of the boys he was with … maybe it would help know where the farm is."

Josiah nodded. "Anything you can remember would help, Mrs. Smith."

She waved her hand at him. "Call me Mabel. I'll see what I can do." Her brow creased. "Maybe there's someone around here that knows who Roy was with." She shook her head. "I just don't know. So many folks my age ain't around anymore. So much has changed."

Josiah stood. "Yes, ma'am it has."

Hazel popped up. "Can you take me for another ride?"

"Hazel! Don't bother the lieutenant!"

Hazel's eyes sought the floor.

"Hazel, I promise I'll take you for another ride sometime, just not today."

She looked up, eyes sparkling. "You promise?"

"I promise."

"I'll be taking my leave now, ma'am, um, Mabel." He turned toward the door, and as he pulled it open, Mabel called out.

"A barn."

Josiah spun around. "What did you say?"

"Roy said they hid it in a barn. Does that help?"

"Thank you. I'm sure it does." He tipped his hat and left. A farm. A barn. He couldn't search every barn for miles around. Besides, some of the barns had been burned down. What if the lens had been in one of those? He lifted his eyes to the sky. *Lord, could I bother you to give me a little help here? Point me in the right direction, please?*

Chapter Eleven

"Sorry, boy, I've got to leave you here today." Josiah stroked the horse's rich brown mane.

Prince chuffed and shook his head as if to say he disliked Josiah's statement.

"I agree. I'd rather spend the day with you too. But I'm only going to town and see if any other lumber companies have offices there, I can save some time and get our job done here. Then we can move on." Away from the aching reminder of what the war had cost him. His home. His town. His love.

Price nuzzled Josiah's cheek.

"I'll be back this evening." Josiah patted the horse's neck, then left the stable and walked down to the wharf, joining others from the fort to board the post yacht, a Navy steam-tug named Rose that would take them to downtown Pensacola. As the boat got underway, Josiah stood near other soldiers by the railing.

"Say, aren't you the engineer in charge of the lighthouse and the new keepers' house?" The tall soldier with the red beard addressed Josiah.

"Yes, I am. Josiah Hamilton." He extended his hand.

"Neal Bradford." Bradford shook Josiah's hand. "Nice to meet you."

The soldier next to him offered his hand as well. "George Moore."

Josiah introduced himself to the rest of the group as well.

"You buying local lumber or having it shipped down?" George said.

“There’s plenty available in the area. I’ve been visiting the lumber mills around here to get quotes.”

“I heard there was a fire at one of the mills,” Neal said.

“At a mill? Or at an office in town?” Josiah asked, recalling the fire downtown at the sawmill office.

“No, not the one downtown. I heard there was a fire at a mill at Molino,” George added.

Alarm shot through Josiah. “Molino? When did that happen? I was there just last week.”

Neal pulled on his beard. “It was recent, just a few days ago in fact, so it must’ve happened soon after you left.”

“Do you know if there was much damage?” Josiah remembered Mr. Hopkins who let him sleep on the floor of the company office of his mill and his son who brought his supper.

George nodded, twisting his lip. “I heard it burned up a lot of their lumber.”

“Does anyone know how it started? Lightning?” Josiah recalled the storm that had passed through the night he was there. But the fire didn’t start that night.

“They think it could’ve been a spark from the smokestack of the boiler. It’s been pretty dry, you know, and windy too. That makes for a dangerous situation,” Neal said, crossing his arms.

Josiah’s gut wrenched to know the Hopkins mill and its workers had suffered such loss. How long would it take them to recover? However, now it looked as if he’d have to rule them out as a supplier. People needed to be more careful. First, the Crawford office downtown and now the mill in Molino. At least, he wouldn’t have to return to Molino. The uneasiness he’d had on the last trip still troubled him.

When the ship docked downtown, Josiah headed over to the Customs House to inquire about local businesses. The clerk inside handed him a list with the names and addresses of three other lumber companies with offices in town. Josiah jotted down the directions to each business and proceeded to find them. Of course, one of them was Mr. Turner’s office. But he’d visit the other two first. Maybe he wouldn’t have to go to the Turner building at all. However, he’d have a hard time explaining his reasons to his superiors for not going there. Especially since the clerk told him what a big enterprise the Turner operation was. Apparently, Mr.

Turner's business had recuperated well from the war.

Josiah walked a block, passing a boarding house, then turned the corner at the bank. Next door to the bank a sign hung for Reynolds Lumber. Josiah entered and spoke with the gentleman inside, giving him the specifications for the buildings. The man peered over the eyeglasses propped on his nose.

"Yes, sir, we can do this for you!" The Reynolds employee spoke in an excited, boisterous manner, using large hand gestures as he conveyed his high energy. "Soon as Mr. Reynolds comes back from his trip to Europe, he can approve my estimate and we can get right on it!"

"Europe? Do you know how long it will be before he gets back?"

"Oh, I expect him sometime next month." The man grinned. "He's over there drumming up business!"

"I see. Well, thank you for your time." Josiah touched the bill of his cap as he left.

Next month? Perhaps another lumber company in town would prefer to do some local business instead of foreign business.

The next office on his list was one block over beside the livery stable. Josiah jumped out of the way to dodge a wagon coming out of the livery as it swerved to avoid a buggy from the opposite direction. He shot a glance at the driver of the wagon as it passed, a young lad who apparently hadn't yet mastered his driving skills.

Shaking his head, he entered the door marked Mendoza & Sons Lumber and Brick.

"Can I help you?" A well-dressed young man with a trimmed mustache and coal-black hair parted down the middle and combed down stood behind the counter.

"I heard you have a lumber company outside of town."

"Yes, sir. We plane wood for other sawmills. Most of our business, though, is from brick-making. Our factory is over on the scenic road, going north out of town." The man eyed the list Josiah had removed from his pocket. "Perhaps I can help you with some brick?"

"As a matter of fact, you can. I'll require quite a bit of brick. Here's the building plans, and you can see where the brick will be on the two properties, both the keepers' house and the lighthouse." Josiah spread out the chart.

The man glanced down at the plans, then back up at Josiah, extending his hand. "My name is Joseph Mendoza. My father owns the company. I'm sure we can handle your needs."

Josiah shook his hand. "Sounds good. Are you the only brickmaker in the area?"

Mendoza nodded. "At this time, yes. There was another before the war, but he left and didn't return. There's also a brickmaker over in Alabama." He drew himself up. "You know, our company has supplied many bricks to the navy yard in the past. I hope we can continue to do so."

"I hope so, too," said Josiah. "When do you think you can quote me a price and time of delivery?" He liked the pride and professionalism Mr. Mendoza conveyed.

"Give us a couple of days to check our inventory and other orders. Will that be satisfactory?"

"That will be fine." Josiah shook hands and left. At least he knew where the bricks would come from. The only remaining office in town for him to see was the Turner business. Sooner or later, he'd have to visit the company. He sucked in a breath and blew it out. He might as well get it over with.

~~~

"Sarah, your father isn't coming home for lunch today. He said he has work to catch up on at the office because of going to the mill yesterday. Will you please take him his lunch?" Mother stood in the doorway as if she weren't allowed to come any closer.

Sarah looked up from the dining room table where she was making an arrangement with the dried flowers she and Anna Grace had picked. "I'd be happy to. I welcome the walk and the chance to see Father's new office."

"Just don't get in his way." Mother turned to walk away. "I'll tell Della to get it ready."

"Mother …"

"Yes?"

"Shall I bring Anna Grace with me?" Sarah placed a piece of glass over her composition and stood. "She'd like to see where Father works too."

Mother twisted her lips as she considered. She was probably
~~~

weighing which was worse—being responsible for her little girl or bothering her husband. Sarah pressed her hands against her skirt, trying to anticipate the answer.

"You can ask her if she would like to go. But if you do take her, please don't let her interfere with your father's work."

Why did Mother always see Anna Grace as an inconvenience?

"She might not want to go anyway and leave the kittens."

"Just let me know one way or the other so I know who's watching her." Mother almost sounded concerned, even though Sarah knew Mother wouldn't be the one to take care of Anna Grace if the little girl stayed home.

"Mother, have you seen the kittens yet?"

Mother paused on her way out the door and looked back. "Not yet."

Sarah pursed her lips. Why wouldn't she go look at them? Mother used to love baby animals, from kittens and puppies to pigs and goats. It was as if she wouldn't allow any joy into her life. Sarah wished she could persuade her mother to go see the kittens, to interact with Anna Grace somehow.

Sarah walked out to the barn and stood below the loft. "Anna Grace? Are you up there?"

"I'm here, Sissie. Come see the kitties! They're playing!"

Sarah climbed halfway up the ladder until she could see into the loft. Anna Grace trailed a piece of straw in front of Sunshine, who batted at it. Anna Grace responded with her little tinkling laugh.

"Anna Grace, would you like to go with me downtown to take Father his lunch?"

Her sister stopped and turned to look at Sarah. "To his office?"

"Yes. But you'd have to leave the kittens here. Can you bear to leave them a little while?"

Anna Grace looked at the kittens then back to Sarah and nodded. "Yes, they'll wait for me till I get back."

Sarah was a little surprised but glad her sister would get to see her Father's office too. When else would she get the chance?

"Let's get the hay off you and get washed up."

Anna Grace had become quite proficient at climbing up and down the ladder, but Sarah hovered beneath her little sister, ready to catch any slip, just as she'd instructed Doc and Della to do in her absence. They went to the pump and rinsed their hands and faces, then shook their hands dry. Inside the house, they grabbed their bonnets, gloves and shawls from the hall tree, putting them on in front of its mirror. Anna Grace waited for Sarah to tie the ribbon beneath her chin before they went back out where Della waited with a covered basket.

"Got some biscuits and a couple pieces of ham, some butter and jelly, and a jar of pickled cucumbers. And there's some coffee in this little crock with the cork in it. Hope it stay hot." She peeked under the cloth. "Oh, and I put a piece of pound cake in too." Della shook her head and muttered. "Never heard of a man who don't come home for dinner!"

It was unusual, since most businesses closed for the noon hour, but Father was spending more time at work these days. Maybe he wasn't accustomed to having his family home and had developed the habit of working through the day. The long hours weren't suiting his appearance very well, however, as he was looking more tired lately. Did he need extra help at the office? Eben stayed up at the mill to handle things there, but Father ran the warehouse and office in town, and Sarah wasn't aware of anyone else who helped him.

Sarah put the basket on her arm and took Anna Grace's hand. They went down the front steps and over to the street, then waited for a carriage to pass before crossing over to the bayside. Seagulls squawked over the waterfront where ships loaded and unloaded their wares onto the docks. The activity from the busy area had always energized Sarah with the sound of men shouting to each other, ship bells ringing and the occasional whistle of steamboats traveling back and forth in the bay.

The waterfront was the hub of life in town, the place where business thrived. Here, the town had regained its strength, and it was easy to forget years had lapsed. Anna Grace was wide-eyed with wonder, and Sarah remembered her own excitement when she too had been a child. For her sister, the experience must be even more amazing, having spent her life up to this time on a farm nowhere near the sea.

Anna Grace looked up at her and grinned, covering her ears. "It's so loud."

Sarah's heart warmed at her sister's amazement. "It is."

They walked another block toward town before turning onto a street that ran between the docks and warehouses. Anna Grace could barely walk straight ahead for turning to look at all the sights on either side of the street, her mouth open in awe.

"Look, Anna Grace! There's Father's building!" Sarah pointed ahead to the two-story red brick structure with letters blazoned on the front—"Turner Lumber and Navy Stores."

"It's so big! Does Father own all of this?" She swept her arm to encompass the whole area.

Sarah laughed. "Oh no. He just owns one of the docks and this building." And the lumber yard, but she didn't want to confuse her little sister any more.

She and Anna Grace walked up to the double doors where an Open sign hung on one of them. Grabbing the doorknob, Sarah pushed the door and they stepped into a large room that smelled of wood and turpentine. A door to their right with "Office" on its frosted glass closed just as they entered. Footsteps sounded across the wood floor inside, then muffled voices. Perhaps this wasn't a good time to knock.

Sarah leaned over and whispered to Anna Grace. "He's got somebody in there right now. Let's wait and not bother him."

"Can we go back outside and count the ships? It smells funny in here."

Sarah glanced at the closed door again and shrugged.

"All right. Let's not go far."

They went back outside and stood in front of a ship with a British flag and watched the activity around it. Sarah tried to answer Anna Grace's questions, while curiosity niggled her conscience. Who was Father talking to? There was a familiar tone to the voice, but she couldn't hear it well. Better not stand around and get caught listening.

Chapter Twelve

Josiah followed Mr. Turner's retreating back to the desk across the room, noticing a stoop to the man's broad shoulders. The older man dropped into a leather-tufted chair behind the desk as if dropping a sack of coal onto the floor. Josiah stood waiting in front of the desk, his palms sweaty as he held his cap before him with both hands.

Mr. Turner's brows creased as he studied Josiah. Was he going to speak to him or throw him out? At least, he'd invited Josiah into his office. Mr. Turner rested his elbows on his desk, clasping his hands in front of him as he gave Josiah the once-over.

"I didn't expect to see you again, Josiah."

Josiah shifted his weight and swallowed hard. "No, sir. I suppose not."

"You're here on business, I presume?" Mr. Turner pulled off his glasses and rubbed his eyes. "I've heard the army is taking bids on the lighthouse and keepers' house."

For once, he was grateful word traveled fast in the community. "Yes, sir. That's correct."

"You have the specifications with you?" Mr. Turner motioned to the padded leather chair beside Josiah. "Have a seat."

"Thank you, sir." Josiah pulled the paper from his coat pocket and sat down. He laid the paper on the desk in front of Mr. Turner. "Here they are."

Mr. Turner put his eyeglasses back on, then lifted the paper, holding it closely while squinting at it. As Mr. Turner scrutinized the information, Josiah studied the man that would've been his father-in-law. From the size of the man's business, he'd recovered well from the war, but the years were showing in his lined face and graying hair, and he appeared to be tired. Mr. Turner blew out a breath and set the paper back down. "I see. We can probably handle it. I'll discuss it with my manager."

"Thank you, sir. Can you give me your estimate by next week?"

"Of course. Can you leave this with me?"

Josiah nodded. "Yes, sir. I made extra copies." And how is Sarah, he wanted to ask. But he knew the question would be unwelcome.

"I see you made lieutenant. Are you with the Corps of Engineers?"

"Yes, sir, I am." He ventured to make conversation to ease the tension and take the focus off himself. "You have a nice facility here." What man wouldn't want to talk about his business, especially if it was successful?

Turner's face relaxed slightly. "Yes, I do. Our business has been steadily growing, especially since I branched out into turpentine and gum. We make barrel staves as well."

"I'm glad to hear that." Was he really? "The navy yard must be a good customer of yours."

Turner's chest puffed out as he leaned back in his chair. "They are, as are some customers in England, France and Cuba."

"How impressive." What more could Josiah say? That he still loved the man's daughter? How ridiculous. But at least they were having a civil conversation. He scooted his chair back and stood. Should he extend a hand?

"Well, I'll leave you to your affairs." He offered his hand. "Thank you for your time."

Mr. Turner stood, looked at the hand, then took it, giving a firm, but quick shake. He pointed to the door. "Do you mind seeing yourself out?"

"No, sir. Not at all." He turned to leave, then paused. "I'll check back with you next Wednesday."

"Fine. It'll be ready." Mr. Turner gestured toward the door. "You can leave that open."

Josiah nodded, then strode out of the office, replacing his cap. He walked out the double doors of the building, taking a deep breath and releasing it once he was outside. Thank God, that was behind him. Words echoed in his head that his father used to say after facing a challenge. “That wasn’t so bad, was it?” Of course, sometimes, it was. Josiah had a feeling Mr. Turner wanted to say more but had held back to remain professional.

As he walked away from the building, he ran into Neal and George from the trip to town. They saluted him. “Greetings, Lieutenant.”

He saluted in return, then paused with them to watch a ship move alongside a dock.

“Was your day productive?” George asked.

“Somewhat. At least I’ve crossed some suppliers off my list.”

“Thought you might like to know we met a fellow in town today from the Perdido Bay area.”

Josiah lifted his eyebrows. “And why would I be interested in that?”

“He told us there were fires at the Perdido mills yesterday.”

~~~

Sarah glanced toward her father’s warehouse as a soldier walked the opposite direction. Her heart skipped a beat. Seeing only the back of him, she could easily convince herself the soldier was Josiah—same height, size, even blonde hair. No. She shook her head. She had to quit thinking she would see him here in town again.

She sighed, then gripped her sister’s hand when she leaned forward to look down at the water. “Be careful, Anna Grace.” Sarah adjusted the basket on her arm. “I wonder if Father’s finished with his meeting?” Hopefully, they had passed enough time. Even though all the activity at the waterfront was fascinating, they needed to get back to Father’s office. “We must deliver his dinner to him. Surely, he is hungry by now.”

“Do we have to go?” Anna Grace peered up at her. “I wanted to go see those ships over there.” She pointed to an area they hadn’t yet visited.

“Yes, we do. We can look at the other ships afterwards.” She lifted the food basket. “Don’t you want Father to get his food?”

“Yes. I’m sorry.” Anna Grace’s lips pushed out into a pout.
~~~

"No need to be sorry. Let's hurry and get back to his office."

When they entered the Turner building this time, the office door was open. Sarah and Anna Grace walked to the door and looked in. Father was hunched over his desk poring over some papers. No one else was in there with him. Sarah tapped on the door frame. "Father? May we come in?"

Father glanced up, a look of surprise on his face. Then as recognition registered, he smiled. "Well hello, Sarah! Anna Grace! Please do come in, ladies." He stood from his seat and came around the desk to greet them, giving each a kiss on the cheek.

"We brought your dinner," Sarah said, motioning to the basket.

"We brought cake!" Anna Grace announced.

"Is that so? Ummm. Sounds delicious." Father smiled down at his youngest daughter. "Just set it down there," Father said, pointing to a place on the desk. He took off his glasses and rubbed his eyes.

Sarah looked at the stack of papers that had held her father's attention. "What are you working on?"

Father waved his hand over the documents. "Just orders, bills, estimates, the usual."

"Do you do handle all of this by yourself? Do you not have a clerk?"

Father shook his head. "I have a shipping clerk, but he just matches up our orders with what we receive or send out."

"So, you do all the rest by yourself?" No wonder Father looked tired. "You seem to have quite a bit of work to do for one person."

"I've always handled it myself. Of course, we've never done as much business as we're doing now. Sometimes I wish there was two of me."

"Father, why don't you let me help?" She restrained herself from picking up one of the papers to examine it.

"Sarah, I've told you before, these transactions are pretty complicated. You don't need to worry your pretty head with this kind of thing."

Sarah gritted her teeth. She was so tired of being told why she couldn't participate in father's business. She lifted the cloth over the basket and began setting each item out on the desk. "You must be hungry."

"I almost forgot about dinner. My stomach quit rumbling long ago." He patted his stomach. "I guess it got tired of waiting."

"We were here earlier, but you had someone in your office with the door closed."

Father's eyes widened, and the color drained from his face. "Did you see anyone here or hear anything?"

Sarah frowned and shook her head. "No, the door was closing as we walked in. I could barely hear anyone speak. Why?"

"I just wondered. The customer wished to have a private conversation, and I assured him no one else would hear it." Father shifted in his seat and appeared uncomfortable.

Why would a customer need such privacy? What kind of business would be so secretive? She studied her father. Was it her imagination or did he look like he'd been caught like a fox stealing chickens?

"Father, your eyes are very red. Mother and I are worried you're not getting enough rest."

He pulled out his handkerchief and began wiping his glasses, pausing to check them. "I probably need to get a new pair of glasses. These are so scratched up, they're hard to see through."

"You must be straining your eyes. I hope you can get some new glasses soon."

"I will. I just have to take the time."

Anna Grace walked to a window overlooking the harbor. "Father, is that big ship out there yours?"

Father glanced at his little girl and chuckled. "No, Anna Grace. I don't own any ships that large." He walked to the window beside her. "However, the things we make go on those ships, then to places far away from here."

"Like Alabama? It's far away." No doubt Anna Grace thought Alabama was very distant after their long journey from there to Pensacola.

Father laughed out loud. "My goodness, no. Much farther away than Alabama!"

"Then I don't want to go there because it takes too long."

Father placed his hand on his daughter's shoulder. "You don't have to worry about going anywhere else, Anna Grace, now that we're home."

"Anna Grace, we better leave now and let Father eat." Sarah reached for her sister.

"Can we go look at the ships again?" Anna Grace said, taking Sarah's hand.

"Yes, for a little while."

"Have you counted them, Anna Grace?" Father asked, with a twinkle in his eye.

Anna Grace nodded with such energy, her blonde curls danced. "Yes, sir. There's fourteen ships!"

Sarah rolled her eyes without letting her sister see her. She looked at her father and shrugged.

"You know, Anna Grace, you are probably correct. I'm certain there are at least fourteen ships out there!" Father said, winking at Sarah.

"See, Sarah. I told you so." Anna Grace tossed her head in victory.

"So you did." Sarah led Anna Grace to the door, then turned around to face her father. "Goodbye Father. We'll see you at supper."

He opened the watch hanging from the chain on his vest, then snapped it shut. "All right. I'll see you ladies at home a little after five."

As they left the building, Sarah said, "Now, where did you say you wanted to go next, Anna Grace?"

"Over there." Anna Grace pointed to the opposite side of the street.

They crossed to the other side where another line of docks connected, each occupied with one or more ships.

Anna Grace pinched her nose. "What's that smell?"

"Fish." Sarah pointed to a boat with a huge pile of fish onboard. "See all those fish?"

"They stink!" The seagulls overhead didn't mind as they swooped lower to try to snatch a free meal while the men on the boat waved them off.

Many of the ships flew flags of different countries, and several foreign languages reached their ears. Sarah sensed the stares of sailors as she and Anna Grace strolled by, burning her cheeks with their attention. Perhaps it was time to go home.

"Mother must be wondering what's taking us so long," Sarah

said, not daring to look in the direction of the sailors as she turned toward home. "Let's go home."

When Anna Grace wouldn't move, Sarah said, "Let's go check on the kittens."

Her little sister's head popped up and she grinned. "I can't wait to tell them about all the ships!"

As they walked home, Anna Grace chattered on and on about all she had seen, but Sarah only half-listened. She couldn't shake the feeling that all was not well with Father. He didn't look well, and he didn't come home for dinner, working long hours. And now the secrecy behind the meeting with his customer. Should she be concerned? Perhaps it was normal for a customer to guard his transactions in privacy. But why did Father look so strange when she questioned him about it? Was he afraid of something or someone?

~~~

Neal was talking, but Josiah didn't know what he said. When Sarah walked out of her father's building, his attention riveted to her. She had the little girl with her again. Her daughter. Had to be. There was a definite family resemblance, although the girl's hair was golden, and Sarah's was a rich brown. Perhaps Sarah's hair had been that color too, when she was as young. Sarah attended the girl like a good mother, from what he could tell. He'd never doubted she would be, with her tender heart, and had expected her to be a good mother to their children one day.

Josiah shook his head, amazed they'd nearly run into each other. What would have happened if they had? Would it have been so awkward? He played the scene over and over in his mind, and every time, he imagined he still saw Sarah's feelings for him in her eyes. And what if she had walked into her father's office while he was there? Would her father have been as cordial or thrown him out on his ear?

His eyes stayed on her as she walked along the waterfront. How would she react if she saw him? If only he had the nerve to go talk to her. But he had no right invading her life. Still, he couldn't help being drawn to her as if there were still an invisible cord connecting them. However, now, he had another reason to
~~~

stay away from her. Knowing how her father felt about him, Josiah realized the opportunity to do business with him might be jeopardized if Mr. Turner knew he still cared about Sarah.

And with the recent fires at the lumber companies, Josiah could run out of possible suppliers and need to do business with Turner Companies. He could not let his personal feelings get in the way of a business relationship, no matter how much it hurt.

Chapter Thirteen

At supper that evening. Father appeared more energetic, although his eyes were still red and tired.

"Did you have a good day at work, dear?" Mother asked, as she passed him the potatoes.

"*Very* good day!" Father helped himself, then set down the bowl. "Of course, the visit from my two lovely daughters was the highlight of my day!"

It was good to see Father so cheerful, but Sarah wondered what brought on the change.

"Did you get caught up on work, Father?"

His brow creased. "No, why do you ask?"

Sarah set her fork down on the plate. "You're in a much better mood than when we saw you earlier."

Father waved her comment away. "Sarah, you concern yourself too much with my business affairs." He placed both hands on the table. "However, speaking of business, I've invited Eben to come to church with us Sunday and join us for dinner afterwards. What do you say, Sarah?"

Sarah grabbed her glass of tea and took a swig. She looked at her father waiting for her response. "Why, I'm glad to hear Eben is going to attend church." What did Father expect her to say?

"Ha. Yes, of course. He's a fine man and a hard worker, so I want you to know him better."

The food in her stomach threatened to revolt. Father was determined to force her and Eben together, whether she liked it or not. She twisted the napkin in her lap and glanced at Mother, hoping for some sympathy on her face, but Mother remained solemn and focused on her food. Did she not understand Sarah's dilemma? Was she in agreement with Father? Sarah's heart sank knowing she had no allies, no one who cared about her feelings. Apparently, they didn't matter. And this was the reason for Father's good mood? Would she ever get what she wanted?

"Excuse me, please." She pushed back from the table and stood. "I need to go to the privy."

Normally, she'd ask Anna Grace if she wanted to go but not this time. She needed to get away by herself. Now. She restrained herself from running out of the room, but once she was outside, she released her emotions and ran across the yard toward the water. The sun was settling down into its watery bed for the night, painting the western sky in a spectacular array of reds, pinks and purples. A lone heron silently stalked the narrow shore, moving away as if to give her privacy.

Sarah stood at the water's edge and watched the heavenly display. "Lord, thank you for showing me your glorious creation, for showing me that beauty still exists in this world." Waves gently lapped the shore as tears trickled down her face while the sky changed from one amazing design to another. The flow of tears increased, and her shoulders shook as she sobbed. "What is Your will for my life, Lord? To be a bored spinster or to be married to a man I don't love?"

As the sun melted into a golden puddle on the horizon, the sky darkened, and the temperature dropped. Sarah pulled her shawl closer and withdrew her lace handkerchief from her pocket to wipe her face and nose. She straightened, took a deep breath and exhaled. "Please give me the strength to do what You want me to do." She turned away from the water, readying herself to rejoin the family. As she glanced toward the house, she was surprised to see Mother standing on the front porch watching her. Did she have any idea how much her daughter hurt, or did she need something?

But as she approached the house, Mother turned around and went back inside without a word. At one time, when she and Sarah had been close, they could talk and laugh together. But that part of her life had vanished long ago, since her brothers' deaths. Mother had shut herself off to everyone, except perhaps Father. Sarah missed the Mother she used to have and prayed someday she'd return, not only for her sake but for Anna Grace as well. Would any of her prayers be answered?

~~~

Sarah opened the front door. "Good morning, Eben."

Eben cleaned up pretty good, as Uncle Harold would say. He arrived at the house Sunday morning spruced up with a clean shave and his hair slicked back. He wore a nice black suit and vest with a white shirt and string tie.

He removed his top hat and ducked to come inside. The man must've hit his head on too many doors. "Good morning, Miss Turner. I hope I got here in time for church."

"Eben! Good to see you." Father walked into the foyer with his hand extended. "We were just about to leave, so you're right on time!"

Mother followed Father and offered a smile. "Good morning, Eben."

"Ma'am." Eben nodded a slight bow.

Sarah glanced around her. "Where's Anna Grace?"

"She better not be out in that barn with her Sunday clothes on," Father said.

"I'll go find her," Sarah said.

"Virginia, would you please check on her and make sure she's presentable?" Father's words were addressed to Mother. Her eyes widened in surprise. Normally, Sarah would be the one to go find Anna Grace, but Sarah got the distinct impression Father wanted to keep her here with Eben.

"Excuse me," Mother said, as she left the room.

Sarah looked out the window and saw Anna Grace coming from the outhouse. She marveled at how well her sister was getting around since they'd moved back.

"Eben, I appreciate you making the effort to join us," Father said.

"Left before the sun came up," Eben stated with pride.

"Where do you normally attend church?" Sarah didn't remember seeing one on the ride to the mill.

Eben cleared his throat, then stuttered. "I … well …"

"There aren't any churches in Milltown, except for the Negro
~~~

church," Father said, helping Eben out.

"Then you must appreciate the opportunity to worship here," Sarah said.

Eben's gaze flickered toward her father as he fiddled with his hat brim. "Yes, yes, I do."

When Mother entered with Anna Grace in tow, Father grabbed his hat. "Shall we go? The church is only a short walk, and the weather is nice today, so we won't need the carriage."

As they strolled toward the brick white-washed church, they were joined by other parishioners on their way to the service. Father greeted everyone they passed with his chest puffed out like a peacock, proud to be accompanied by his family. The bell tolled in the belfry atop the arched entry doors as they entered the church. When they reached their family pew, Father motioned for Sarah to enter, then for Eben to scoot in beside her before the rest of the family settled onto the bench. Eben sat close to her, a little too much so for Sarah's comfort, but the short pew didn't allow for much extra room. Anna Grace usually sat on Sarah's lap so she could see and also to make room for everyone, but Father reached for her and sat the little girl on his lap instead. Sarah eyed her father curiously, but he smiled and faced the pulpit.

Eben bounced his hat on his knee—either he was nervous or anxious as he glanced around the congregation. Whichever, he did not appear to be comfortable, and he certainly didn't exude the confidence he'd had at the lumberyard. How long had it been since he was in a church? She almost felt sorry for him and had a fleeting desire to make him feel more comfortable or settle him down by taking his hand like she would if he were a child. Sarah guessed from his reaction to her question that he hadn't been in church for some time and perhaps felt guilty about it. Or maybe he was just uncomfortable because he didn't know anyone there besides her family. Whatever the reason, he acted like a caged animal, eager to get out.

One good thing about the service was that she and Eben wouldn't have to talk to each other. But she was uncomfortable with the impression others might have because he was sitting in their pew, and right next to her. People might assume they were courting! She tried to move farther over so she wouldn't be touching him, but there was no place to go and no way to keep her full skirt from making contact with his trousers.

When the service was over, people took turns speaking to the rector as they exited the building. Father paused in the doorway.

"Dr. Scott, I'd like to introduce you to my manager, Eben White. He runs the mill for me."

Dr. Scott nodded and shook Eben's hand. "Welcome, Mr. White. Will you be joining us on a regular basis?"

Eben glanced at Father and appeared unsure how to answer.

"Perhaps not every week, as he has to drive from Milltown."

"I see." Dr. Scott looked at Sarah and gave a knowing smile. "Perhaps the drive will be worth the trouble."

Eben's face turned beet-red, and Sarah's face heated as well.

"Can I pull the rope?" Anna Grace caught them off-guard, and they jerked to see her. She pointed to the rope that hung down from the belfry which was tied to a cleat on the side of the wall.

Dr. Scott chuckled. "I'm afraid that wouldn't be a good idea right now. People might think church was starting all over again, and they'd be mighty confused."

Father took Anna Grace's hand. "We better go before the temptation is too great."

Anna Grace stuck out her bottom lip. Dr. Scott leaned over to her. "Tell you what. If you get here early next week, I'll let you help me pull it."

Her eyes grew wide and her face brightened. "You will?" She looked up at Father. "We must get here early next time, Father!"

Father chuckled. "We can do that if you are dressed and ready to go and not visiting kittens." He glanced at the rector. "Anna Grace has been engrossed with some new kittens in our barn."

The rector smiled. "I see. Well, they can be very entertaining, can't they?"

Anna Grace nodded vigorously. "Yes, sir. Do you want to come to our house and see them?"

Dr. Scott chuckled and put his hand on her shoulder. "I'm sorry, but I can't do that today. I have dinner plans but maybe another time."

"Maybe you can come to our house for dinner and see them!"

Mother's face turned pink, and Father spoke up. "Why that is an excellent idea, Anna Grace, if the rector's available." He addressed the rector. "Check your appointments and let us know when you're free. We'd be honored to have you."

"I'll do that. Thank you very much." The rector looked down at Anna Grace again. "We'll see you here next week—early."

Father pulled her away before she could continue talking and started walking home. Eben frowned as he waited for Sarah to join him before he followed Father. Since Eben didn't offer to make conversation, she thought she'd give it a try.

"How did you like the service?"

He responded with a slight shrug. "Fine."

"Was it similar to churches you've attended before?"

He glanced at her with a raised eyebrow. "I suppose so."

"Where did you attend before?" She was being nosy, but she didn't care. She wanted to know how serious he was about his faith.

"A country church in Georgia. Where my folks brought me. It wasn't very big."

So, he had been to church before but as an adult? "Oh, I didn't realize you had lived in Georgia."

"Most my life."

"So why did you move here?"

Another shrug. "Needed work."

She had more questions but was tired of working so hard to get answers. When she didn't say anything else and allowed silence to exist, he cleared his throat.

"Your little sister—is she always like that?"

His question wasn't accompanied by a smile. A spark ignited in Sarah's chest. "Like what?"

"Interrupts grownups like she did back there."

"Interrupt? I wasn't aware she interrupted anyone." Sarah's anger simmered.

"Way I was raised, young'uns didn't say anything to grownups. Unless the grownup asked them."

"Oh? Well, that's not the way I was raised nor is Anna Grace. We treat the children in our family like they're just as important as adults."

"But they're not."

Sarah was seething now. "And why not?"

"They don't do work or do anything to put food on the table. Grownups have to take care of them, so they should show respect."

"Anna Grace is *not* disrespectful." Sarah wasn't interested in continuing the conversation any farther, especially since she was about to completely lose her temper. How dare he speak about Anna Grace that way? They had reached the edge of the Turner property, and Mother and Father started up the steps to the front door. Father, still holding Anna Grace's hand, turned around and smiled, oblivious to their heated discussion.

"You two coming?"

Sarah nodded, then had an idea. "Anna Grace, come here. I want you to show Mr. Eben your garden."

Anna Grace let go of her father's hand and hurried as best she could to Sarah. Taking Eben's hand, the child pulled the surprised man toward the rear of the house.

"What…why…I don't …" he stammered, at a loss for words.

"Come on, Eben," Sarah said. "You must see this."

Will they reached the garden, Anna Grace let go of his hand. Green sprouts were visible in the rows. "See?" Anna Grace said, waving her hand through the air.

"What am I supposed to see?" Eben asked.

"This, Eben, is how Anna Grace is going to put food on our table."

Chapter Fourteen

With great effort, Sarah went out of her way to be polite during dinner. She and Eben were so different in the way they were raised and the way they thought. Why couldn't Father see the void between them? She just couldn't believe he thought they would make a good match. Or did he just want a man to pass his holdings to? His lack of belief in her ability threatened to crush her confidence. But she wouldn't let it. She had to prove to Father she could provide value to his company, even if she was a woman.

After dinner, Father asked Eben to step outside on the porch. "I know it's Sunday, ladies, but I need to speak to Eben about some things before tomorrow. Please excuse us."

Sarah was more than happy to be free of the man, as well as, the forced company.

"Can I go see the kittens now?" Anna Grace begged.

"Of course. Let me help you out of your church clothes, then we'll go see them." Sarah and Anna Grace went upstairs to the bedroom they shared and changed clothes. Sarah put on her daywear as well, even though she was certain her parents wouldn't approve while they still had company. But why should she get her best dress soiled climbing into the hayloft? Besides, she wasn't trying to impress Eben.

When they came back downstairs, Mother was sitting on the sofa. Mother's eyebrows lifted. "Sarah, did you forget you have a guest?"

"No ma'am. Father is busy with *our* guest. And frankly, I'd rather spend time with kittens. I'll be in the barn with Anna Grace, if anyone needs me." She started out the side door, then paused to look over her shoulder. "You're welcome to come too, Mother. What else do you have to do?"

Mother's brow creased. "I have to be hospitable. That's what the lady of the house does."

"Then I'm glad that's your job and not mine."

Mother opened her mouth to speak, but Sarah went out before giving her a chance. She felt a little guilty for being impertinent to Mother, but she still had the ability to make some of her own choices, whether her parents approved or not. Even if they weren't big choices. Anna Grace was down the stairs and headed to the barn already by the time Sarah got outside. The voices of the men talking around the other of the veranda seized her attention.

She stopped and listened, holding her breath against the cigar smoke wafting through the air. Did Eben smoke cigars? Mother didn't approve of them, so Father never smoked them, at least, not at home. Maybe this nasty habit would be a mark against Eben as far as Mother was concerned. Good. She needed Mother on her side.

The conversation wasn't clear, but she caught a few words. "Army," "lighthouse," "bid." She connected the words and deduced Father's company had bid on something to do with the lighthouse. Since the army was in charge of the lighthouse, the bid must be for the army. Despite Father's displeasure with the army's presence, he wouldn't turn away a solid business opportunity. But had Father already done the bid or was he asking Eben to do it for him? His frustration over the payroll gave her reason to be concerned about Eben being capable of handling as much paperwork as Father needed him to. But there wasn't anything she could do to help Father if he didn't let her.

Footsteps shuffled on the porch indicating the men were moving, so she scurried down the back stairs and out to the barn as fast as possible. She didn't want to be discovered listening, plus she didn't want to be seen either. Right now, she just wanted to disappear.

~~~

Josiah rode Prince down to the edge of the narrow bayou
~~~

bridge and waited for a wagon to come across from the other side. Today, he was visiting yet another mill north of town. There were only two more lumber mills yet to visit, and then he'd have to make a decision. He'd be glad when this part of the job was over. The choice should be simple enough—best price for best quality and prompt delivery—but the fires had frustrated the process and eliminated some choices.

He was eager to get the construction underway. And the sooner the construction was done, the sooner he'd be finished with his assignment. And then what? He'd been so glad to return to Pensacola, but now he realized his reasons weren't realistic. He was a fool to think there was going to be another chance for him and Sarah. Why had he been so certain she was still waiting for him? Even though her father had disapproved, Josiah had hoped that they'd be able to overcome his objection when they were older, and the war was over.

But even now, knowing how hopeless the situation was, he couldn't get Sarah out of his mind. In fact, ever since he'd seen her, his feelings had resurfaced stronger than ever. But she was another man's wife now. Wasn't it a sin to covet another man's wife? But he rejected that thought because Sarah had been a friend before they were engaged, in fact, the best friend he'd ever had. And as a friend, he just wanted to talk to her. Was that so wrong?

Prince snorted and shook his head. Josiah glanced around the bayou. Was there some danger present? Sometimes, an alligator could be lurking in the reeds, but they weren't usually seen during this time of year. The back of his neck crawled the same way it had when he'd ridden past the farm house in the country.

Josiah stroked the side of Prince's neck. "What's wrong, Prince?" Someone was watching him again. But who? And why? Bushes rustled behind him and he spun to look. A man walked down the path toward him. Although he didn't know the fellow, he looked familiar. Where had he seen the man before?

Dressed in shabby civilian clothes and wearing a dirty slouch hat, the unshaven man nodded as he approached. "Too much traffic today?"

What? Josiah spun around and realized the man had referred to the bridge traffic.

"It's not too bad, considering our choices."

"Better than swimming, haha." The other man chortled at his own joke.

Josiah affected a smile as the man joined alongside. The last wagon passed, and both men attempted to go forward at once.

"You go ahead." The other man motioned.

Josiah tightened his hold on Prince's reins as they stepped onto the wooden bridge. Prince acted antsy but followed Josiah's unspoken command. Josiah had already discovered the horse didn't like bridges, but was that what was bothering the horse? Or could it possibly be the man Josiah had been talking to? Josiah walked Prince gingerly across the bridge.

The other man appeared beside them, walking in long strides as if to keep up, and Prince grunted another time.

"I'm going over to do some work this side of Pensacola." The man pointed to the other shore. "You?"

It was none of the fellow's business, but then Josiah's mission was public information. He looked at the man and answered. "Just north of Pensacola. Gibson's Lumber Company."

"Sure. Fine folks, the Gibson's."

Josiah studied the man whom he figured to be slightly older than himself, but his unkempt appearance made him look much older. Scraggly brown hair stuck out from under his hat, and he wore a loose vest under his baggy jacket. He was cocky, exuding a confidence that belied his social status. A wad was stuffed inside his cheek and he spit brown juice over the side of the bridge, then wiped his mouth with the back of his hand.

"I didn't catch your name, sir. I'm Lieutenant Josiah Hamilton." Josiah held tightly to Prince's reins as if the horse might bolt. He certainly didn't want to shake the man's dirty hand.

"Rafe Nettles." He gave a nod.

"Mr. Nettles, are you employed at the navy yard?"

"Used to be. I do a little bit of everything, fix things, carpenter and such."

Josiah couldn't help but wonder why he didn't work at the navy yard anymore. If he had to bet on it, he'd say the man was let go from the yard. He didn't strike Josiah as one who took orders from his superiors.

"I'll keep that in mind if I need something fixed," Josiah said, with no intention of ever hiring the man.

As they approached the other side, Josiah scanned the overgrown banks, noticing an old Negro man wearing a straw hat fishing nearby. Josiah turned up the trail to the north, then glanced over his shoulder at Rafe Nettles. "Good afternoon, Mr. Nettles."

Nettles waved and grinned. "You have a good one at Gibson's, lieutenant."

The man seemed especially friendly, yet his smile didn't meet his eyes. Why did he want to know where Josiah was going? People didn't usually discuss their plans with strangers. Josiah rode up over the ridge and took the right-hand fork in the road, glad to put some distance between he and the Nettles fellow. Perhaps Josiah was being too judgmental, but his intuition told him the man was unprincipled. Josiah believed he had a knack for assessing someone's character, so he trusted his gut about Nettles. And if he was right about Prince's mood, the horse agreed.

The Gibson lumber mill was about ten miles north which would take around two and a half hours to reach. The road he traveled was on the western edge of Pensacola where houses were scattered at random. Most of these homes had good-size gardens, since there was more land between them. When his family had lived in town, they'd kept a garden a few blocks away on Garden Street where most townspeople kept theirs. The houses downtown were built too close together for gardens, so the household help tended the family gardens, bringing fresh vegetables back with them. The only exception to this custom was the Turner house which sat on a whole city block by itself.

Warmth filled Josiah's chest at the memory of Sarah, and the way she'd enjoyed tallying the number of tomatoes or beans or whatever was growing in the garden behind their house. The warmth evaporated, leaving behind a cold emptiness. Why did everything remind him of her? If only he could stop those thoughts from coming.

When he reached the Gibson mill, he didn't see an office. He inquired of the nearest worker where Mr. Gibson might be. The man ran off and after some time, another harried-looking man hurried across the lumber yard toward him.

"Can I help you?" The man didn't bother to introduce himself.

"Are you Mr. Gibson?"

"No, sir. Mr. Gibson ain't here. He's gone away on some kind of personal business."

"I see. I needed to talk to him about possibly supplying lumber for the renovation of the lighthouse and building of the keepers' house. Are you his manager? Perhaps I can leave the specifications with you and you can give them to him when he returns."

The nameless man held up his hands in protest. "No, sir. Don't leave that with me. Mr. Gibson, he takes care of all the paperwork. I might lose it. Mr. Gibson will be back next week if you want to check back with him."

Another trip next week. Would this job ever get finished? Josiah tipped his cap. "Thank you, sir. I'll come back another time."

The man hurried away without another word. Josiah shook his head, then pulled the reins and turned Prince to leave. "Well, I guess this was a wasted trip, Prince." He leaned over and patted the horse on the neck. "Sorry, boy," as if the horse was the one frustrated.

They headed back the way they'd come, reaching the edge of the bayou around mid-afternoon.

"Your friend didn't stay long."

Josiah jerked his head toward the man who spoke, the Negro he'd seen earlier that day. He sat on a stump, a cane pole in his hand and a string running from it into the water.

"My friend?" Josiah arched an eyebrow.

"That fella you was talkin to this mornin'." The man lifted his pole to look at the hook on the end, then tossed it back out in the water. "Yes, sir. He done went right back over after you left. Must've forgotten somethin'."

Was he talking about Rafe Nettles? "I wouldn't know. I just met the man this morning," Josiah said.

"That right? I seen you two talking and figured you knowed each other."

"No, just going the same direction." Or were they? Nettles said he had work to do. Perhaps he did forget something. Josiah shrugged. The man's business was not his concern, but Josiah could've sworn he'd seen the man before. However, there were lots of people around the navy yard he'd seen, so why should it bother him?

When Josiah reached the other side, he had an urge to go back to Mabel Smith's house. He tied Prince up at the fence and looked around for sight of Hazel. Not seeing her, he walked to the front door and knocked. He heard shuffling on the other side before Mabel opened the door.

"Lieutenant Hamilton! Fancy seeing you today. Come on in." Mabel stepped back and let him in.

"Your lady friend was here earlier. She's right nice." Mabel pointed to a chair then plopped down in hers.

"Excuse me, my lady friend? I'm afraid I don't know who you mean." Josiah sat in the appointed place. Seemed like he had more friends than he was aware of.

Mabel chuckled. "You mean, you got more than one?"

Josiah's face heated. "I don't—I mean, what was her name?"

"Let's see." She tapped her forehead. "Lizzie, yes, that's it. She said she's the new lighthouse keeper's daughter."

"Yes, I know Lizzie. So she came to visit you, did she?"

"Yes, she brung me some tea too. Wasn't that nice?"

"Why did you say she was my lady friend?"

"I seen you two sitting together in church. Besides, she said so."

Josiah's shoulders tensed. "She did? What exactly did she say?"

"Just that you and her talked about the house you was going to build for her and such."

He allowed himself to relax a little. "Well that is true. I am building the keepers' house and Lizzie and her parents will live there."

Mabel grinned. "Um huh. She said you two was gonna fix up your old house in Pensacola and live there."

"She said that?" Alarm raced through Josiah. What had he said to Lizzie to make her think that?

"You didn't?"

Josiah shook his head. "I'm happy with the house they provided me here at the fort. It's perfectly acceptable." Perhaps Mabel was confused. He'd clear it up with Lizzie later. "So what else did you talk about?"

"Just you." Mabel chuckled again. "She sure is smitten. She's right proud of you too. Told me about your job and how important you are. Your ears must've been burning."

Josiah's collar tightened. "I didn't know I was such a conversation piece."

Mabel nodded, rocking in her chair. "She's so nice. Said she was helping you."

"Helping me?"

"You know, helping you find that thing what went in the lighthouse that you've been looking for. She asked me if I remembered where it was."

His pulse quickened. "And did you tell her anything?"

"Just what I told you."

He leaned forward and lowered his voice. "Mabel, I appreciate your help. And Lizzie's. But I need to ask you a favor." How could he say this? "Since finding the lens is a government directive, we need to keep the information just between you and me. I'll talk to Lizzie and thank her for her help."

Mabel grew serious. "I didn't mean no harm, lieutenant."

"Oh no, no harm done." Yet. "Just please only talk to me about the matter. Please?"

She nodded, then opened her eyes wide. "I just remembered something!"

"Yes?"

"Roy said something about Molino. Yes, now I remember. He had a friend who lived somewhere near Molino. Maybe that's where the barn was."

Molino? That was one place he'd not expected to see again.

Chapter Fifteen

"Here's some turnips, Della. I washed them off outside." Sarah plunked the heavy basket on the kitchen table.

Della turned from the stove and wiped her hands. "Where's your little helper?" She glanced around the room.

"If you mean Anna Grace, you can guess where she is."

"In the loft with them kittens, huh?" Della chuckled. "Looks like she gave up on being a farmer real quick."

"Maybe not, but at least for now the kittens are more entertaining."

Della peered into the basket, handling the turnips. "These are pretty. They should taste real good."

Della took a large bowl off the shelf and grabbed a knife. Soon, purple and white peels curled onto the table top.

"Della, may I ask you a question?" Sarah began emptying the basket, placing each turnip on the table.

"Sure you can, Miss Sarah. But I might not have the answer."

"When Eben was here, you acted like you didn't like him."

Della didn't answer but continued to peel, tossing the peeled turnips in the bowl and keeping her eyes focused on what she was doing.

"Well? Do you like him or not?"

The cook shrugged. "It's not my business to like him or not." She still wouldn't make eye contact with Sarah.

"Please, Della. Do you know Father is trying to match me up with Eben? He thinks I should marry him!"

Della grunted. "What you wanna do?"

"I don't want to marry him! But I'm trying to see Father's side and trust his judgment. I really don't know Eben, but wouldn't Father want me married to a reputable man?"

"I think so, if he thinks the man is a good man."

"Della, why won't you look at me? Is there something about Eben White I should know?"

Della stopped what she was doing and holding up a turnip in one hand and the knife in the other, faced Sarah. "Miss Sarah, I jus' hear things, that's all."

"What kind of things? Please, Della, tell me."

"I hear he's not fair with the men, or maybe it's just the coloreds."

"What do you mean by 'fair?'"

"They don't get paid the same for the same work." Della shook her head. "But I hear sometimes even the white folks don't think their pay is right neither."

The memory of Eben hiding the papers on his desk ran through Sarah's mind. Was he trying to hide a discrepancy in wages?

"Has anyone spoken to my father about this? If Eben isn't paying his workers fairly, then Father should know."

"Who's gonna talk to him? Most folks just want to keep their jobs. Besides, they think Mr. Turner knows what's goin' on."

Sarah jerked back. "They believe my father would intentionally cheat them out of an honest day's work?"

Della shrugged again. "He do own the company, so he must let Mr. White pay the workers what he wants to pay them."

"I don't think Father would be unfair. Doesn't he pay you fairly? And Doc?"

Della nodded. "He do. We think he pays us good." She resumed her task peeling the turnips.

"Maybe I should speak to Father about it."

The cook paused again, and her eyebrows shot up. "Oh no, Miss Sarah. You don't want to do that."

"Why on earth not? I'm sure Father would rectify the situation."

"No, no, Miss Sarah. I shouldn't have told you anythin'. If Mr. Eben hears people been talkin', especially, people like my Zeke, it could be big trouble. Zeke's got a family to feed. He's got to keep his job, even if he don't like things."

"But couldn't he work for another lumber mill that would pay him better?"

"And how he gonna get there? He'd have to move his whole family. He lives right next to the mill in Milltown. Please, Miss Sarah, don't say nothin' to your father."

Sarah frowned. She hadn't thought about the ramifications. But she wanted to help.

"But there must be something I can do."

"I don't know what. Besides pray about it. That's alls I can do, and maybe that's enough."

"I will, Della. Believe me, I will. And will you pray for me too?"

"Pray for you?"

"Yes, Della. Pray that I make the right decision about Eben." Sarah wanted to give Eben the benefit of the doubt, but her instinct told her he was aware of what he was doing. And she also knew that she was the only one who could tell her father. But she had to have proof. How was she going to get it? She had to figure out how to get her hands on the paperwork.

~~~

"What have you found out about the lens?" Captain Stewart sat behind the desk in his office. Josiah sat across from him to report his progress thus far.

"The person I spoke to said it was hidden in a barn somewhere around Molino. That's all I know for now."

"So we'll start searching every barn from Molino out about five miles."

"That will take some time."

"It will, unless we get lucky and find it right away." The captain clasped his hands on his desk and steepled his fingers. "Lieutenant, have you heard about the fires at several lumber companies?"

"Yes, sir, I have heard of some. It's pretty dry around here."

"You're right about that. However, don't you think it's interesting that the fires have started mainly at lumber mills? And even more interesting, the ones you've visited?"
~~~

Josiah's back stiffened. "The coincidence had not occurred to me, sir."

"Well you should know, there's been some talk."

"Talk, sir?" Josiah's palms sweated against his legs.

"Talk about your connection to the fires. Now I know they didn't start until a little time passed since you had visited them, but you must say, it looks odd."

"Sir, you don't think I had anything to do with those fires?"

"No, Lieutenant, I don't. There must be a rational explanation." The captain glanced out the window and sighed. "Is there anyone who would want to make you look responsible for the fires?"

"No, sir. I can't imagine why anyone would do that."

"Do you have any enemies here?"

"Not that I'm aware of." Did Sarah's father count as his enemy? Would he go to such lengths to impugn Josiah's character?"

"The question is, what would anyone gain by such deeds?"

"I can't imagine, captain, unless they were trying to rid themselves of competition." Alarm quickened his pulse. Was Mr. Turner devious enough to sabotage his competitors?

"So, have all the mills you've visited had fires?"

"I'm not sure, sir." There was Gibson's. He'd visited Mr. Turner at his downtown office, but so far, he hadn't heard of the place catching on fire. Josiah fiddled with the brass buttons on his jacket, finding one loose. He'd have to ask the laundry to secure it next time he took the uniform in.

"Well I'm going to conduct an investigation and find out. Have you narrowed down your list of possible suppliers?"

"Yes, sir. I didn't get to see the owner of the last mill I visited—he was out of town. I was going to check with him again next week."

"Where is he located?"

"Couple of hours north of Pensacola."

"And the name of the place?"

"Gibson's Lumber Company."

"Gibson's?" Captain Stewart looked down at the paper before him, then back up at Josiah. "Seems that they had a fire a couple of days ago."

Josiah's stomach soured. "Oh, no. Do you know if they had a lot of damage?"

"Enough to set them back awhile. Plus, some workers were injured trying to put it out."

Josiah's gut wrenched and he closed his eyes. *Lord, what is going on?*

"So, you see how bad this looks for you."

"But sir, these fires happened *after* I visited them, not *during* my visit."

"Nevertheless, you appear to be connected. So, every mill you've visited has had a fire. Which lumber mills have you not visited?"

"Turner Lumber, sir," Josiah mumbled with his head down, then lifted it to look the captain in the eyes. "I mean, I've been to the office downtown, but I've never actually been to the mill up in Milltown. I hope they don't have a fire too."

"Well, if I didn't know better, I'd say you want Turner to get the business, since they're the only one that hasn't had a fire."

"Sir, I've known the Turners a long time, but I can't say we're friends. You know he was a Confederate and I wasn't."

"Of course, the other scenario is that Turner has been trying to keep his competitors out of business so he gets it all."

"Sir, no matter how I feel personally about Mr. Turner, I believe he's an honorable man and would not stoop to such depths."

"Perhaps not. But at this point, you both look guilty." Captain Stewart pushed back from his desk and stood. Josiah stood right away as well. The captain pointed at Josiah. "I know you're innocent of any wrongdoing because I know you as a man of integrity. But if there's an investigation, other people who don't know you may judge you simply on the basis of the evidence they have."

"Yes, sir. I appreciate your support. What should I do now, then?"

"Have you received a bid from Turner?"

"No, sir, I'm supposed to check back this week."

"Then I suggest you go get the bid."

Josiah saluted. "Yes, sir." He turned to leave, but when he reached the door, the captain spoke again.

"Lieutenant Hamilton?"

"Sir?"

"You should warn Mr. Turner about the fires, in case he hasn't heard, which I'm sure he has."

"Yes, sir."

"He might like to know he's under suspicion."

"Yes, sir."

"Good day, lieutenant."

"Good day, captain." Josiah saluted and left. He needed to get to Pensacola as soon as possible. Hopefully, the steamer was at the dock. He checked his pocket watch. The boat should arrive in the next half hour. He went to the stables to get Prince, saddled him and mounted as fast as he could.

As he trotted across from the stables to the Navy Yard, he spotted Lizzie. He needed to speak with her but didn't want to lose any time right now. Too late, she saw him and waved him over. He couldn't pretend he didn't see her, so he rode to where she was standing with another young woman. As he approached, the two giggled and whispered. His jaw tightened as his face grew hot.

"Good morning, Lizzie. Ma'am." He touched the brim of his cap and gave a polite nod to the other woman too.

"Good morning, Josiah." Lizzie's grin spread from ear to ear. "I haven't seen you in such a long time."

"Has it been that long?" It had only been a few days since the last time he saw her in church, but he didn't have time to debate it.

"Too long." She batted her eyes and swayed. "This is my friend, Mary."

"Nice to meet you ma'am." He touched his cap again.

"You don't have time to get off your horse and escort us?" Lizzie whined.

"I'm sorry, but I really must catch the next steamer to Pensacola."

Lizzie puffed out her lips in a pout.

"But I do need to talk to you soon," he said, hoping she wouldn't get the wrong impression.

"Oh?" Lizzie's eye's brightened and her smile returned.

"Yes, perhaps later today if I get back early enough. I'll come to your house. Will you be home?"

"Of course, I'll be home. Home waiting for you." Both girls

giggled again.

Josiah gritted his teeth but spoke as politely as he could. “Good, then I’ll see you when I return.”

He tipped his cap, then rode away, reaching the wharf just in time to board the post yacht before it left. He pushed his irritation about the encounter with Lizzie aside to focus on his next task. He had to prepare himself to meet with Mr. Turner again.

Chapter Sixteen

The kittens climbed all over each other as they wrestled and attacked their siblings. Cottonball lived up to her name being a fat ball of fluff. She waddled into Anna Grace's lap and curled up, purring. Sarah had never seen her little sister so happy. She loved the kittens and they seemed to love her too. The mother cat was content as well, having grown comfortable with Anna Grace's presence.

Smoky pounced on Cottonball, disturbing his rest, then began biting on his sibling's ear.

"Smoky! You stop that!" Anna Grace picked up Smoky and pointed her finger in his face. "That's not nice." She put him down, and he bounded over to Sunshine and jumped on her.

"I'm afraid they might fall out of the loft," Sarah said.

"Doc says he's building them a box, so they won't."

Downstairs they heard Doc whistling as he entered the barn, then the ladder creaked.

"Ladies, you up there? I got this here box for them cats, so they don't fall off."

"We're up here, Doc." Sarah unfolded her legs and stood, then walked over to the ladder and peered down at Doc holding a wooden box. "I'll take it. Thank you, this should keep them corralled a little while, at least."

"I think it will. When they'se big enough to climb out of it, they'll be big enough to bring down and put someplace else."

"Thank you for making it for them, Doc." Sarah took the box and put it where the kittens were. "Anna Grace, let's put them in the box and so they can get used to it. Gently, now." Of course, the large wooden box made it more difficult for Anna Grace to reach the kittens too.

Doc watched, then started back down the ladder.

"Doc, did Della tell you I saw Zeke when I went up to the mill? He looks like a very strong man."

Doc chuckled, holding onto the ladder. "He sure 'nuff is strong! Has to be for that job. It's hard work."

"He has three children?"

"Yes, ma'am, he do. Two little girls and a baby boy."

"Do you see them often?"

"No, ma'am. We don't have a horse or wagon, and it's pretty far up there," Doc said. Sarah recalled the long buggy ride she had taken to and from the mill. Doc added, "And Zeke don't have any, so he can't come visit us neither, 'less he hop a ride with some other folks. Too bad, or his granma would be sendin' them food and clothes all the time. Della loves doin' for them grandchildren."

"Why don't you ask Father to take things to them for you?"

Doc chuckled. "No, Miss Sarah, we not gonna put Mr. Turner out like that."

"But he has to go that way."

"Thank you, ma'am, but we'll see Zeke and the family for Easter, prob'ly."

"Easter? Why, that's still two months away!"

"Don't you worry your head 'bout us, Miss Sarah." He climbed back down the ladder and dropped to the floor of the barn. "We be fine," he said as he walked away.

Maybe Doc and Della wouldn't ask her father to take things with him for their children and grandchildren, but she could ask him. Better than that, she could take them herself. Doc didn't want her to get involved, but Sarah was sure she could convince Della of her idea. Her plan wasn't entirely unselfish, however. If she accompanied her father again, she'd have to go to the mill, and once she was there, she'd figure out how to see Eben's payroll ledger for herself. She had to get to the bottom of the problem. If she could just get her father and Eben out of the office while she was there… She'd figure something out.

~~~
~~~

Josiah stood in front of the two-story building steeling himself for his next meeting with Mr. Turner. He glanced from side to side to see if anyone else was approaching, then sucked in a deep breath, exhaled and straightened his shoulders.

He hated the thought of another confrontation with the man and prayed this meeting would go as well as the last. However, how could he bring up the fires and the suspicion that hung over the man's head? And his own? Josiah could see how someone might believe he and Mr. Turner were in cahoots together. But the idea that the two of them could partner in anything was almost laughable. Still, the conversation must be had.

Josiah opened one of the double doors and stepped inside. Mr. Turner's office door was open, so he looked inside to see if Mr. Turner was there. The man leaned over his desk, pulling his graying beard and rubbing his eyes alternately. Mr. Turner slammed his fist down on the stack of papers in front of him and Josiah jumped. He rapped his knuckles on the frame of the door.

Mr. Turner jerked his head up, frowning and peering over the glasses on his nose. Recognition crossed his face, and he sat back. "Hamilton. I assume you've returned for that bid."

"Yes, sir, I have. Is it ready?"

Mr. Turner reached for another stack of papers and held it aloft. "Here it is. Come on in."

Josiah crossed the floor and took the papers from Mr. Turner's hand. He wasn't asked to sit down, so he continued to stand.

"Thank you, sir." Josiah quickly glanced over the papers while Turner watched him.

"Is everything in order?" Mr. Turner asked, removing his glasses and rubbing his eyes.

Josiah hadn't planned to review the bid in front of Mr. Turner, but the man waited for a response. Josiah scanned the numbers, surprised at the lack of neatness and the way some of the numbers ran together. Some of the calculations didn't look correct either. It would be impossible for the company to supply the material with such a low estimate. Surely, Mr. Turner didn't do the bid himself. How could the man be so successful with such incorrect, messy paperwork and ridiculous prices?

"Is something wrong?" Mr. Turner replaced the glasses and

eyed him with a pinched forehead.

"Sir, did you do this yourself?"

"Yes, but my manager looked over it too. Why?"

How could Josiah tell the man he'd made mistakes? "Sir, let me take this back with me and take my time going over it. If I have any more questions about it, I'll let you know."

"Fine, then. Have you gotten many bids?"

"Well, sir, funny you should mention that." He glanced at the chair behind him. He needed to sit down for this.

"Funny? How so?"

"Well, actually sir, it's not funny, it's peculiar."

"What are you talking about, Hamilton?"

Josiah couldn't think of another person other than his parents who addressed him in such a way, not putting "lieutenant" in front of his name. But he couldn't complain. He didn't have Mr. Turner's respect. But at least, the man was talking to him.

"May I sit, sir?" Josiah motioned to the chair.

Mr. Turner waved his hand. "Of course. Go ahead."

"Sir, there's been some strange goings-on."

"What kind of things?"

"Have you heard about the fires at the other lumber mills in the area?"

Turner leaned back in his chair. "I've heard of a couple—well, the Crawford fire here in town and one other. You mean there's been more?"

"Yes, sir."

"Who could be doing such a thing?" Turner shook his head. "We better post a couple of guards at our place."

"Yes, sir. That would be wise."

Mr. Turner sat up straight. "Are you saying you haven't gotten many bids due to the fires?"

"Yes, sir."

"There's at least a half-dozen lumber mills around here. Just how many of them have had fires?"

"All of them, sir. Except yours."

"Are you accusing me of having something to do with those fires?"

"No, sir. I don't think you would ever do anything like that." Josiah paused, glancing down at his feet, then back up at Mr.

Turner. "But there are rumors because your place hasn't had a fire."

"So, I suppose we should have a fire so I don't look guilty. Is that what you're proposing?"

"No, of course not, sir. I don't want your property to be harmed."

"Then what are you suggesting I do about this situation?"

"Sir, do you think there's someone who works for you who might have started the fires, maybe to help your business?"

A look of alarm crossed Mr. Turner's face and he drew himself up. "Why no indeed not! I can't think of anyone who would do that." Turner's expression gave Josiah the impression that the man did have someone in mind but didn't want to admit it to Josiah.

Should Josiah mention that he himself was also under suspicion? Would it help relieve Mr. Turner's conscience, or would he also suspect Josiah?

Josiah stood. "Well, sir, I thought you should know about the situation. I'm in a difficult position with only one bid. Not that I don't want you to have the business, but it doesn't seem fair with the other companies unable to participate."

Mr. Turner's eyebrows lifted. "This situation looks bad on you, too, doesn't it?"

"Yes, sir. It appears that, well, that you and I might be working together to guarantee you get the business."

Turner laughed out loud. "Imagine that. And here I was, wondering if we *could* work together."

Josiah relaxed his shoulders and smiled. "I've wondered the same thing, sir."

"So we're in agreement about something."

"Yes, sir. But I also think we agree about something else."

"What's that?" Turner frowned.

"That we need to find out who's responsible for the fires and put a stop to them before someone is killed."

"You mean, there have been injuries?"

"Yes, sir. People trying to put out the fires have been burned, but so far, not too seriously."

Mr. Turner leaned forward. "Look, Josiah. I may be a competitor, but we all need each other. We're rebuilding this city, and people need work, the city needs workers to live here and customers who will buy our goods. Of course, I want to prosper, but I want others to as well, so we'll have a healthy economy. Whoever is starting these fires is not just a threat to the lumber companies, he's a threat to the very prosperity of this city!"

"Sir, I appreciate your position. I've always believed you were an honorable man."

Mr. Turner cocked his head, studying Josiah. He probably never expected to hear Josiah say such a thing. To be honest, Josiah was surprised he admitted his feelings to the man. However, when he planned to marry Sarah, Josiah was happy to know her father had such integrity.

"Thank you, Josiah. I'm glad you feel that way. I do try to be a good, Christian man in my business and in my life."

"Yes, sir. I've always thought so."

Mr. Turner stood and extended his hand. "Thank you for being honest with me about everything, Josiah."

Josiah shook his hand. "That's the only way I know to be, Mr. Turner."

As Josiah left the building, he glanced up at the sky. *Thank you, Lord.* But one thing still bothered him. Given Mr. Turner's honesty, how could he allow such an incorrect bid to be presented?

Chapter Seventeen

"Della, next time I go to the lumber mill with Father, I'll be going past Zeke's neighborhood and might even see Zeke again. I thought there might be something you'd like me to take to him or his family." Sarah stood in the threshold to the kitchen holding Della's basket before collecting the day's yield from the garden.

Della paused in her stirring and glanced up at Sarah with widened eyes. "Did you say you'd take somethin' to Zeke's family for me? Mr. Turner gonna let you do that?"

"I don't see why he wouldn't. I'll just tell him I want to do it for you."

Della shook her head slowly and resumed stirring the beans cooking on the stove. "I don't want to get you in no trouble. Or me too. Or Zeke."

"Why should my taking something get anyone in trouble? I'll tell Father I suggested it. Besides, I want to go back to the mill, and this would give me another reason to go." Sarah felt a twinge of guilt admitting her other motive.

Della put a hand on her hip and glanced out of the window and back at Sarah. "Uh huh. Now I understand. You up to somethin', ain't you?"

Sarah tried to hide a smile. "Let's just say, I want to kill two birds with one stone."

The cook chuckled. "You gonna try to fix things at the mill, ain't you?"

With a shrug, Sarah said, "I just want to look over the books. You know I'm good with numbers, and I can see what's in the ledger."

"And how you gonna do that? You think them menfolk gonna throw open they books and let you read their figures?"

"Maybe. Maybe not. But I have to at least get there. If I can just find a way to keep them busy a while…"

"You a brave girl, that's the truth. Just please, if they want to know why you so curious, don't let Zeke's name out."

"I promise, I won't. I want to help, and I think I can." Sarah stepped closer to Della. "So what can I carry up there for you?"

Della looked up at the ceiling and puffed out a breath. "Well, I made two dresses for the little girls and some gowns for the baby. Got some beans and jelly I canned and can send them too. Elmira, Zeke's wife, she need a new apron, so I'm gonna send her one of mine."

"I'm sure they'll be very happy to receive whatever you send. Can you give me directions to their house?"

"Sure can. When you goin'?"

"I'll ask Father tonight. Maybe he'll let me go tomorrow."

"Tomorrow? Then I needs to get here real early with the things. Maybe I'll bake a loaf of bread you can take too."

"All right then. You go ahead and get your things ready, and I'll talk to Father at supper. What time are you going home today?"

"I'll make sure I leave after y'all get through with your supper, so I'll know if he says 'yes' or not." Della's eyes brightened, then misted over. "Miss Sarah, you a good woman to care about what happens to other folks, especially my family. I'll pray you find out what you needs to know, and that your Father won't get angry with you."

"Thank you, Della. I need those prayers. I don't know what's going on, but I'm going to find out, one way or the other. I truly don't believe Father has any idea something is wrong, so I have to be able to prove it to him when I discover the problem."

When Father returned home that evening, he appeared to be very tired as usual, but the crease in his forehead denoted worry.

"Is everything all right, Charles?" Mother asked at the dinner table.

"I don't know. I mean, I think all is well with our lumber mill, but I've heard others are having trouble."

"Trouble, what kind of trouble?"

Father glanced at Sarah and Anna Grace as if he unsure he wanted to answer in front of them.

Father laid down his fork. "Do you remember the fire downtown at Crawford's?"

"Yes, we had just gotten back home." Mother passed a plate of bread to Sarah. "Is Mr. Crawford all right? His family is well, aren't they? I saw his wife at the mercantile today."

"Yes, they're fine. But it seems there have been more fires—at other lumber companies."

Mother's eyes widened with fear, while Sarah stopped her spoon on the way to her mouth, waiting for Father's next words.

"Charles, are you concerned about our mill, that there might be a fire?"

"Perhaps. I'm going there tomorrow to talk to Eben about having some guards posted."

"Oh dear," Mother said, her hand across her chest. "So, these fires have been intentionally set? Why would anyone do such a malicious deed?"

Father shook his head. "I don't know. It doesn't make sense. If someone were disgruntled with their company, they might cause trouble with that company only. But with all the lumber companies? No, it doesn't make sense."

"I'm sure no one who works for you would ever do such a thing, since you treat your employees so fairly," Mother said.

Sarah stared at her mother who had no inkling there was any unrest at the company. Would unfair wages be a cause for a fire? She was even more convinced she had to go the mill and see those books to protect her father's company.

"I'm sure Mother is right," Sarah offered, hoping to ease her mother's anxiety so she'd be open to Sarah's suggestion.

"We've been fortunate," Father said. "I've heard of employees at some companies walk off the job and strike. I've always thought that was a foolish thing to do when one needs to work."

"I agree," Sarah said. "You have loyal employees like Zeke and Eben."

"That's true," Father said, rubbing his eyes.

"Dear, you should go to bed early tonight for that long ride tomorrow."

"I think I will." Father pushed away from the table.

Sarah took her chance to ask before he left the room. "Father, may I please go with you tomorrow? I promised Della I'd take some things to Zeke's family for her next time I go with you."

Father lifted his eyebrows and Mother looked at her with surprise.

"You did, did you?" Father tapped on the table. "Did Della ask you to do that?"

"Oh no, she'd never do that. I offered. She mentioned her grandchildren because Anna Grace reminded her of them. She told me she had made them some clothes but didn't know when or how she'd get them delivered. Since their home is on the way to the mill, I offered to take them for her."

"Sarah, perhaps this isn't a good time," Mother said. "It sounds like there could be some danger."

"Mother, I'll be fine. I'll be with Father all the time. He can drive me right up to their shanty and I'll drop off the things. Then I'll go with him to the mill. I won't even go outside the office at the mill, just to be safe. Besides, no one would start a fire when everyone is around."

"Well …" Mother cast an anxious glance at Father. "Do you think she'll be safe, Charles?"

Father studied Sarah, then sighed. "I think she'll be fine. She'll stay right by my side."

"If you say so, then all right."

"Can I go this time?" Anna Grace asked.

"No, I'm afraid not," Father said. "But maybe someday you can."

Sarah couldn't imagine when that would be, but she was thankful her father was gentle in his answer to his little girl. Meantime, Sarah couldn't wait to go tell Della she could go.

"Excuse me," Sarah said. "I'll let Della know we'll be going to Milltown tomorrow so she can bring the things I need to take in the morning."

"I'm heading to bed." Father stood. "Sarah, be ready by sunrise tomorrow."

"Yes, sir, I will." Sarah quickly took up the dinner plates and silverware to be washed, then hurried out the door to the kitchen.

~~~
~~~

Josiah stood on the wharf supervising the unloading of brick from the steamship. Stacks were loaded in carts, then carried to a wagon with two mules waiting to haul them up the hill. Today, Josiah had the satisfaction of seeing some phase of his work accomplished. Mendoza had been able to deliver the bricks needed, so at least the repair work on the lighthouse could proceed. Although a small fire had started at the Mendoza planing mill, it was quickly put out with minimal damage. The brickmaking part of the company was not affected.

The planing mill would not have been sufficient to supply all the lumber Josiah needed anyway. For now, he was thankful the company could supply the bricks. This was only the first load, as several thousand bricks would be needed to complete both the lighthouse and the keepers' house. Construction on the house couldn't begin until the lumber was procured, and that contract still waited to be settled.

The mules strained to pull the first wagonful through the sand toward the lighthouse where it would be unloaded again.

When the last load left the dock, Josiah followed it up the hill. Keeper Ponder stood by the stacks of brick, surveying the unloading. As Josiah approached, the keeper turned to greet him.

"Good to see some progress, lieutenant. I was beginning to wonder when some work would begin." The keeper crossed his arms and rocked back on his heels.

"I agree. At least we can do the repair work on the lighthouse where the cannon shot damaged it."

"Good. And the house? When will construction begin on it?"

"Can't say just yet. We've had some delays with the lumber."

Ponder's eyebrows drew together. "What kind of delay? The weather hasn't been a problem."

"No sir. Just some problems at the lumber mills."

"Hmmph! I would think they'd want the business."

Josiah didn't feel the need to share any more information about the fires with the man. No doubt the keeper would have an opinion about how to solve the problem, and Josiah didn't want to hear it.

"Excuse me," Josiah said. "I need to verify the quantity." He walked away from Ponder as his eyes roamed over the brick, hoping his estimate for the work was correct. He'd ordered a total of 45,000 bricks for the entire project. This was only the first third of the order. A few people from the navy yard had come to see the bricks unloaded, excited about the new construction they represented and almost as eager. Josiah assumed some bricklayers he could hire might be among the onlookers.

Hearing laughter coming from a group to his left, he was surprised to see Rafe Nettles. When their eyes met, Nettles lifted a hand and grinned. Odd to see him here. He didn't mention having bricklaying experience, and Josiah wouldn't want to hire him anyway. Remembering what the old fisherman said, Josiah wondered why Nettles had returned to this side of the bayou so quickly. The man's presence bothered him, but Josiah couldn't explain why.

Standing off to the opposite side, Lizzie Ponder caught his eye. She waved with enthusiasm as if she hadn't seen him for ages. He gave a half-hearted wave back, then returned his attention to the bricks, verifying the last load. Now that his work for the day was done, he needed to speak with Lizzie.

He made his way over to her while she waited with a grin.

"Hello Lizzie."

"Hello, Josiah. I was hoping you'd notice me." She smiled demurely, then pointed to the stacks. "That's a lot of bricks."

"It certainly is," Josiah said. "We'll get a lot more before we build your house."

"And when will that be?"

"Soon, I hope." Josiah motioned away from the bricks. "Do you have time to take a short stroll?"

"Yes, of course." She lost no time tucking her hand inside his elbow, acting as though she'd laid claim to him.

"Lizzie, I understand you've been to see Mrs. Mabel Smith."

"Who?" She lifted her eyes toward the sky as if trying to recollect the name and feigning innocence, in his opinion. "Oh yes, I did."

Josiah took his time formulating his statement. "I didn't realize you knew her."

"Oh, I know her from church. She's a nice lady."

"Yes, she is." He considered his words, trying to choose them wisely. "Did you tell her you were helping me?"

Lizzie nodded. "Umhum. I did. I think it's only right that I should help you."

An uneasy feeling crawled up Josiah's shoulders. "And that's because…"

"Why, because you're fixing the lighthouse and building our house, of course."

"I do appreciate your desire to help me, Lizzie. However, I'm the one being held responsible for the project, not you."

"And I want you to succeed." She smiled up at him, fluttering her eyes.

"Thank you, but perhaps you shouldn't get involved in some things."

She angled her head at him. "What things?"

"For one, finding the missing lens. There may be people who don't want me to find it, and if they hear I know where it is, they might move it."

She touched her finger to her lip and glanced to either side. "Oh. Then I'll keep it a secret."

"Keep what a secret?"

"Where the lens is, of course."

"And you know where it is?"

"Just that it's in a barn in Molino like that lady said."

Josiah suppressed his agitation with her. He lowered his voice. "That's something you shouldn't discuss with others. Especially since we still don't know exactly where it is. But talking about where it might be could interfere with our finding it. Do you understand?"

She nodded with vigor and squeezed his arm. "My lips are sealed."

He wanted very much to ask her about what Mabel Smith said Lizzie told her about rebuilding his parents' house, but what if Mabel was confused about what she said? "Lizzie, did you say anything else to Mrs. Smith about us, you and me?"

Lizzie glowed. "Oh, I don't remember exactly. But you know some things women want to keep to themselves…especially about their men friends."

Heat flushed his face. "Lizzie, I need to be honest with you. I haven't kept company with a lady since before the war. I was once engaged, but the war ended that."

Lizzie' face darkened, and the look on her face was somewhere between angry and sinister. Then she brightened again and pouted her lips. "I'm so sorry. That must have been so sad for you."

"It was." His mind drifted to Sarah's face and his heart swelled with yearning.

"What happened to her? Did she die?" Lizzie patted his arm, and her face showed real concern. "I know how it feels, to lose someone. My intended died too."

He was taken aback by her bold confession, not to mention the suggestion that Sarah had died.

"No, she didn't die. In fact, she lives right here." The surprise on Lizzie's face made him wish he hadn't told her. "You see, our engagement was ended by her father because I fought for the Union and he was a Confederate sympathizer."

"And she lives here? Now?" Lizzie's agitation bordered on anger and alarm.

"Yes. I don't know when her family moved back, but I saw her recently." Did Lizzie flinch?

"I mean, I saw her from a distance. I believe she's married and has a child. I haven't spoken to her since before the war." Why did he feel the need to explain to her? Yet, she seemed upset to hear about Sarah, and he didn't want her to have any misconceptions. Why, it sounded as if he were spying on Sarah. What if Mr. Turner heard anything remotely hinting at that?

Lizzie's shoulders relaxed slightly. "Oh. Then it's a good thing you and she have forgotten each other now. No need worrying about the past. After all, we have the future to look forward to." Lizzie grinned, looking at him with a gleam in her eyes.

So she thought he'd forgotten Sarah? If she only knew how impossible that was. But he wouldn't tell her otherwise. He should have forgotten about Sarah, just as she'd forgotten about him. His chest squeezed at the notion that she really had forgotten about him. He was such a fool to believe she hadn't. However, even though he and Sarah were no longer engaged, he and Lizzie weren't either, nor were they even courting. So why did she act like they were?

Lizzie appeared to be very sensitive, and he feared upsetting her. So, what was the harm if she had set her sights on him? He hadn't asked to court her, so was it necessary for him to tell her he had no interest in doing so? For the time being, he thought it'd be best to just humor her. What could it hurt? There was no one else who'd be affected.

"Yes, and speaking of the future, I hope we can get started on your home soon. The new keepers' house will be very nice."

"The keepers' house?" Lizzie looked confused.

"Yes, so you and your family will be able to move and have more room."

Lizzie's forehead creased. "I thought you were having problems finding the lumber to build it."

"I have been, but I'm about to narrow down my decision." How did she know he was having problems finding the lumber? He didn't remember discussing that with her. But it was a small community, and news about the fires probably traveled fast.

"Then I suppose you'll be able to start rebuilding your old house."

"My old house? You mean, my parents' home in town?"

"Yes, I can't wait to see how it will look when it's new again."

"But…I…"

"Excuse me, Lieutenant. The Captain wants a word with you." The young soldier appeared at Josiah's side with a salute.

"Where?"

The soldier motioned back toward the bricks. "Over there."

"Tell him I'll be right there."

"Yes, sir!" The soldier turned on his heel and marched away.

Josiah patted Lizzie's hand and gently removed it from his elbow. "Please excuse me, Lizzie. We'll have to continue our conversation later."

She grinned. "Of course, Josiah. I'll be right here, waiting for you."

He tipped his hat and spun around. Why did his conversations with her leave him more confused than ever?

Chapter Eighteen

Sarah looked down at the note in her hand with the directions she'd scribbled from Della. Turn down the second alley on the left, then turn right at the next. The house would have a little weathervane on the roof, which would be easy to find, if she could see over the shanties in front of her and the clothes hanging out between them. She shuffled the weight of the basket on her arm.

"Sarah, I don't know why I allowed you to talk me into this," Father said, casting glances all around him. "We don't know exactly where the house is."

"I thought you said you knew." Sarah sidestepped a child running past. "Besides, if we can't find it ourselves, I'm sure we can ask someone. Everyone here probably knows everyone else."

"Hmph." Father certainly looked out of place wearing his fine suit in the middle of this poor area. Sarah glanced down at her own dress, almost embarrassed by the difference in what she had and how little these people possessed.

"Father, you could have stayed with the buggy. I didn't need an escort."

"You most certainly do. I wouldn't let you wander around this area by yourself."

Sarah spotted the rusted weathervane on the roof ahead. A baby cried inside the house, and Sarah hesitated to knock on the partially open door.

"Well, are you going to just stand there? Let's get this over with." Father pounded on the doorsill.

"Coming," A high-pitched woman's voice responded.

The door slowly creaked open, and a young Negro woman wearing a dingy white turban and apron over a plain muslin dress looked out. She had a baby on her hip and two little girls clinging to her dress. “Can I help you?” asked the woman, her dark eyes wide with wonder, mirroring the expression on the little girls’ faces.

“Are you Elmira, Zeke’s wife?” Sarah asked in a soft voice so the woman wouldn’t be any more frightened than she already appeared to be.

She nodded. “Yes’m, I’m Elmira.” She squinted at Sarah’s father. “You Mr. Turner?”

Father cleared his throat. “I am. Zeke works for me.”

Elmira glanced from Sarah to her father as fear filled her eyes. “Is Zeke all right?”

“He’s fine.” Sarah reached out to touch the woman’s hand. “We didn’t mean to alarm you.

I’m Sarah Turner and this is my father.”

“I seen Mr. Turner before, but he don’t remember me.” She nodded to Father, her eyes cast down.

“I’m sorry, I don’t. Bad memory, you know.” Father put a finger to his head.

Sarah lifted the basket to show Elmira. “Della sent some things for you. You know she works for us.”

“Yes’m, I do.” She eyed the basket. “What things she send?”

They hadn’t been asked in, so Sarah set the basket down on the floor in front of Elmira, squatted beside it and lifted the cover. She pulled out a plain little dress made from flour sacks and held it up in front of one of the little girls peering from behind her mother. “This looks like it would fit you,” Sarah said.

“A new dress? Josie, look there what yo grandma made you.” Elmira patted the girl’s head.

Sarah pulled out another, identical dress. “And one for you too.” She showed the other little girl that clung to Elmira’s other leg.

“Tess, you got a new dress too,” Elmira spoke down to the child.

Sarah stood, placed the dresses back inside the basket and handed it to Elmira. “There’s a gown in here for your baby too. Plus, she sent a loaf of bread, a jar of pickles and a few other things."

Elmira shifted the child on her hip as she took the basket, tears in the corner of her eyes. "The good Lord bless her. Please tell Della we be so grateful." A tear left a trail down her face.

"We will. She'll be so pleased to know we were able to get them to you."

"The Lord bless you nice folks too. You'se real nice to bring this to us. Zeke will be happy 'bout it too."

"Good. Well, we need to get going now." Father took Sarah by the arm, his discomfort obvious to her.

"Goodbye," Sarah said, as they turned to leave.

"Bye," Elmira said to their backs.

Father practically pulled Sarah down the alleys back to the carriage, sweat popping out along his hairline even though the day was cool. "Well, that's done." He helped Sarah into the carriage, then hopped in beside her, slapping the reins to start the horses.

"Thank you for allowing me to do that, Father. I know you were uncomfortable." Sarah studied her father's face.

"I'm just not used to those situations." Father kept his focus ahead. "Your mother used to do things like that though. I called her a 'good Samaritan,' like the one in the Bible."

"She did?" Sarah searched her memory. A vague image of visiting a poor family in town came to her mind from long ago. "Oh, I think I remember. She used to go see the elderly people who couldn't get to church, didn't she? I'd forgotten about that."

"That's right. She did."

"Why did she quit?"

Father shook his head. "Your mother hasn't been the same since your brothers died. But you know that, don't you?"

"Yes. I wish she would go back to being the way she used to be."

"I thought Anna Grace would pull her out of her mourning. In fact, that's one reason we named her 'Grace,' for God's grace giving her another child. But when she realized Anna Grace was crippled, Virginia thought God was still punishing her."

"I don't know why she would feel that way. She has to know it wasn't her fault about Anna Grace or about the boys' passing."

"I've tried to convince her. But she still blames herself that the boys got sick. She let them play outside and they got the vapors."

"But I played outside too, and I didn't get sick."

"I know. But maybe you were inside more. I really don't understand why some people got the fever and others didn't. So many in Pensacola died." Father glanced at Sarah, his eyes misted. "I'm just thankful you didn't."

Sarah placed her hand over her father's. "Me too, Father." She wanted so badly to say she would take the place of his sons but knew that would be impossible, much as she wished she could.

They entered the lumber yard and drove up to the office as before. The workers didn't seem to be as busy, but they exchanged glances and cast a wary eye on her and Father. The office was locked, and peering through the window, it was evident no one was there.

"Hmm. Wonder where Eben is? He doesn't usually lock the office in the daytime."

Father stood on the platform outside the office with his hands on his hips, surveying the yard. A man in overalls hurried over.

"Good morning, Mr. Turner, Mr. White's not here."

"Did he leave you in charge, Mr. …?"

"Yes, sir. Homer Sims is the name. I'm the foreman here."

"Well, Mr. Sims. Where is Mr. White? Do you know when he'll be back?"

"No, sir. He said he had some business to take care of. I figured he went down to Pensacola."

"I wasn't expecting him in town. Did he leave you a key to the office?"

"Yes, sir, but he told me not to go in there unless there was a fire."

"A fire?"

"Yes, sir. He said if there was a fire, I was supposed to get the records out of the office."

Father frowned, his lips forming a straight line. "Give me the key, please."

"Yes, sir." The man pulled the key from his pocket and handed it over.

Father unlocked the door, and he and Sarah went inside. Sarah scanned the room, noticing a leather folder with a string tied around it on the corner of the desk. The musty office appeared as if no one had been there all day.

"Sarah, try to make yourself comfortable. I'm going to take a walk around the yard and check on things. I don't know how long I'll be."

"You go ahead, Father. I'll be fine. I have a good view of everything from here."

Sarah couldn't believe her good fortune. Now she had the office all to herself and could finally get a good look at the paperwork. She glanced through the window to make sure Father had gone away before she grabbed the leather folder. Her fingers hurried to untie the string and open the folder before pulling out a sheaf of papers.

One thing for certain, Eben had poor penmanship. It took some effort to decipher his writing. In addition to the sloppy writing, the pages were smudged from multiple erasing. Some of the ledgers appeared to be for inventory, with amounts of logs listed by dates. Other ledgers recorded shipping, noting which company had picked up a certain number of logs. She finally got to the bottom of the stack and found ledgers with employee names listed. There must have been forty employees recorded, what their job title was, and how many hours they worked.

On the far right side of the ledger was an amount which she determined to be how much each man earned. It didn't take long for her to realize the amounts were not the same. Obviously, not all the men were paid the same amount. Sarah assumed different jobs were paid at different rates.

But when she studied the numbers and compared them, nothing made sense. Not even men with the same job were paid the same. The amounts appeared to be very arbitrary. Even though the number of hours worked wasn't consistent, her calculation showed an inconsistent hourly pay rate as well. What was going on here? No wonder the men were upset. They never knew what they were being paid. But why was Eben paying them this way? Was he showing favoritism?

Sarah decided to look at the other lists for comparison. She found errors in the inventory too. Then she reviewed the shipping ledgers. They also had errors. From what she could tell, Eben just wasn't good with his numbers. How could they do business this way? Surely, some of their customers would notice discrepancies, unless no one knew the difference and just trusted him. True, there were many uneducated people who worked in the industry, but sooner or later, the ones who were smart enough to check the figures would find the errors. And then the Turner business reputation would be at stake.

How could she tell her father though? She knew he would be angry with her for snooping in his business, but wouldn't he want to know? She lost track of time as she perused the documents. When she found what looked like an estimate, she paused. Once again, the numbers didn't add up. The company could lose money if this was a bid. If only she could handle the bids. God had given her a good head for numbers, so didn't He expect her to use it?

Steps sounded outside the door and she jumped, hurrying to stuff the papers back into the folder. The door opened just as she retied the string. Father stepped inside looking worried.

"Is everything all right, Father?"

"I don't know, Sarah. I could feel some tension in the air from the workers, and I don't know if it was simply because I'm here or something else. I also don't know why Eben left the mill today. The supervisor told me Eben leaves at least once a week to 'take care of business,' whatever that means. I'd sure like to find out what kind of business he's taking care of. I told the foreman to tell Eben to contact me as soon as possible."

"Father, do you think there's anything dishonest about his affairs?"

The angry glance Father gave shocked her. "Eben has *always* been trustworthy."

Maybe he had been, but Sarah suspected Father was having doubts about his trustworthiness now. Father was concerned about his manager's absence, but perhaps he should have been more concerned about the man's poor arithmetic.

Chapter Nineteen

"Lieutenant Hamilton." Captain Stewart returned Josiah's salute. "Does this load meet your approval?" The captain's arms were across his chest as he nodded toward the bricks.

"Yes, sir. They all seem to be accounted for and in good condition."

"Fine. I'll post a guard in the area to make sure they're not tampered with." He faced Josiah. "You've finished your visits to the lumber mills?"

"Yes, sir. Or at least to their offices in town."

"And Turner is the last one you saw?"

"Yes, sir." Josiah's collar tightened. "Is there a problem sir?"

"No, I suppose not. You did get an estimate from them?"

Josiah swallowed hard. "Er, yes, sir. I need to go over it more carefully though. I've only looked at it briefly."

"And as far as you know, they haven't had any fires?"

"Not that I know of." Josiah almost said, "not yet," but pushed the negative thoughts away.

"Did I hear something about fire?" Mr. Ponder strolled up. "What fire?"

Captain Stewart and Josiah exchanged glances before the captain spoke.

"There have been some suspicious fires at area lumber companies."

Mr. Ponder paled. "Was anyone hurt?"

"Not seriously, thank God," Josiah said.

Ponder looked down at the ground and shook his head. "Thank

God indeed." He glanced up at Josiah. "I suppose these fires have something to do with why the construction hasn't begun."

"That's correct," the captain said.

"So what if you can't get the lumber around here? What will you do?" Ponder asked.

"We can have it sent down by ship from the north," Josiah said. "It will take longer for the lumber to arrive, but it's our last alternative. I'm sorry the lighthouse and your home are being delayed, sir."

Ponder frowned, then cleared his throat. "Yes, well, I am too." He scanned the area, then glanced at Josiah. "I'm sure Mrs. Ponder and Lizzie will be disappointed to hear about the problems as well."

"No need to discuss it yet, Mr. Ponder," Captain Stewart said. "We're trying to get to the bottom of this. It appears that some people don't want these projects to be completed."

"Why wouldn't they?" Ponder asked. "You don't still suspect any Rebel involvement, do you?"

The captain shrugged his shoulders. "It's possible. But the governor's request to keep federal troops in the state even after Florida was readmitted has pretty much eliminated any trouble from former Confederates."

"Like the problem locating the lens, I assume." Ponder said.

"Perhaps," the captain said.

"Say, do you think the same people that hid the lens are setting the fires?" Ponder asked.

"Seems doubtful, since the lens was stolen seven years ago when the Confederates left, and the fires are recent."

"But what if some of the same people came back?" Ponder's face contorted. "Those blasted Rebs!"

"Mr. Ponder, let's not go jumping to conclusions," Captain Stewart said.

"Well it makes perfect sense to me," the lighthouse keeper said. "They're still trying to sabotage us."

"There could be other explanations," Josiah offered. "What if there's a disgruntled lumber worker who's out to get revenge?"

Ponder cocked his head. "Now that's a strange notion." He stroked his beard. "Guess it's possible." He mulled over it a minute. "What if one lumber company is trying to get rid of its competition?"

Captain Stewart glanced at Josiah, whose stomach churned at the suggestion. The captain had suggested Mr. Turner could be guilty of such actions.

"We're considering all possibilities," the captain said. "If you'll excuse us, Mr. Ponder, Lieutenant Hamilton and I need to discuss some things."

"Sure thing. I hope you find the culprits and hang them!" Ponder turned on his heel and stormed off as Josiah's gut twisted in knots.

He and the captain watched Ponder stomp away. Josiah was surprised to see Lizzie still standing where he'd left her, apparently watching him the whole time. When her father approached her, he grabbed her by the elbow and turned her around, forcing her to walk with him. No doubt he didn't want her standing around with all the men. What had she told her father about him? Did he think they were courting? No, he couldn't, because Josiah had never asked permission. Still, what she'd said to Mabel Smith was disturbing.

"Lieutenant?" Captain Stewart got his attention. "What is your relationship to that young woman?"

"Sir?" Josiah looked over at the Ponders' retreating backs.

"Miss Ponder."

"None, sir. I mean, other than friendship, there's nothing more."

"My wife heard that Miss Ponder has designs on you."

Heat crept up Josiah's face. "She has?"

"You know how women talk. Apparently, Miss Ponder has talked about you frequently."

Josiah looked up at the sun, wondering when it had gotten so hot. "Sir, I haven't intentionally given Miss Ponder the impression we are anything but acquaintances."

Captain Stewart laughed and clapped Josiah on the shoulder. "Don't worry, lieutenant. She can't force you to court her."

"No, sir, I suppose not. But how can I convince her I have no intentions? I don't want to hurt her feelings." Or make her angry, remembering the glare she gave him at one point in their conversation. He certainly didn't need to be the object of Mr. Ponder's anger.

"My advice is to just continue to act as honorably as you have been. Stay busy and steer clear. Eventually, she should realize your position. Or maybe she'll find someone else who interests her more."

If only that would happen.

~~~

The silence was unbearable. Father was fuming, but Sarah was afraid to ask him any questions. He was like a steam kettle getting ready to spew hot steam into the air, and Sarah didn't want to get burned by it. They travelled several miles before she could take the silent tension no more.

"Father, you seem angry. Is it unusual for Eben to leave the mill?"

He stared straight ahead. "Not that unusual, but I normally know when he has to go somewhere, since it's probably to Pensacola to see me or conduct business in town."

"So, is there anything wrong with him leaving?" Father's anger seemed excessive, considering his trust in Eben.

"No, Sarah, as long as someone is watching the business."

"It seemed that Mr. Sims was left in charge."

"Hmmph!" Father snapped the reins.

"Is there another reason you're angry, Father? There must be something else on your mind to upset you so."

Father gave her a quick glance, then blew out a breath. "I'm concerned about the fires that are being set at the lumber yards. I wanted to talk to Eben and make sure he increased the guards around our yard and make sure no one suspicious has an opportunity to do harm to our property."

"Do you think the fire at the Crawford office is connected to the other fires?"

He looked at her with eyebrows raised. "Yes, I suppose that fire could be connected to the others. But most have occurred at the mills themselves. Eben needs to be aware of the severity of the threat to our business."

"Do you truly believe someone would start a fire here, too? Doesn't Eben know about the fires already? Surely, he didn't intentionally leave the business exposed to danger." Was she really
~~~

defending Eben?

"I suppose you're right." Father's shoulders relaxed.

"Father, you've been so tired lately. I think you should see the doctor."

"I don't need a doctor. Maybe I am a little tired. I've been very busy."

She understood his frustration more than he realized. Father depended on Eben so much to help him share the workload, and to find him missing was like a punch in the stomach. But Father couldn't possibly know how unreliable Eben's numbers were. And if she told him now, wouldn't that just increase his worry?

"Does Eben ever help you with the paperwork?"

He lifted an eyebrow. "Yes, some of it. Why do you ask?"

Now what? She readied herself for his response.

"I saw some papers in the office."

"You did? By accident, I assume."

She didn't answer so she wouldn't lie.

"I found them on the desk." In a folder, but she did find them on the desk.

"So you looked at the papers. What kind of papers were they?"

"Nearest I could tell, there were different kinds of ledgers."

"You know what I've told you about getting involved in the business. But I know you were bored and needed something to do while you waited for me."

"Yes, sir, that's true." Maybe he was too tired to get angry with her.

"I assume you were looking at inventory ledgers. Is that what you were looking at? Did you find them interesting, or did you just see a bunch of numbers that have no meaning to you?"

"Yes, I believe some of them were inventory ledgers." She touched his arm. "Father, you know I am good with my arithmetic, don't you?"

"Yes, Sarah, you've always had a good head for numbers. Why do you ask?"

"Because it appeared that many of the calculations were wrong. Incorrect."

Father stopped the carriage and faced her. "Are you sure about that?"

"Yes. I checked over them several times. Have you ever checked Eben's figures?"

Father frowned. "Not often. I assumed he knew simple arithmetic."

"I don't think he does. There were several ledgers—some for shipping, some for payroll, and they all had errors."

"I need to verify what you're saying, but it's too late to turn around now and still get home before dark. You should have told me when we were there."

"But Father, you were already so angry, I was afraid to tell you I looked at the papers."

"Yes, I can see why you wouldn't want to tell me then. Looks like I'll be going back to the mill tomorrow and look at those papers myself."

"I could go back with you."

"No. I think it's best you stay home."

"Could you bring the papers home and let me help you look at them?"

"Maybe. If I think I need another pair of eyes to look at them, you'll be the first to know."

"Yes sir." At least he was considering letting her go over the papers. "Father, how long has Eben been handling these ledgers? Have you ever had a bookkeeper?"

"Used to. Before the war. But he didn't come back. When I returned, Eben had just come back too, so I hired him to run the mill. I never questioned his arithmetic."

"Have any of your customers ever questioned the numbers?"

Father sobered. "Maybe a couple of times."

"What happened?"

"One of the customers complained that our prices were too high compared to other lumber companies, so we lost their business."

"And did you check the prices to see if they were right?"

He shook his head. "No, I just assumed they wanted cheap wood and settled for an inferior product."

Sarah repressed a sigh, sensing Father's regret already. What good would it do to remind him of mistakes made in the past? If she could only prevent more errors from happening. And what about the payroll? That was a whole different story. He needed to know about that too. One thing at a time. She'd let him dwell on what she'd told him so far. He needed to see the errors on the inventory first, then he might review the other figures and find the problem himself.

Chapter Twenty

Josiah went back over the figures on the Turner estimate as he had already done several times. Shaking his head, he pounded his fist on the desk. How did Mr. Turner arrive at such figures? Or maybe he wasn't the one who filled it out. Turner mentioned having a manager that looked over it. Surely, Turner was smarter than the person who did this. He couldn't believe Mr. Turner had examined the bid carefully.

One thing for certain, Josiah couldn't turn in the estimate as it was. He needed to take it back to Mr. Turner and go over it with him. Josiah blew out a breath. Why was this project so difficult to complete? In the past, he'd never had an issue completing his work and doing it well, even finishing ahead of schedule, as he preferred. His superiors had always been pleased with his work. But now, he felt like a bungling fool who couldn't manage the simplest job.

Why did he feel like he was in a battle? Was someone really trying to prevent him from completing his work? If so, why would anyone do that? Ponder believed the Confederates were behind all the interference. But Josiah wasn't so sure. He accepted the fact that there were still subversives, but overall, the Pensacola area had made more progress toward restoring the peace and prosperity of the state. Even those who had fought on the other side needed to work and regain a normal life. People like Mr. Turner who saw the necessity of laying former hostility aside for business' sake.

Josiah put the Turner bid in his leather pouch to take with him, then left his desk and went outside. The aroma of fresh-baked bread wafted through the air from the bakery, reminding his stomach that it was lunchtime. He strode over to the mess hall and took his place in line. Conversation from other soldiers buzzed around him and he caught words like "fires" and "Rebs" drifting in conversations. Josiah's ire rose as he overheard various rumors passed from one man to the other. While he was aware the information was not personal, Josiah stung with self-consciousness because his job was in the middle of the activity. Not wanting to engage with anyone about the topics, he hurried through his meal of stew and hot rolls. An idea struck him as he was about to leave, so he grabbed an apple from the bowl on the table and dropped it in his pocket before approaching one of the servers.

"Can you fix me a couple of extra plates, please, to take to some people?"

The server nodded, hurried off and returned with a burlap tote sack he handed to Josiah. Josiah thanked him, then left for the stables to get Prince. When Prince saw Josiah, he nickered his hello. "How are you today, Prince? Look what I brought you." Josiah withdrew the apple from his pocket and offered it to his horse. Prince nickered again before chomping down on the apple while Josiah stroked his forehead. "You're very welcome." Josiah strode to the equipment rack and retrieved Prince's halter, reins and saddle and returned to ready Prince for the day.

Josiah tossed his saddlebag over last, then mounted the horse and headed down the hill toward Warrington. From the fort's position at the top of the hill, he could see all the way across the sparkling blue water of the bay to the white sand of the barrier islands where Fort Pickens sat on one side of the pass and Fort McRee on the other. The view was breathtaking and inspiring at the same time. *This is the day the Lord hath made.* The word of the Psalm went through his mind. *Let us rejoice and be glad in it.* Indeed, he was thankful to be in such a beautiful place, no matter what his situation was.

Prince trotted down the road to the neighborhood where Mabel Smith lived, then stopped in front of her house where Josiah dismounted and taking the tote sack of food, went up to Mabel's door. He knocked a few times before a voice answered. "Come in, it's open."

Josiah removed his cap and walked inside as Mabel was

getting up out of her rocking chair.

"Hello Mabel. Please sit down." He motioned with his hand for her to sit. "I brought you some supper." He took the food out of the bag.

Mabel pointed to the small table in her kitchen. "Put it in there. It smells good. Thank you for thinking of me again, lieutenant."

"You're welcome." He pointed to a chair. "May I?"

"Go ahead. What's on your mind today? You find that thing for the lighthouse yet?"

"No, ma'am. Not yet."

"Well, I don't remember nothing else about it. Sorry. How's your ladyfriend?"

Josiah's face heated, but he held his tongue. "She's well. Has she been back to see you?"

Mabel nodded and rocked. "Yes. She stopped by yesterday. Asked me questions about you."

"Me? What sort of questions" Why would Lizzie ask Mabel about him? Mabel really didn't know him very well.

"She wanted to know about some lady you were supposed to marry a while back. For some reason, she thought I knew the lady. But I told her I didn't know anything about your private life."

Josiah clenched his fists at his sides. Why did he even tell Lizzie about Sarah?

"There's really nothing to know. All that is in the past, and I haven't even talked to the lady in question for years."

"I think Miss Lizzie has a jealous streak. She didn't like the fact that you had been promised to someone else before her."

He gritted his teeth and tried to speak civilly. "I can't do anything about the past, so it's best left there."

"I agree. I tried to tell her that too. Told her 'let bygones be bygones.' Some people cross your path just to get to the other side, and you can't help it."

Cross paths…Josiah remembered why he was there. "Speaking of people crossing paths, Miss Mabel, have you ever heard of someone named Rafe Nettles?"

Her eyes widened, then darkened with anger. "I guess I have! That snake was one of them boys that got my boy in trouble!" Mabel grimaced and pretending to spit. "Why're you asking about him?"

"I met him recently and was just curious."

"You best stay away from the likes of him. He's no good."

"Yes, ma'am. I'll do that."

Mabel's forehead creased. "You say you met him around here?"

"Yes, ma'am."

"So he's back in town, huh? I thought he was long gone when he high-tailed it out of here in '62. Surprised he didn't get hisself killed during the war."

"Apparently, he was one of the fortunate who survived."

"Well I hope he don't come 'round my house. He knows what I think of him. I warned Roy to stay away from him, but he wouldn't listen. Now my boy is dead, and that scoundrel came back."

"If you don't mind my asking, why don't you like him? What did he do?"

"He always had some hair-brained scheme that would get Roy in trouble with the law. I told Roy he was bad company."

"I'm sorry to hear he was such a bad influence on your son. But he must've been a devoted Confederate."

Mabel looked at him and twisted her mouth. "You could say that, all right." She leaned forward, lowering her voice as her eyes darted from one side of the room to the other. "He might be the one that talked Roy into stealing that piece from the lighthouse. In fact, he might even know where it is."

~~~

Ever since she got up that morning, Sarah had been thinking about her trip to the mill. For once, Father was considering letting her look over the paperwork. She tried to imagine what he would do when he saw Eben's figures. What would Eben do when Father confronted him? Would he know she was the one who'd discovered his errors snooping around his desk? Would Father fire him? Sarah had scarcely been able to think of anything else since she returned from the mill with Father, conceiving various possible results.

She'd been out on the veranda soaking in the warmth of the
~~~

morning sun, praying and thanking God for the chance to help her father. Right after breakfast, Anna Grace had gone to see the kittens, but Doc said he'd watch her get into the loft, so she didn't follow. *This is the day the Lord has made. Let us rejoice and be glad in it,* the words of the Psalm came to her mind as she viewed the shimmering water of the bay. She suddenly realized she hadn't reported back to Della about delivering the gifts to her grandson's house and meeting Elmira and the children.

The screen door slammed behind her when she hurried in to the kitchen, and Della jumped, her hand covering her heart.

"Lawd, chile, you done scared me to death."

"I'm sorry, Della. I just wanted to tell you that Elmira was very grateful for the things you sent."

"So you met Elmira. Did you see the children too?"

"Yes, they were all with their mother. Elmira's pretty, and those girls look just like her."

Della chuckled as she kneaded the dough. "They do. The boy, he gonna be long and skinny like his pa."

How could she know the baby she saw on Elmira's hip would be tall?

"Well, I'm glad we could carry those things to her for you. She was deeply touched."

"You'se mighty kind to offer. I'm kind of surprised your father let you."

"He's got a kind heart underneath, even though he doesn't show it." Sarah walked to the window and looked outside, then spun around. "Della, Father said Mother used to visit people who needed help and bring them food and other things. I can barely remember that. Do you?"

Della took a glass, turned it upside down and began cutting circles in the dough. "Sure do. I used to make up baskets of food for her to take. Folks around here thought she was an angel or somethin'."

"I wonder why she doesn't do things like that anymore? I understand she's been grieving the boys' deaths but seems like she just stopped living."

"I know, Miss Sarah. Sometimes people get so stuck in grievin', they quit livin'."

Sarah looked back outside. Her mother came out of the barn

and walked to the pump where she washed her hands. "There she is now. Wonder what she was doing in the barn?"

"Don't know for sho, but last time I sees Anna Grace, she had her mother's hand and was pullin' her toward the barn."

Hope flooded Sarah with excitement. "She was? Do you think Mother went to see the kittens?"

A smile tugged at the corners of Della's mouth. "Could have. Your momma was hangin' clothes on the line, and Miss Anna Grace, she come out of the barn, cryin'. That's when they went back to the barn."

"Oh my. I wonder if something happened to one of the kittens?" Sarah turned toward the door. "I should go find out."

Della's hand fell on Sarah's arm, holding her in place. "You just wait right here, Miss Sarah. You let your momma take care of it. She needs to be the one Anna Grace go to sometimes."

Sarah halted, stunned by Della's words. It took a moment for the truth to sink in. If she stayed out of the way, Mother might give Anna Grace more attention.

"I suppose you're right. I'm just so used to seeing about Anna Grace. I mean, Mother never pays her any mind."

"Maybe your momma needed time to grieve. I know she been grievin' a long while, but could be time she's pullin' out of it." Della looked Sarah straight in the eyes. "And you needs to move out of the way and let her."

"You know, I was so worried about leaving Anna Grace alone for the first time when I went to the mill with Father."

"And you come back and everythin's fine. Ain't that so?"

"Yes, and I must admit, I was a little surprised."

"Even a baby bird gots to leave the nest 'fore he can fly. And your momma, well, she was a good momma to you and to your brothers, wasn't she? The momma inside her is still there, just hidin' 'cause it was 'fraid to get hurt again."

"Della, you're a wise woman. I never thought about things like that. I just knew I didn't like the way they'd turned out."

"They's some things you can change and some you can't. You has to know the diff'rance. And you know you can't change a person. No, you not that pow'rful. Only God be that strong."

Sarah pondered what Della said. No, she couldn't change the people in her life. But could she change their mind? What about

Father and his records? Perhaps she could do something about the records, if Father allowed it.

"Della, when I went with Father, I had an opportunity to look at some of the ledgers. They were very questionable, and I can see how the employees could be upset about their pay."

"So, that Mr. White, he's being partial?" Della's mouth formed a straight line. "I knowed somethin' wasn't right. Zeke, he's smart, and he know too."

"I mentioned the ledgers to Father, and trust me, he didn't know they weren't correct. But I don't think it's just the salaries that are wrong. Della, I saw a lot of things wrong with every record, even the inventory of logs. I fear Mr. White might not be good with numbers. Maybe he's not intending to be unfair. Maybe he just doesn't figure the pay correctly."

"Hmmph! You don't say. So who's gonna fix it? Who's gonna make the numbers right?"

Sarah tried to keep from smirking. "I am. Father doesn't know it yet, but I'm going to set things straight if it kills me."

Della chuckled a deep, throaty laugh. "Well, I'd like to see you do it. What you think that Mr. White gonna do when he finds out his work is wrong? You think he'll be mad at you? You think he's gonna want to marry a woman who thinks she's smarter than he is?"

Sarah put her hands on her hips. "You know, I don't really care what he'll think. And marrying him is the least of my concern. What's important is being correct. My father's reputation is at stake."

"I don't know how you gonna do it, but I'see gonna pray you figure it out."

"Thank you, Della. I really do need your prayers." After all, only God could work this out.

Chapter Twenty-One

"Excuse me, sir." Josiah peered into the partially open door.

Charles Turner stood at the window of his office looking out at the harbor. He spun around.

"Josiah. I didn't hear you come in."

Mr. Turner looked haggard, his lips turned down and his posture slumping. What had taken its toll on the man? Too much work?

"I'm sorry to surprise you, sir. I knocked on your door but didn't hear an answer and let myself in."

"Well, what are you here for? Did you make a decision on that bid?"

"Not yet, sir. I thought you might want to make some corrections on it first."

Turner raised his eyebrows. "Corrections? Why would I want to make corrections?"

Josiah opened his leather pouch and pulled out the paperwork. He glanced down at it and back at Mr. Turner. "Mr. Turner, sir, I'm sure it's an oversight, but there are some errors in the calculations."

"Let me see that." Turner frowned and reached for the paperwork.

Josiah handed it over while Mr. Turner retrieved his eyeglasses from the desk and put them on. Squinting, he studied the bid. He looked up at Josiah.

"Can you show me exactly where you think there are errors?"

Josiah leaned over the desk and pointed to some figures in the right-hand column. "Well, here is one. I don't believe you meant to list this amount as $300. It should cost more than that."

Turner rubbed his red eyes and peered at the place Josiah had indicated. "Why, that's $800, not $300!"

"Sorry sir, but it looks like a '3' to me."

"Maybe you need glasses, Josiah."

"Beg your pardon, sir. My vision is near perfect."

Turner pounded his fist on the paper and steeled a glare at Josiah. "Is that so?"

"Yes, sir. The Army doctor said so when he gave me my eye test."

Turner pulled his beard some more while staring at Josiah, making Josiah wonder why the man hadn't pulled the whole beard out. "So, if this bid has so many errors, why didn't you just refuse it?"

"Because sir, I'd like to do business with you, but I can't approve that bid. And secondly, I don't think you intended the bid as it is. I'm sure you would lose money if we accepted that bid. Plus, some of the calculations are just wrong. I know you're busy, but perhaps you have someone else who can review it and correct it."

Mr. Turner lifted an eyebrow, studying Josiah as if considering what Josiah had said, but didn't answer right away. Heaving a sigh, Mr. Turner's shoulders sagged.

"I suppose I should have someone else look at this. My eyesight has been getting worse, I'm afraid. I got new glasses, but I still can't see well. I think I might have cataracts." He waved his glasses in the air. "You're right. I don't want to submit a bid full of errors, and I certainly don't want to lose money. I appreciate you giving me a chance to fix it. Some people might take advantage and go with the lowest bid."

"Yes, sir. I realize that. But it wouldn't be the decent thing to do. The government might like to take the lowest bid, but my parents taught me to have principles and be fair."

Turner shook his head. "I'm afraid this isn't the only bid that's gone out wrong. I thought my manager would catch any errors, but he hasn't. I don't understand it, either. And I don't think he has any problems with his eyes."

"What about a bookkeeper? Have you considered hiring one?"

"The one I had before the war didn't come back. Between myself and my manager, we've been handling the estimates all right, at least until now."

"Sir, I'd help you with it myself, but I'm afraid that wouldn't be ethical."

"No, of course not."

"Don't you have anyone else who could check it for you?"

Turner pulled his beard again. "I might, I just might."

"Do you know how long it would take to get the other man to take care of it? My time is running short to get this lumber procured. Otherwise, I'll have to buy from outside the area, and that is my last resort."

"I understand your situation." Turner turned to stare outside the window again. "All right. I'll take care of it. I'm sure she can get to it right away. We'll have it ready by the end of the week."

She? Josiah raised his eyebrow. There was a woman bookkeeper in town? Things had changed here even more than he realized.

~~~

Anna Grace couldn't stop talking at the supper table. She was so excited about the kittens, even more because Mother had finally seen them.

"Mother says her favorite is Sunshine!" Anna Grace grinned as she looked at Mother.

"Is that right?" Father glanced at Mother, whose eyes showed the faintest glimmer of mirth. "And which one is your favorite, Anna Grace?"

"Well, it used to be Sunshine, but since that's Mother's favorite, I think mine is Cottonball."

"What happened today to upset you? Della said she saw you came out of the barn crying."

"I was scared 'cause I couldn't find the kittens. I was afraid they'd all climbed out and fallen or run away."

"So where were they?" Sarah asked, putting her fork down.

Anna Grace looked over at Mother. "We think Mouser moved them. I don't think they could climb out of the box yet," Mother said. "We found them in a corner of the barn behind some hay
~~~

bales."

"Why do you think she moved them?"

"Mother said something must've scared the momma cat, so she moved them."

"I think she moved them because they were almost able to climb out of the box and she knew if they did, they'd fall out of the loft," Mother said. "Now they're on the ground where they can't fall."

"But is that really safer? Couldn't they be stepped on by the horses?"

Mother frowned at Sarah. "No, the horses are in their stalls. And I'm sure the momma cat will teach the kittens to stay away from them."

"Horses are pretty smart too," Father said. "I've seen them around little chicks, and they seem to watch their step around small creatures."

"Well that's good to know." Sarah tamped down her excitement over seeing the exchange between Mother and Anna Grace. Would that have happened if she'd gone down to the barn and intervened? Della was right. It must've been the right thing to do. She had to get out of the way so Mother would spend more time with Anna Grace.

"Sarah, I need to speak to you after dinner," Father said, lifting his glass to take a drink.

"Yes, sir. As soon as I help Mother clear the dishes."

"I can help," Anna Grace said.

"Yes, Anna Grace can help," Mother said. "She's getting to be a big girl now."

Sarah's mouth fell open. Did she really hear her mother give Anna Grace credit for something?

"Yes, she is," Father said. "Which is a good thing because I need Sarah's help now."

He did? The surprises kept coming.

Father pushed away from the table. "Excuse us, please. Sarah, let's go out on the veranda."

Sarah stood, dumfounded. Had Father said he needed her help? She glanced at Mother and Anna Grace. "Please excuse me."

When Sarah joined her father, he was leaning over the porch railing, staring out at the waters of the bay as dusk settled in. The moon had just begun its ascent over the water.

"Yes, Father? What is it?"

"Sarah, you asked, rather begged, to help me with some of my paperwork. Today I realized I ought to give you the opportunity."

"What happened? Did you see Eben yet?"

"No. I haven't seen him yet and I'm afraid I still need to make another trip up there this week … unless he shows up here first. I told that foreman to tell Eben I needed to see him."

"So, do you want me to go back with you and go over the ledgers?"

"Not yet. There's another matter that needs to be handled sooner." Father searched the sky as stars popped out in the darkening night.

"What other matter?"

"The federal government is asking for bids on lumber and other materials to build a new lighthouse keepers' house and do some repairs at the lighthouse. I turned one in, but it was rejected."

"Rejected? Was it too high?"

"No, well, it just had some miscalculations on it, and they asked me to re-submit it."

"Father, you know I'd love to look at it. But why can't you fix it? Are you too busy?"

"I am busy, yes, but to be honest, I'm having trouble with my eyes. Even with my glasses, things are blurred. I think I have cataracts, but I'm not ready to have the doctor poking around in my eyes yet. I had hoped Eben could help me, but after what you told me about the other ledgers, I'm not sure I want him to look at it. Besides, this needs to be done right away, and I don't know when I can speak to Eben about it."

"Oh, I see. So where is it? When can I look at it?"

"It's at my office. I almost brought it home with me, but I figured you could use my office where you have a place to work. I have plenty of other things to do, shipments to oversee, and so on."

"So, I can come tomorrow?" Sarah wanted to jump for joy.

"You certainly may. Right after breakfast, you and I can go together." Father faced Sarah. "Will you be willing to do that?"

"Absolutely!"

"I thought you might be," Father said with a smile easing across his face.

"Thank you, Father." Sarah threw herself against her father's broad chest.

He patted her on the back and chuckled. "You sure are excited about doing arithmetic," he said. "Not too many people get so enthusiastic about such a thing."

"I suppose it's rather unusual. I've never known anyone else that loved numbers as much as I do."

"Oh, you know one."

"Who?" Sarah pulled back and searched his face.

"Me. You share my attraction for numbers. Which is why I'm willing to let you help me. It is greatly distressing, even embarrassing, to know something left my office with my approval that wasn't done correctly. I've always prided myself in accuracy and quality work. To know something came from my company that was inferior is simply unacceptable."

"I can imagine your concern, Father. I'll do my best to straighten it out."

"I'm confident you will."

Sarah looked up at the clear night sky and thought her heart would burst from joy. *Thank you, God.*

~~~

The morning air was cool and crisp the next morning when Sarah walked down the street with her father. Already, she could tell the difference in his mood as if a burden had been lifted from him. Ship bells and shouts greeted their ears as they turned alongside the wharves alive with activity. She could feel the men's stares as they walked past the ships docked in the harbor, but with Father alongside her, she was safe and protected. Her heart swelled with pride and anticipation, and she walked a little taller knowing she could contribute to Father's work.

Father unlocked the front door to his building, and they stepped inside. Light spilled in through the windows, making the wood floors shine, and brightening the dark interior. He opened his office door where dust danced in the sun's rays penetrating the window. Father pointed to his desk. "You go ahead and sit there. The paperwork is in the top drawer."

Sarah pulled the drawer open and found the paper. Laying it
~~~

on the desk, she noticed immediately that the lines were all skewed. “Do you have any clean ledger sheets?” she asked.

“Right there beside you. You can tear pages out of that book if you need to. Some sharpened pencils are in the desk as well.”

Sarah grabbed a pencil and began going over the paper.

“You go ahead and take your time. I want to make sure it’s done right this time.” Father bent down by the fireplace in the room. “I’ll get a little fire going for you. It gets pretty chilly in here in the mornings.” He stood and brushed off his hands. “I’ll either be in the warehouse or out on the dock, but I’ll be back in time to collect you for lunch. Will you be all right here by yourself?”

“Of course. Don’t worry about me. I’ll have plenty of company with these numbers.”

Father grinned, then left the office, closing the door behind him.

Sarah glanced around the room in amazement. Here she was in the fine office of the owner of a lumber company. Who happened to be her father. Who happened to trust her to help him with his work. A thrill rippled through her. Her prayer had been answered. *Lord, help me straighten these errors out so I can prove myself to my Father. And if I do, maybe he’ll let me do this more often.*

Sarah opened the clean ledger book and began to copy the various amounts of lumber and other stores from the bid in a column on the left side of the paper. Next, she noted the price per item. These amounts she would have to verify with Father, but she soon found out that multiplying the amounts needed by the prices shown resulted in much different amounts than were on the bid Father gave her to fix. No wonder it was wrong. Poor Father. He really was having trouble with his eyes, and he’d been relying on Eben to correct his mistakes. Yet Eben obviously wasn’t capable of doing that, based on the work she’d seen at the mill.

She worked on the bid all morning, taking an occasional break to stand up and stretch, looking out the window as she did. The energy from the wharves invigorated her, and she felt as if she was participating alongside the sailors and merchants she saw. Her contribution, though small, was just another piece in the puzzle of the industry that surrounded her and filled her with satisfaction. She had just finished her calculations when Father tapped on the door and stuck his head in.

"Are you getting tired or hungry?"

"Tired, no, not at all. But hungry, now that you mention it, yes."

Father stepped into the room and pointed to the papers on the desk. "How much have you managed to decipher so far?"

"I've recalculated the whole thing, but I need to go over the prices of the goods with you to make sure I got them right."

"We can do that after we eat." He motioned for her to come. "Mother is expecting us."

Sarah stood and came around the desk. "I love your office, Father. I feel quite at home here."

Father chuckled as he closed the door behind her. "Does that mean you're planning to take over the business?"

"You'd never let me get away with that!" Sarah smiled as she took her father's arm when they went outside the building.

As they headed down the street toward home, they passed a man and woman standing on the corner engaged in conversation. They both stared at her as she passed by, eyeing her curiously. Sarah adjusted her bonnet and glanced down at her skirt to see if anything was askew with her appearance. Or maybe they were looking at her father and not her. Surely, that was it. So why did she detect a scowl toward her from the fair-haired woman?

Chapter Twenty-Two

"Sir, I may have some information that could help us find the lens," Josiah stood at the entrance to Captain Stewart's office.

"Have a seat and tell me about it, lieutenant." The captain pointed to the chair across from his desk.

"Sir, I met a man that might have been involved in the theft of the lens. His name is Rafe Nettles."

"And he admitted knowing about it?" The captain clasped his hands on the desk.

"No sir, he and I have not discussed it. However, the lady I've been speaking to, Mabel Smith, who said her son had participated in the theft, told me he and Nettles were associates."

"She's the one who said the lens was hidden in a barn somewhere around Molino?"

"Yes, sir."

"So where is this Nettles fellow?"

"I'm not sure where he lives, but I've seen him around here several times. In fact, he was at the lighthouse the day we unloaded the bricks."

Captain Stewart sat back and covered his mouth with his hand. "Hmm." He moved his hand and said, "Pretty bold fellow if he's still around. Wonder if he's planning some form of sabotage?"

"I wonder that myself, sir. He strikes me as an unsavory character. Mrs. Smith was surprised to hear he was back in town."

"Perhaps we should bring him in for questioning."

"Perhaps, but I doubt he would tell us the truth."

"Too bad we can't follow him around and see where he goes.

But we'd be a little obvious."

"Sir, we might not have to."

"And why is that, lieutenant?"

"Because I think he may be following me."

"That so? Well, then, you need to lead *him* to the lens."

"Sir, but I don't know where it is."

"Hear me out. Although we've searched the area already, we didn't find it. You can go back to Molino under the auspices of meeting with the lumber mill up there again. I know they suffered damage in the fire, but I'm sure they'll reopen as soon as possible. If Nettles is following you, we'll follow some distance behind so we're behind him. If you get near the lens, he's sure to make a move to stop you from finding it."

"I suppose it's worth a try," Josiah said. "And then you'd arrest him?"

"That's right."

"When should I leave?"

"Give it a couple of days so we can let the word out that you're going back to Molino. I'll arrange for some other men to be ready to follow you. Why don't you go on Thursday? Meanwhile, you can drop a few hints around the area about your plans so the word will get back to Nettles."

Josiah stood and saluted. "Yes, sir. I'll be at the stables Thursday morning right after breakfast."

Captain Stewart stood too. "Fine."

Josiah started to leave, but the captain spoke again. "Before you go, I wanted to ask how things are going with that last bid. Is it ready?"

"Not just yet. I had some questions about it, so I brought it back to Turner."

"And when do you expect to pick it up?"

"Early next week. I gave him until the end of the week to resolve the discrepancies."

"Good. We need to get this assignment handled."

"Yes, sir. I agree."

Josiah left the office and decided to walk toward the lighthouse. If Nettles or Lizzie were in the area, he'd make sure they heard about his trip the next day.

However, when he reached the lighthouse, only a couple of

guards were present, standing near the bricks. Josiah glanced around, looking for someone else, but when he didn't see anyone, he decided on a whim to climb the steps of the lighthouse to the top.

One hundred seventy-seven steps later, he pushed out the door to the gallery and stepped outside. A brisk breeze blew at the top of the lighthouse as he walked around the lantern room, surveying the land below and around for miles. He could see every ship that came through the pass going to and from the harbor through the pass. To the southeast, Fort Pickens commanded the end of the island closest to the pass. On the southwest side of the pass, the badly damaged walls of Fort McRee gave testimony to the onslaught of battle during the war. But now the fort was empty, and the sand was reclaiming the pensinsula. Peace had resumed its dominance of the area, and the view from the tower made Josiah appreciate the benefits of being a lighthouse keeper. Perhaps he should apply for one of the positions some day.

Once many years ago, he and Sarah had stood on this gallery and admired the view. Before the war, before cannons fired at each other across the bay, before neighbors chose sides against each other, before the two of them had been forced to end their engagement and their future together. Peace had indeed returned to the area but not to his heart. It was like the crumbling walls of Fort McRee, defeated by the battle, even though his side had won. Was there any comfort in winning the war but losing the battle?

He turned away from the gulf view and moved around to the back of the gallery which faced land and viewed the massive brick walls of Fort Barrancas, imposing on the summit of the highest point of land on the post. He looked toward the navy yard and the houses of Warrington, reminding him of Mabel Smith, her son Roy, and Rafe Nettles. A few live oak trees still stood, survivors from the bombardment in 1862, and through their canopy, he detected movement.

The flash of a woman's blonde hair shone in the sunlight. Was that Lizzie? He peered through the trees, wishing he had a telescope. Then he saw the man. Standing very close to the woman, he wore a slouch hat and a familiar-looking brown jacket. Rafe Nettles. With Lizzie? Now he remembered where he'd seen the man the first time. He'd been talking with Lizzie one day, the person she'd referred to as a friend. So how long had they been friends? The thought made him uneasy. From all he'd heard about Nettles, he wasn't a man an honorable woman would fraternize with. Did she know of his reputation?

Lizzie couldn't have known him a long time, since she'd only arrived in the area recently. But if she was indeed consorting with him, Joshua could use that to his advantage. He'd make sure he told Lizzie what he wanted Nettles to find out. Now was a good time to test his assumption.

He climbed back inside the lantern room and down the ladder, then trotted down the spiral stairs, hoping to happen upon the couple when he exited the building. When he stepped outside, he spotted them about fifty feet away near the trunk of one of the trees and headed in that direction, trying to appear as nonchalant as possible. Nettles saw him coming and said something to Lizzie before walking briskly away. Wonder why he didn't stick around to speak to Josiah? He'd been friendly on the two previous occasions when they'd seen each other.

"Lizzie! I was hoping to see you!" Josiah fought guilt about his statement since he'd actually been hoping the opposite.

Lizzie beamed her delight as he approached. "You have?" She gave him one of her coy smiles. "I was hoping to see you too!"

"Is that so? What did you want to see me about?" Josiah attempted to contrive a reason to back up what he'd said.

"I wanted to ask you to go on a picnic this Saturday." Lizzie grabbed hold of the crook in his arm and tilted her head to view him, batting her eyelashes. "You don't have other plans, do you?" The look in her eyes dared him to say he did.

"What a coincidence! I was thinking of taking you out on a sail, that is, if the weather is warm enough." He secretly wished it wouldn't be.

"Ooh, that would be so nice." She twisted a loose strand of hair, then her face brightened. "I have an idea! Why don't we sail over to the island and have a picnic over there?"

"That's a splendid idea, Lizzie." Maybe it would rain. Remembering his plan, he said, "I'll be ready for a pleasant outing. I've spent so much time riding around the countryside, and I've still got more to do."

"You do? I thought you were finished seeing all the lumber

mills," she said.

How would she know that? He hadn't given her any such details.

"Well, actually, I'm going back to the one I first visited, the one in Molino."

Lizzie's brows pinched together. "Molino? I heard a fire put them out of business."

"It did, temporarily, but it seems they're going to reopen soon and might be able to take on our business." He leaned over and lowered his voice. "I might find the missing lens while I'm gone."

She looked surprised. "Do you know where it is?"

"Not exactly, but I have a general idea."

A shadow crossed her face. "When are you going?"

"Tomorrow. I'm leaving early tomorrow morning." Was she taking the bait? "I should be back by Saturday though. So we can go sailing, of course."

Her face brightened again. "I can hardly wait."

"I'll have to reserve one of the post sailboats, of course." He assumed a look of surprise. "As a matter of fact, I better do that right away to make sure we have one. There are only a couple, and the officers have first choice."

"But you're an officer, aren't you?"

"Yes, one of six here. But what if the others get ahead of me?" He gently pried her hand loose from his arm. "I need to make haste to the wharf." He smiled as he pulled away from her. "I'll call for you around noon on Saturday."

"I'll be ready," she said.

As Josiah hurried away from her, he looked around for Rafe but didn't see him. Would his plan work? Would Nettles fall for his trap?

The next morning, Josiah saddled Prince and met the other soldiers at the stable who would be following him.

"Make sure you stay about half a mile behind me. Don't leave here for about 30 minutes. We don't want our suspect to realize you're following me."

"Yes, sir." The soldier saluted.

Josiah headed north toward Molino, his ears and eyes alert to anyone else on the road. He traveled several miles before Prince snorted. Josiah stopped and leaned over the horse's neck. "What is it, boy?"

Prince shook his head and snorted again. Josiah glanced around but didn't see anyone. He clucked to Prince, and they continued on the hard-pack dirt and sand road. Horse hooves sounded behind them, and Josiah looked over his shoulder, hoping the other soldiers weren't in view. Pretty soon, a lone rider came galloping through at a fast pace. Josiah glanced at the chestnut horse with white markings as the rider sped by, barely glancing at Josiah, intent on the road in front of him.

Josiah tried to get a look at the man as he passed them. A hat was pulled down low over the sandy blond hair of the young man, around eighteen or nineteen, who had facial hair resembling peach fuzz. Was the man running from something or just in a hurry? Had he seen the other soldiers?

"Was that what you heard, Prince? The other horse coming?"

Prince shook his head as if answering. They rode for another hour, then Josiah stopped to dismount, stretch his legs a little, and take a drink from his canteen. He studied the woods near the road, noticing the thick palmetto undergrowth. It would be difficult to pass through that stuff without a machete unless there was a trail. He listened for the sound of someone else in the area but barely heard a bird chirp. He climbed back on the horse and continued his journey. After a while, he spotted the farmhouse where he'd thought he was being watched before, but this time there was no movement.

Was Nettles near him? He wasn't sure the man had followed him, and the only way to know was to stop and see if he caught up or wait for the other soldiers. He decided to stick to the plan, so he continued up the road to Molino. When he reached the town, he went straight to the lumber yard, or what was left of it. Burned logs, evidence of the fire that the company had suffered, sat in ashy piles. A newly built shack stood near the remains of the former office. As he rode in, he spotted Mr. Hopkins walking toward him.

Hopkins raised his arms in surrender. "Lieutenant, I'm afraid we won't be able to fill your order after all." He gestured toward the burned lumber. "Guess you can see we've had a little setback here."

Josiah's gut wrenched. "I'm sorry to see that, Mr. Hopkins."

"Yep, me too. Gonna take us a while to get back on our feet.

Good thing you weren't in the office when it caught on fire."

Remembering the night he slept in the building, Josiah repressed a shudder. What if he had been in there then? Would someone have set fire to it? Or did they wait on purpose? It was a small consolation to know he didn't suffer the same fate as the lumber yard. Yet guilt ate at him knowing his visit may have prompted the fire.

"Yes, sir. I guess I should be thankful for that."

Hopkins' teenage son strode up and pointed a finger at Josiah. "You're bad luck!"

Mr. Hopkins scowled at his son. "Luke! You mind your manners! The lieutenant didn't have nothing to do with the fire."

Luke Hopkins put his hands on his hips and steadied Josiah with a glare. "Yeah? So how come the fire happened after he came here?"

Hopkins looked at Josiah. "Sorry, Lieutenant. Luke needs to control his tongue." Luke stormed off. "He's pretty bitter about the fire. Whoever started the fire shot his dog."

Josiah felt sick. "I'm so sorry. No wonder he's so angry. Do you have any idea who started the fire? Do you have any former employees who might hold a grudge?"

"No, sir. Most all my workers have been with me a long time. It'd be pretty foolish for any of them to burn down the place that provides their livelihood, now wouldn't it?"

Josiah nodded. "It would indeed."

Did Mr. Hopkins know about the other fires? Had word gotten this far? If he knew, he might actually blame Josiah too.

"Well, sorry you made the trip up here today, but I need to get going. We have a lot of work to do here, you know."

"I won't keep you any longer." Josiah tipped his cap. "I'll pray you can get your business back up and running soon."

"Prayers can't hurt." Hopkins gave a slight wave as he turned to walk away. "Good luck with your search."

When Josiah rode out of town, he met the other soldiers waiting. They saluted, looking rather sheepish.

"Did you see Rafe Nettles?"

"Yes, sir. He was riding with another man."

"And did you see where he went?"

"No sir." The soldier cleared his throat. "We came around a

bend and he was gone."

"Both of them?"

"Yes, sir."

Now he was certain the ruse was a waste of time. An idea hit him.

"Do you remember what the other man looked like?"

"Yes, sir. Young, blond hair hitting his shoulders."

"I saw him. He passed me, riding his horse at breakneck speed."

"They must've split up," the soldier said.

"So it seems. I think Nettles hid somewhere until you passed but sent the other man on ahead."

"Sorry we lost them, sir." The soldier's face bore genuine regret.

"That's all right, soldier. Looks like Mr. Nettles is a pretty savvy fellow. I believe he sent the other man ahead knowing I wouldn't recognize him."

"But why was he running?"

"Apparently to warn someone else that we were coming. Or maybe to distract us."

"Sir, do you think Mr. Nettles is around here somewhere?"

"No, I don't. I wouldn't be surprised if he was back in Pensacola by the time we get there."

Josiah felt like he was a player in a poker game and Nettles was his opponent. And right now, Nettles had called his bluff.

Chapter Twenty-Three

Sarah was going over the new ledger sheets she'd completed when someone knocked on the door. She looked up to see Eben standing in the doorway, his eyes wide with surprise.

"Hello, Eben."

The man fidgeted with his hat as he glanced nervously around the room as if he'd find Father hiding among the bookcases.

"Miss Sarah." He gave her a slight bow of his head. "I'm looking for your father."

"Yes, well he's out back or on the wharf. I believe he's expecting you."

He swallowed hard, then his eyes narrowed. "What are you doing here? Waiting for him?"

"No, actually. I'm doing some work for him." Apparently, Eben never considered that possibility.

He motioned to the papers on the desk. "You working on figures?"

"Yes, I am. Father's had a lot of work to do by himself, so I offered to help him." She hoped Father wouldn't mind her telling Eben that much, as long as she didn't disclose more.

Eben raised an eyebrow and smirked. "He already has help. He has another *man* to help him—me."

A thousand comments flitted through Sarah's mind, none of them good or nice. Oh, how she wanted to let him know how ineffective his help was. Just because he was a man, he thought he was sufficient. Well, he wasn't. But it wasn't her place to say so. She bit her lip to keep from letting her true thoughts come out.

She crossed her arms. “Unfortunately, Eben, you’re too far away to help him here.”

“Well, I’m here now. I can take that off your hands.” He nodded to the ledgers.

Father’s voice behind him said. “That won’t be necessary.”

Eben paled and turned, stepping aside to admit Father into the room.

“Sarah, would you please excuse us? Eben and I need to talk.” Father moved around the desk while Sarah stacked the papers and moved them to the side, then stood up and backed away so he could have his chair back. “Eben, have a seat,” Father said.

As Sarah moved toward the door, she glanced at Father, and he gave her a nod. “Close that door behind you, please.”

She grabbed her gloves, bonnet and shawl from the table by the door as she left. Father needed to have this conversation with Eben in private, but she was tempted to stand outside and listen. No, she couldn’t do that. Father wouldn’t be pleased to know she eavesdropped. She had to trust that he would tell her what happened afterwards. What could she do now? She couldn’t go home yet because she wasn’t finished with the paperwork.

She decided to go outside and get some fresh air while she waited until they were finished. She pulled on her gloves and tied on her bonnet before wrapping her shawl around her shoulders and going outside. The sun had warmed the day, but there was a cool nip in the air, especially when a gust of wind blew off the water. Meandering down along the side of the building to a sunny spot out of the wind, she stopped to watch the activity on the docks.

She glanced up at the building and saw Father’s form through the window, waving his arms around. He must be giving Eben a severe scolding. The man certainly had a lot to answer for. Why was he gone from the mill and where had he been? No doubt Father was disappointed to find out the man he most depended on wasn’t where he needed him to be. Still, much as she didn’t particularly like the man, she didn’t doubt his loyalty to Father. But where had he been going?

And now that the fires had been reported at other lumber mills, Eben needed to be at their mill even more than ever.

A shocking thought struck her. Could Eben have been the one to set the fires at other mills? Would he do something so devious to their competitors? No matter how things looked, she couldn't believe Eben was that mean-spirited. He didn't strike her as the crafty sort. And although he'd made mistakes on the ledgers, Sarah didn't believe they were intentional. Perhaps he didn't even know they were wrong.

She glanced back up at the window, wondering if the discussion was still going on, but didn't see Father anymore. How would she know unless she could see the front door when Eben left? She ambled back to the front, her mind going over the ledgers she'd been working on. Lost in thought, she strolled a ways down the street, keeping an eye on Father's building. She reached the end, then turned back, hoping she'd passed enough time. The sensation of being watched made her glance quickly around. Perhaps Eben had left and wanted a word with her. Yet he was nowhere in sight.

Was she imagining things? She slowly scanned the area again, then her eyes fixed on the person standing in the shade of a tree. It was that blonde woman again, the one she'd seen with the man that morning. What was she doing here and why was she watching Sarah? Were they acquainted? An uneasiness ran through her shoulders. What was it about that women that bothered her so? She had an inclination to go introduce herself and dispel the mystery, yet Sarah had the distinct impression that she should stay away from the woman.

When she returned to the office, the door was open, and Eben was gone. Father sat at his desk with his back to the door, staring out the window.

She removed her things and laid them down. "Father?"

He looked over his shoulder at her. "Come in, Sarah."

"What happened?"

Father turned his chair around to face her, his face that of resignation. "I told Eben I was concerned that he left the mill without my knowledge and made him aware of the fire danger."

"What did he say? Did he tell you where he was?"

"Not exactly. He apologized for not being there, but said he had some personal, private matters to take care of."

"And he wouldn't tell you what they were?"

"No, but he seemed earnest, and I have to respect the man's privacy." Father rested his arms on the desk. "I don't believe he's done anything immoral or improper regarding the business. He was quite concerned to hear about the fires and didn't know there had been so many."

"What about the ledgers? Did you ask him about those?"

Father nodded. "I told him I saw them, and they were illegible. I also said I would be going over them when I go back up there."

"Was he angry about that?"

"No, not exactly angry, yet he did seem concerned."

"So he's gone back to Milltown?"

"Yes, he left right away when he heard about the fire danger."

"Father, do you think it's unusual that our mill hasn't had a fire while others have?"

"I've thought about that, yes."

Should she venture her concern? How would Father react? She took a deep breath and steeled herself. "Do you think Eben could be capable of setting the other fires?"

Deep furrows formed in Father's forehead and he pulled on his beard, steadying her with his gaze. "I have asked myself the same question, Sarah. I don't want to believe he is. I've considered myself to be a good judge of character, and Eben has never given me reason to suspect him of anything so malicious. I can see how someone would question his motives as well as his whereabouts, but I prefer to give him the benefit of the doubt. At least for now." Father blew out a breath. "You know, people could consider me guilty as well."

"You? Why?"

"I could have told him to do it."

Sarah shook her head. "You'd never do anything like that!"

"You and I know that, but not everyone around here knows us so well. What if one of the other mill owners accused us?" He gazed at the cold fireplace in the office. "I just pray there won't be any more suspicious fires—anywhere."

"I'll pray for that too, Father. Don't worry. You're highly respected in town, and I don't believe anyone would ever doubt your integrity."

A hint of a smile brightened his face as he looked at her, warmth in his eyes.

He picked up the stack of papers Sarah had moved aside on the desk. "Now, let's get back to the business at hand. Are you finished with these?"

"Almost. I wanted to review them with you to make sure I copied the right thing, then I wanted to rewrite the whole bid and make it very neat before you give it back to the army."

"Sounds good to me. Would you like to go over them now?"

"Yes, I would, if you have the time. They are waiting for this, are they not?"

"Yes, they are. I told them they'd be ready by the end of the week."

"And so they will." Sarah would make sure the government bid was clean and professional and most importantly, correct. She wished she would be able to hand the bid over to the army herself, knowing it was her work and she was proud of it.

"Excellent. Thank you, Sarah. You've been a great help to me."

Sarah beamed. "Father, you know I love doing this kind of work, and I'd gladly do more."

"Well, you might have that opportunity. Chances are I'll bring the ledgers from Milltown back home with me. I need to find out what's on those papers and I'd like to have your eyes to see them."

Sarah tamped down her enthusiasm with great difficulty. "I'd be happy to, as you know. But I feel the sooner, the better. If your workers aren't being treated fairly, that should be rectified. People's families depend on it."

Father raised his eyebrows. "I'm beginning to suspect you know more about my business than I do." He gave her a wink.

Sarah smiled as her face warmed. "I'm working on it."

"Hmm. Guess I better stay on my toes."

"All I really want to do is ease your load and help you get more rest."

Father studied her intently. "You sound like your mother now. Or like she used to."

"That means a lot to me, Father." Sarah sat down in the chair across from the desk to begin reviewing the paperwork.

"Let's get to work. Shall we?"

How Sarah loved to hear those words.

~~~
~~~

"So you think he was on to you?" Captain Stewart stood behind the desk in his office.

"I'm afraid so, sir."

"And the other rider. You believe they're accomplices?"

"It would be my guess, sir."

"Do you think you'd recognize the other man if you saw him again?"

"Let me think about it. I didn't see him that well with his hat pulled so low, but he was young with light-colored hair. Maybe one of the other soldiers remembers something unique about him."

"Maybe he'd be more cooperative than Nettles, if we could catch him."

"That's a possibility, sir. I'll check with the others and see if they can remember anything about the rider."

"You do that. lieutenant. Report back to me what you find out."

"Yes, sir." Josiah saluted and about-faced. When he reached the door, he halted and turned back around. "Sir, there was something about the horse that just came to my mind."

"What's that?"

"He was a chestnut brown with some white markings. In fact, I believe half his face was white and the other half was brown. Perhaps we can search for a horse marked that way."

"Good idea. I'll tell the other officers to tell their men to be on the lookout for the man you described as well as the horse with those unusual markings."

Chapter Twenty-Four

When Sarah and Father returned home, they found Anna Grace and Mother sitting in the rocking chairs on the front porch.

Anna Grace waved as they walked up to the house.

Sarah glanced from her sister to Mother. "What are you two up to?"

"Just rocking." Anna Grace grinned.

Sarah lifted an eyebrow. "That's all?"

"And waiting for y'all to come home."

Mother barely smiled, yet her eyes held a mystery.

"Why?"

Anna Grace looked at Mother, who nodded, then the little girl pulled something out from under her apron and held it up. Four small squares of fabric were sewn together. "Look what I made!"

Sarah reached for the cloth. "You sewed this, Anna Grace?"

Her sister's head bobbed up and down as her grin stretched across her face. "Yes, I did! I'm making a quilt for my doll's bed. Mother's showing me how to quilt."

Sarah couldn't hide her surprise. "Why, that's wonderful. Let me see those stitches." Sarah studied the fabric with the crooked stitches. "That's very nice work, Anna Grace."

"Mother told me to make little tiny stitches." Anna Grace beamed with pride.

Father reached for the fabric. "Let's see that." He examined the handiwork. "Very well done, Anna Grace. Did you just learn how to do that today?"

She bobbed her head again. "Yes, sir."

"Well, it looks like all my girls have been very productive today."

Sarah was amazed but incredibly happy to know Mother had spent time with Anna Grace. Her little sister was ecstatic. But would Mother continue to give her attention, or was this only because Sarah hadn't been around to entertain the little girl?

Mother stood and straightened her skirt. "Are you two ready for supper?"

"I am." Father opened the door, holding it for them to enter.

Mother went inside, while Anna Grace slid out of her chair. Sarah reached out to steady the rocker so she wouldn't fall, offering her hand to her sister out of habit. "I can do it," Anna Grace said.

Sarah fought rejection from the remark but pushed the feeling aside. She should be glad that her sister was achieving more independence.

"Of course you can," Sarah said.

After they were seated at the table, Father said grace and they passed the food.

"Do y'all know someone my age with blonde hair, kind of thin and shorter than me?"

Father and Mother looked at each other and shook their heads.

"I can't think of anyone off the top of my head that fits that description," Father said. "Why?"

"I saw her this morning when Father and I walked to the office. She was talking with a man, and they both watched me."

"Are you sure they were watching you?" Mother asked.

"I wasn't sure at that time, but it felt like they were. And then this afternoon while I waited outside while Eben was at the office, she was there by herself. But she stared at me again."

"Don't you think it's possible she was looking at someone or something else?" Father said as he lifted his fork to his mouth.

"It's possible, of course. Actually, I hope she was because it was very uncomfortable being watched."

"Well, I'm sure you were just being self-conscious." Father swallowed some tea.

"Maybe so." Sarah hoped so anyway.

"So Eben came to see you today?" Mother asked.

Father nodded. "Yes, he did."

"And did you find out where he's been?"

"No, not really. He said it was a personal matter, and I thought it rude to pry."

"Was he aware of the fires?"

"No, he said not. But once he heard, he showed real concern and left quickly to get back to the mill."

"I'm sure there's a reasonable explanation," Mother said, wiping her mouth with her napkin. She looked at Sarah. "Sarah, did you make some progress with Father's paperwork?"

"Yes, I did." She glanced at Father. "We did."

"Sarah has been a great help today. I'm thankful she was available."

"So are you finished with the work?"

"Yes, the bid is ready for the army to pick up. He plans to come get it next week."

"So Sarah doesn't need to go to the office tomorrow? If not, perhaps she can help Anna Grace with her quilt."

A weight fell on Sarah's shoulders, and she glanced from Mother to Anna Grace. Was she pulling away again and letting Sarah take over? "Are you going to be here, Mother?" Sarah asked.

"Yes, I'll be here in the morning. Mrs. Browning, one of the ladies I met at church, dropped by today. She invited me to her house for lunch tomorrow to meet a few other ladies, and I accepted."

"Why, that's excellent, dear. I'm glad to hear you're getting to know some people in town."

Sarah was pleased to hear the news as well, yet still afraid to believe Mother had come out of her gloom. Much as she wanted to go back to Father's office and do more work for him, she didn't mind staying home if it meant her mother was going to socialize.

"Are you going to wear a new dress?" Anna Grace asked Mother.

Mother blinked a few times. "A new dress? Why do you ask that, Anna Grace?"

The little girl shrugged. "It sounds like you're going to a party. And I thought you'd want a party dress instead of your old black one."

Mother gaped, and Sarah held her breath, waiting for her reaction. Would Mother ever wear anything besides black again?

"Why, that's a good idea, Anna Grace," Father said. He reached over and placed his hand on Mother's arm. "I bet you have a couple of dresses in your trunk you could wear."

Sarah scanned her memory trying to recall what Mother wore before black.

"Like the pretty one in the picture?" Anna Grace pointed to a photo on the wall of Mother and Father on their wedding day. "You were really pretty in that dress."

Father chuckled and Mother allowed a smile to appear on her face. "Why, that's a wedding dress, Anna Grace. You only wear dresses like that on your wedding day, the day you get married," Mother said.

"However, your mother does have some dresses that are almost as pretty, don't you, Virginia?" Father sought Mother's face.

"Yes, I think I do. I'll have to dig through my trunk and see what I have that's acceptable."

"Can I see?" Anna Grace implored.

Mother glanced at each of them. "I suppose it will be all right. If there is anything in there worth wearing and the bugs haven't gotten to them. Sarah, you and Anna Grace clear the table and then you can help me choose something. I'm sure everything in that trunk needs some freshening before it can be worn."

Anna Grace clapped her hands. "I can't wait to see!"

"Before you ladies get carried away with clothes, I'd like to make a suggestion," Father said.

They all gave him their attention. "What is it, dear?" Mother said.

"The weather has been warming up this week, so I think Saturday will be a good day for the picnic we talked about. Why don't we sail over to the island and have one?" Father said.

Anna Grace jumped up and down. "Yes! Can we, Mother?"

Mother shrugged. "I suppose so."

"Then it's decided. You get everything ready when you come back from your soiree tomorrow, and I'll procure the boat."

Mother frowned. "Soiree? Charles, please."

He gave her a wink, picked up the newspaper and began to peruse it.

Sarah wondered if she was having a dream or had accidentally entered someone else's home. It had been a long time since her Father had appeared so happy, even longer since her mother had been so relaxed. Whatever was happening, Sarah whispered a "thank you" to God for the change in her family's atmosphere.

~~~

Upstairs in Mother and Father's bedroom, the old trunk creaked open as Mother lifted the hinged lid. Sarah sat on the bed as Mother searched through layers of clothing while Anna Grace sat on the floor peering into the trunk. Mother lifted a beige satin dress with brown stripes and held it up. "What do you think?"

"I think it's fine, Mother." Anything would be an improvement over the black.

"Mother, I like this one!" Anna Grace reached in and fingered the lace on a pale yellow, lightweight muslin dress. "It's so pretty!"

Mother eyed the dress but shook her head. "The fabric is too sheer for this time of year."

Anna Grace stuck her lips out in a pout.

Sarah pointed to a dark blue fabric. "What about that one, Mother? Is that a dress?"

Mother lifted the dress out and shook it. The dress had fabric with navy blue stripes of satin on a navy background and a white lace collar. "Maybe this one will do." She held it up in front of her as she looked at her reflection in the cheval mirror.

"I like it," Sarah said, as Mother laid the dress on the bed.

Anna Grace rifled through the trunk, searching for another choice. "Mother, you have more than dresses in here."

A look of alarm covered Mother's face and she rushed over to the trunk. "I believe we have enough to choose from." She pushed Anna Grace's hand out of the way and closed the trunk, acting as if she didn't want the little girl to see the rest of the contents. She straightened, then blew out a breath and faced them. "So, shall it be the blue or the beige?"

"Beige!" Anna Grace said.

"I like either, Mother. I've always been partial to blue, but the beige is pretty as well."

"I think the blue will be appropriate. The beige might still be
~~~

too much of a summery material for now."

"You didn't like any of mine!" Anna Grace complained.

"I'll wear the others another time. Will that be acceptable?"

"I guess so." Anna Grace's eyes were downcast, then she brightened and looked up at Mother. "Can I fix your hair?"

"Fix my hair? Anna Grace, I don't think you can braid my hair." Mother's hair was very long and seldom seen down except when she brushed and washed it, but most of the time it was parted down the middle and braided, then put into a chignon with a hairnet over it. "Tell you what though, I'll let you brush it in the morning."

Anna Grace's eyes lit up. "I can?"

Sarah doubted her little sister had the patience to take the time to brush Mother's hair, something Sarah herself liked to do when she was younger. Mother would sit in a chair with her hair hanging behind it, almost to the floor. Brushing her hair could be an arduous task.

"Yes, you can help me brush it."

Anna Grace seemed satisfied, and Mother had agreed to wear a different dress color. Although the dress was still dark, the blue was a welcome change. The gloom that had hovered over their home for so long was beginning to lift.

~~~

Josiah escorted Lizzie on his arm down the wharf to the sailboat tied up beside it. He saluted the two young soldiers onboard who would be sailing the craft. Josiah was perfectly capable of handling the boat by himself but wanted company for propriety's sake. Mr. Ponder had escorted them as far as the wharf, Josiah believed to assure himself that his daughter had adequate escorts for the trip.

On his other arm, he carried the basket Mrs. Ponder had prepared for them to take. He handed the basket to one of the men in the boat who set it down on the bottom, then he and the other soldier helped Lizzie step into the boat. When she was safely in, he untied the rope holding the boat to the wharf, and tossed it into the boat before jumping in himself. He and Lizzie settled themselves on a side bench as they slowly moved away from the pier and out
~~~

into the open water of the bay.

Soon the sails caught the wind, and the boat moved smoothly through the water, barely bouncing in the gentle waves. Lizzie snuggled as close to him as she could as soon as they were out of her father's view, too close for his comfort, but he resigned himself to humor her. Even though he'd rather not be with her, he had decided to stay friendly in hopes he could discover more information about Rafe Nettles and what their connection was.

The day was beautiful, and he contented himself with enjoying the scenery and warm winter weather. He tried not to think of Sarah and the times they had sailed together on this same bay, but how could he help it? Yet, being with someone he didn't care for took away some of the pleasure from the outing.

"When will we stop for the picnic?" she asked, fluttering her eyelashes up at him.

"Are you hungry already?" He smiled at her. "I thought we'd spend some time enjoying the sail before we stop at the beach by Fort Pickens for the picnic. Is that all right with you?"

"Of course, as long as you can keep me warm, I'm perfectly comfortable."

He forced a smile but hid the fact that he was gritting his teeth. How ironic that she feigned being cold while exposing too much of her skin in such a low-necked dress. "Maybe you should pull your shawl closer together," he said. She grinned as if she thought his comment was humorous and not to be taken seriously.

Glancing away, he waved at other boaters.

"Do you know everyone out here?" Lizzie asked.

"Oh no. It's such marine friendliness to acknowledge others who are out on the water too."

"Truly? Well you better not be waving at some other woman in those boats." Lizzie's smile didn't match the look in her eyes. He didn't appreciate her warning or her jealousy, but he saw what Mabel had said about her. If only this afternoon would pass quickly.

~~~

Sarah held Anna Grace's hand onto the wharf, despite the girl's assertion that she could "do it herself." Maybe she could, but
~~~

Sarah cringed at the thought of her little sister stumbling, then falling into the water.

Father helped them and their picnic supplies into the sailboat before casting off and manning the sails himself. He was quite adept at sailing, having done so his whole life. Sarah was capable of helping him if necessary, but he preferred to handle the craft alone. Soon they were gliding through the bay, joining other boaters enjoying the pleasant weather. Sarah's heart was full seeing the relaxation on both her mother's and father's faces, such a change from the last sail.

"Where are we going to stop for our picnic?" Sarah asked. "Fort Pickens?" The fort had been a familiar destination when they lived here years ago.

"No. Not Fort Pickens." Father's expression turned serious, and Sarah remembered the fort had remained in enemy hands during the war, firing on the Confederate army across the bay. Apparently, the fort was now a traitor too, and Father didn't want to go anywhere near it. "No, I thought we'd stop to the east of the fort where the sand is softer to sit on."

They hadn't sailed long before Father let the sails down and beached the boat, hopping out to drag it up higher on the sand. He helped the women out, then picked up Anna Grace and handed her to Mother. Sarah retrieved their picnic basket and an old quilt to spread out on the sand. She and Mother caught the corners of the quilt and laid it on a dry place where the sand was deep and comfortable as a feather bed to sit on.

They each found a place to sit, as Mother and Sarah passed out the food Della had packed. Anna Grace made sure each person had a napkin. Soon they were feasting on fried chicken, pickles and cold biscuits with honey. There were two Mason jars of sweet tea that they poured into tin cups and drank while watching the other boats pass by, waving as if they were all friends.

When they'd finished, Anna Grace took off her shoes and stockings to make soft impressions of her little toes and feet in the sand. She bent over to pick up a seashell. "Look how pretty!"

"Let's see." Sarah observed the cone-shaped pink seashell with light brown spots. "Ooh that *is* pretty. Let's see what other pretty ones we can find."

Sarah stood and ambled alongside her sister, her eyes focused on the sand, bending over frequently to pick up a shell.

"Sarah, look! That shell is moving!" Anna Grace pointed to the sand.

Sarah picked up the moving shell. "This is a hermit crab. See? There's a little crab in here carrying the shell on his back."

"Can we keep him? Please?"

"No, he needs to live on the beach. He'd die if we brought him home. You don't want that to happen, do you?"

Anna Grace shook her head. "No. That would be sad."

"So let's put him back so he can go see his friends." She set the crab down on the shell and it scurried away.

Anna Grace giggled. "He must be in a hurry to see his friends."

Sarah paused to straighten and stretch her back. As she gazed out at the bay, a sailboat passed in front of her. Her breath caught. There in the boat sitting very close to a woman was Josiah.

She stared in disbelief, not believing her eyes. But it was indeed he, the sandy brown hair, the chiseled chin with the cleft she once adored. She could almost see his sky-blue eyes. There was no doubt she was looking at her former fiancé.

She glanced at the woman beside him and recognized her as well. She was the blonde woman who'd been near Father's business. The one who'd been staring at her. Sarah was glued to the spot, her emotions churning inside, confusion giving way to disappointment. Then he looked her way and their eyes met and she knew he saw her too.

"Sarah, why don't you wave at that boat?" Anna Grace said, waving.

She'd forgotten about Anna Grace. She glanced down, bereft of words. "I … forgot."

But she hadn't forgotten. She'd never forget. But he'd forgotten her. Obviously, he was married, and the woman was his wife. No one else would have been sitting so close to him.

Chapter Twenty-Five

She'd seen him. Of that he was certain. He couldn't believe Sarah was there on the beach in front of him. So was her daughter and her parents. But where was her husband? Had he died in the war? She wasn't wearing mourning clothes, but maybe enough time had passed for her to be out of them.

And she'd seen him with Lizzie. What must she think? No doubt that he and Lizzie were a couple. The idea made him ill.

"Who was that?" Lizzie asked.

His head jerked toward her. "Who?"

"That woman back there on the beach. The woman you were staring at."

"I was staring? I'm sorry, I didn't mean to. I must've thought she was someone I knew."

Lizzie scowled, obviously unhappy with his behavior. Did she sense he was lying?

"When are we going to have our picnic?"

"Our picnic? Yes, of course, we're going to stop soon." He motioned to one of the soldiers. "Pull up by Fort Pickens."

The man acknowledged him, and aimed for the fort, away from the place where Sarah's family was. Josiah had lost his appetite completely, yet he couldn't let Lizzie know how seeing Sarah had affected him. He had to keep Lizzie happy and pretend nothing was out of the ordinary. But was he that good an actor?

"Are you sure you didn't know her? She was looking at you too."

"Who? Oh, you mean that woman back there. Perhaps I

reminded her of someone she knew too." He faked a laugh. "Ah, here we are. Let's go have a picnic!" Josiah mustered all the enthusiasm he could. He told himself this outing was part of his job and nothing more, an information-gathering exercise. But he had to be careful to earn her trust or she wouldn't tell him anything. Funny that he wanted her to trust him when he didn't even trust himself. Pretending he didn't know Sarah was like pretending he didn't know his own name. But somehow, he had to block thoughts of her from his mind and focus on his mission.

"This looks like a good spot! What do you think?" he said as he helped her out of the boat.

She scanned the area, then pointed to another place down the beach. "How about over there?"

"Sure. That's an even better spot!" He grabbed the basket with one arm and her hand with the other. "Be back after a while, gentlemen. You just relax and enjoy yourselves." He dearly wanted to invite them to share the picnic, but suspected Lizzie would prefer to be alone, which is why he'd told them ahead of time to be sure to eat lunch at the mess hall.

They sauntered down the beach to a place of Lizzie's liking, and he smoothed the sand with his hand so they could use the spot for their picnic. Lizzie's mother had packed a tablecloth, so they spread it out and sat on the edge of it. He watched Lizzie take the food out, some bread and jam and two boiled eggs and a jar of pickled okra. A jar of lemonade was included as well, but no cups, so he assumed they were both supposed to drink from the jar.

"I'm famished! Aren't you?" Josiah feigned hunger, patting his stomach and eyeing the meager feast.

"Maybe a little." Lizzie scooted closer, legs folded and leaning toward him. Her shawl had slipped down so that it only remained held on where it was secured by her arms. He cut his eyes away from her and toward the food, avoiding what he thought was supposed to entice him.

He selected an egg and offered it to her. "Would you like one?"

"No, thank you."

Josiah peeled the egg and ate it, then grabbed the jar of lemonade to wash it down. "How about some bread?" He picked up the bread and broke off a piece, then searched the picnic basket for a spoon to use with the marmalade. He pretended he was famished, just to avoid eye contact or conversation with her.

Wiping his mouth with his handkerchief, he said, “Lizzie, aren’t you going to eat?” She’d stared at him the entire time he ate. “I feel rather foolish eating everything by myself.”

She shrugged and glanced at the selection, then picked up the jar of okra and handed it to him. “Would you please open this for me?”

“Of course.” He handed her the open jar and she withdrew a piece of okra, then began nibbling on it, reminding him of a squirrel nibbling an acorn.

Josiah glanced across the bay in the direction of the lighthouse. “Pretty soon, you’ll be living over there and be able to look over here from your new house by the lighthouse.”

Lizzie’s gaze followed his. “Wouldn’t you rather live in town? In your old house away from the fort?”

Her question startled him. “Not really. All my business is around the fort, and the officer’s house is adequate for me.”

“But what if you get married? Maybe your wife won’t want to live there.”

Josiah practically choked on the bread he was eating. “Most army wives live where their husbands are assigned.”

“But what if you quit the army?”

“I haven’t considered leaving the army any time soon. I don’t know what other job I’d do.”

Her face darkened. “I’m sure there are other occupations you could have.”

“I don’t know what, but in the meantime, I need to finish the task at hand before I’m assigned somewhere else.”

“You mean the task of finding lumber or the missing lighthouse part?”

“Both.”

“Are you any closer to finding either?”

“Yes, as a matter of fact, I’m about to wrap up my search for a viable lumber source. I have one more place to go.”

She lifted an eyebrow. “Is that so? It must be far away, or you would have been there already.”

“You’re right that the actual mill is pretty far away—on the Blackwater River northeast of Pensacola. But they have an office in town, so I don't have to go all the way to the mill."

"What's the name of the company?"

"Turner Lumber Company."

Why was she so interested? Suddenly, Josiah wished he hadn't told her anything about the lumber.

He looked for a way to change the atmosphere and the subject. A seagull hovered overhead, and he broke off a tiny piece of bread and tossed it up in the air. The bird swooped to catch it. Soon other seagulls in the area found out about the free food and joined him. He threw another crumb up and laughed when the birds cawed and fought to catch it. Soon a flock of birds were above them, squawking and competing with each other for the crumbs he tossed up.

At first, Lizzie seemed amused by the birds' antics. But as more birds joined the others, she grew annoyed, especially when they swooped too close to her head. She held onto her bonnet with both hands as if the birds would steal it. The more aggressive the birds became, the more Josiah laughed, knowing how uncomfortable she was, but glad that at the same time, she was distracted.

A splat of seagull mess landed on her dress and she screamed, waving her hands at the birds. "Shoo! Go away!"

When they didn't, she pleaded with him. "Would you please make them go away?"

He quit tempting the birds, stood and waved his hands. "Go! Get on now!" The birds flew a short distance away and settled on the beach, keeping an eye on him in case he offered more food. He stretched. "I'd like to go for a walk. Wouldn't you?" He reached for her hand and she took it, then he pulled her to her feet.

They strolled a little way with her attached to his arm as usual. He stopped to pick up a seashell and held it up to show her. "This is a nice one, isn't it? Would you like to keep it?"

She eyed it curiously, then took the shell from him and dropped it between her breasts where it disappeared, giving him a grin. He tried to hide his surprise, but decided not to pick up any more shells, fearing they'd meet the same fate.

Perhaps this was a good time to ask her questions.

"Lizzie, do you know someone named Rafe Nettles?"

She avoided his gaze and glanced away. "Who?"

"Rafe Nettles."

She tapped a finger to her mouth. "Hmm. I'm not sure. Why?"

"I met him last week, and he looked like the same fellow I saw you talking to a couple of times."

Her brow creased and she pouted her lips. "Maybe I have talked to him and didn't know his name." She batted her eyelashes at him. "You know, there are a lot of men around the fort, and many of them speak to me."

Josiah feigned jealousy. "Is that right? So you have many men vying for your attention? Well, now, since you're such an attractive woman, I supposed that doesn't surprise me."

Lizzie grinned, showing pleasure at being complimented.

"I guess that Rafe fellow stood out because you told me you were old friends. Since you haven't been here very long, I wondered if you knew him when you lived somewhere else."

Her face reddened. "Did I say that? What I meant to say was that he reminded me of an old friend."

She was lying about Rafe. And she had lied about their relationship to Mabel Smith. What else would she lie about?

"I see. Well, since I thought you were friends, I was hoping you could give him a message for me."

"A message? What message?"

"He knows a lot of people around here, and I saw a horse the other day I really like and would pay top dollar for it. He was friends with the rider, so I thought he could tell the man I wanted to buy it."

"I thought you had a horse."

"I do." Hopefully, Prince wouldn't find out what he said. "But that horse was really special. The face was half brown and half white, and I heard horses marked like that were very lucky. I've always wanted one myself and I want to talk to the owner about it." *Lord, forgive me for lying.*

"You'd pay a lot of money for it?" He had her interest.

"Oh yes. They're very valuable."

"Well, if I ever see that—what's his name, Rafe? —I'll be sure to tell him."

"Thank you. I'd really appreciate that."

A gust of wind blew sand all over them, and she sputtered and shook her dress. "Can we turn back now?

"Yes, of course. Let's get everything picked up and head back to the boat. We don't want to be out here too late. It feels like it's getting colder."

~~~

"Sarah, what's the matter?" The screen door closed behind Mother as she joined Sarah on the porch. "You haven't been acting the same ever since the picnic."

Sarah shook her head. "I'm just not feeling well." Much as she wanted to talk to her mother, she didn't know where to start. Mother had been so obsessed with her own grief for the past years, Sarah had kept her feelings to herself. How could Mother offer her any sympathy? It wasn't as if Josiah had died. But even so, she had grieved her loss, the kind of loss Mother wouldn't understand. After all, Mother had married her sweetheart with her parents' blessing, unlike Sarah.

As soon as they'd gotten home from their outing, Anna Grace had gone to play with the kittens, but Sarah had gone out on the veranda. She wanted to be alone with her thoughts as she tried to sort out her feelings. Now that she'd seen Josiah, Sarah struggled with a mixture of feelings. Her questions had been answered, so she knew he was alive and had returned to Pensacola. Yet, what should have brought her joy only brought more loss now that she knew he had married.

Mother put her hand on Sarah's arm. "Sarah, what is it? Please tell me. I know something has upset you."

Sarah glanced up at her mother and seeing the compassion in her eyes, let the tears flow. "Mother. I saw Josiah. He was in a sailboat that passed by the beach." Sarah choked out the words and sobbed.

Mother drew her close into a hug. "Are you sure it was Josiah?"

"Yes. He looked straight at me."

"Did he acknowledge you?"

Sarah shook her head. "No, he was with a woman. She must've been his wife."

"Are you certain?" Mother patted her on the back.

"It had to be. She was sitting so close to him."
~~~

They stood in silence for a few minutes while Sarah sobbed. Mother pulled her handkerchief from her pocket and handed it to Sarah. Sarah wiped her eyes and blew her nose, then took a deep breath and stepped back. “All these years I hoped that somehow we could get together. Even though Father made us break our engagement, I hoped that someday things would change, that Josiah hadn’t stopped loving me. When the war ended, I thought that maybe Father wouldn’t be angry anymore, and that we’d all come back to Pensacola and our lives would return to normal. I’ve been such a fool, hoping for the impossible.” She began sobbing again, letting her head fall against Mother’s shoulder.

“I’m sorry, Sarah. Truly, I am. Sometimes we can’t go back to the way things used to be.”

Mother was talking about the boys’ deaths now. Of course, life hadn’t gone back to normal for her. But Sarah had held onto hope all this time. Why? *God, why didn’t I give up? Why couldn’t I have fallen in love with someone else?*

“I kept hoping I’d get a letter from him. Even though Father was against us, I thought Josiah would try to let me know he still loved me. I should’ve known better than to continue waiting for him when I never heard from him again.”

Mother was silent, letting Sarah cry. It gave her some comfort to be able to share her pain with her mother. After all, Mother knew about misery. But Sarah made a promise to herself right there, that she wouldn’t live in agony the way her mother had for so long. Just because she was suffering, she didn’t have to make everyone else suffer too. No, it was time to give up hope. At least hope for her and Josiah. Perhaps it was time to put her hope somewhere else.

Chapter Twenty-Six

On a hunch, Josiah went back to see Mabel Smith. When he rode up to her house, he was surprised to see her sitting in a chair on the small front porch.

Wrapped in a heavy shawl, she waved from a sunlit area.

"Good morning, lieutenant."

He dismounted and walked toward the gray-haired lady. "Good to see you out here, Mrs. Smith."

"Got tired of being cooped up in that house and it looked pretty warm out here in the sun. It's right nice."

"Yes, it is. Still a little cool at night, but very pleasant during the day."

"So, what's on your mind, lieutenant?"

Josiah leaned against the porch column. "Sorry to bother you again with my questions, but I don't know who else to ask."

"I don't mind your questions. Just sorry I don't have all the answers."

"Well, I saw someone the other day with Rafe Nettles and wondered if you knew who it was."

"I might. What did he look like?"

"Younger, blond. Didn't get a very good look at him. He was on a horse riding pretty fast."

"Hmm. You know, Rafe had a little brother. Don't recall his name right off. He was too young to join up in '61, but he'd be probably 17 or 18 now. Worshipped the ground Rafe walked on and followed him around like a puppy. He was mighty upset when Rafe left for the war and he couldn't go too."

"Did he have blond hair?"

"Oh yes, tow-headed like cotton when he was a little fella. He'd do anything for Rafe."

No doubt he would, even aid his brother in hiding the lighthouse lens, Josiah wagered. Maybe he'd be interested in selling his horse.

~~~

"Miss Sarah, I saw your papa leave for Milltown this morning. He didn't want you to go with him this time?" Della asked, when Sarah came in with the breakfast dishes and put them down on the work table.

"No, he wanted to go over the paperwork with Eben by himself. I wish I could have gone because Father's eyesight is failing, and I could help."

"He probably knows you could, but you know men, they likes to do it themselves." Della picked up her knife in one hand and a sweet potato in the other and began peeling.

Sarah leaned against the door and sighed. "I know. I just hope he brings the paperwork back home with him so I can go check it."

Della raised an eyebrow as her focus shifted from her work to Sarah. "Are you feelin' well, Miss Sarah? You looks tired."

Sarah fought the urge to give in to her sadness in front of Della. She'd resolved to keep from spreading it to others, and she meant to keep her resolve. She straightened, glancing out the window at Anna Grace in the garden with Doc. "I'm fine. Just worried about Father and the business."

Della shook her head. "Never seen a woman so worked up about men's business before."

"Why is it 'men's' business? I don't think of it that way. It's our family's business, which is important to all of us."

"You'se right. Guess I never had a head for such things. I takes care of the inside of the house and Doc, he takes care of the outside of the house. It keeps us out of each other's way." Della grinned and chuckled.

"You don't ever get bored?"

"Ha! I'm too busy to get bored. But when I gets caught up at home, I make things like the clothes I made for Zeke's children."
~~~

The mention of Zeke took Sarah's mind back to the mill. "You know, Della, I wish I knew where Eben went when he leaves the mill."

"He come here, don't he?"

"Not all the time. He was gone when we were there last and when Father questioned him about it, he said it was 'personal' business. His foreman didn't know where he went either."

"Why do you care about that?" Della dropped the peeled potato to the bowl on the table. "Why you want to know the man's business?"

Sarah stiffened. "I'm only concerned because it affect's Father's business when he's not there." Sarah crossed her arms as she turned to stare outside. "But I do wonder if his activities are entirely upright."

"What you think he be doin'?"

Facing Della again, she said, "There've been fires at some of the other lumber companies."

Della's eyes widened. "You thinks your father's mill might have a fire too?"

"Father has been concerned about that, and he's told Eben to post extra guards to make sure it doesn't happen."

"You mean somebody been settin' them on purpose?"

"It appears that way, especially since it's only been lumber mills."

"Why would somebody do that—put those poor workers out of a job?"

Sarah shook her head. "No one knows. But it just seems peculiar that our mill is the only one that hasn't had a fire."

Della put down her knife and fixed her eyes on Sarah.

"You thinkin' Mr. Eben been settin' fires at the other places so your father's mill get more business?"

"The thought has crossed my mind. But when I suggested it to Father, he wouldn't hear of it. He trusts Eben and thinks he's too honorable to do such a thing."

"And you don't?"

"I don't know. I supposed I should trust Father's judgment, but there's just too many unanswered questions, like where Eben goes when he leaves the mill and won't tell anyone about it."

"I sees what you mean." Della resumed her chore. Then she

paused, knife and potato mid-air. "Maybe somebody could follow him."

Sarah jolted. "Who? Certainly not Zeke, since he's got to be working too."

"Hmm, I'll think on it. Let me talk to Doc and Doc can get the word to Zeke somehow. Maybe Zeke can ask a friend to follow the man."

"I wonder if that can be done without getting caught."

"There's ways, I bet, especially if Mr. Eben don't know the person that follows him."

"You know, Della. I doubt Father would approve of the idea, but I'd certainly like to know. If Eben's whereabouts are honorable, then why wouldn't he tell anyone what they are?"

"That's what I wants to know too."

~~~

Mother, Sarah, and Anna Grace finished their noonday meal and cleared the table. "Anna Grace, would you like to read with me?" Sarah asked her sister as she straightened the table cloth.

Mother raised her eyebrows, but Anna Grace clapped her hands together. "Yes, will you let me read too?"

"Absolutely." Anna Grace's "reading" consisted of her repeating what Sarah had just read, but she seemed to be recognizing a few words now.

Sarah lifted the heavy Bible from the sideboard and put it on the table, pulling it toward her so Anna Grace could look on as she sat on her knees in her chair. Sarah opened the book to a place marked by a ribbon, then glanced up.

"Mother, will you join us?"

Mother looked at the two of them, then nodded. "Yes, that would be nice."

"Here's where we left off last time in the book of Romans. 'For this, Thou shalt not kill, Thou shalt not steal, Thou shalt not bear false witness, Thou shalt not covet; and if there be any other commandment, it is briefly comprehended in this saying, namely, Thou shalt love thy neighbour as thyself.'" Anna Grace stumbled with the words as she tried to read along, following Sarah's finger across the page.
~~~

"Why did Jesus talk so funny?" Anna Grace asked.

Sarah bit back a smile, but Mother looked surprised.

"I think the apostle Paul is repeating Jesus here, but I agree, the words are not like words we use. But we can still understand them. Do you know what it means when it says, "Thou shalt not…?""

Anna Grace bobbed her head, then pointed her finger at Sarah. "It means "Don't do that!"

Sarah's heart was touched by her little sister's version. "That's right. So what things does it say not to do in this verse?"

"Don't kill. I'd never kill anything."

"That's right. What else?"

"Don't steal. That means don't take something from somebody that's not yours."

"Correct. Are there any other words you don't understand?"

"What's 'covet'?" Anna Grace put her finger on the word.

"It means to want what someone else has more than you want what you have, that you think about it too much." Sarah's heart pricked. Was that the way she felt about Josiah's wife because she wanted Josiah? *Lord, forgive me.*

"Oh. What do those words mean, 'bear falz wit…ness'?" Anna Grace sounded the words out. "A bear?"

Sarah giggled. "Not that kind of bear. It means to say bad things about someone that aren't true."

"I wouldn't do that! That's not nice!"

"I'm glad to hear you wouldn't. Do you see any other words you know?"

"There's 'love.' You're not supposed to love?" Anna Grace tilted her head and pursed her lips.

Sarah glanced back at the page. "Look, there's no 'not' in front of 'love.' So that means you *are* supposed to love, in other words, it says to love your neighbor."

"I don't know my neighbors."

Mother spoke up. "That means to love other people, like our friends at church."

"Like Della and Doc?"

"Yes, like Della and Doc."

"Mother, can we go meet our neighbors so I can love them too?"

Mother gave her little girl a warm smile. “Yes, perhaps, someday, we’ll call on them and introduce ourselves.”

“This verse means if you really love others, you won’t do those other bad things,” Sarah added.

“I can spell ‘love.’ L-O-V-E.’” Anna Grace crossed her arms in obvious pride.

“That’s wonderful. And a good word to know,” Mother said.

For a family, yes, that was a good word to know and to show. Mother was beginning to show love to Anna Grace, albeit in a reserved manner. But Anna Grace didn’t seem to be bothered by Mother’s lack of affection. Mother was paying attention to her, and that seemed to be enough.

But love outside their family only reminded her of Josiah and the love she’d lost. In her mind, she saw him breezing past in the sailboat with another woman, just as if Sarah had never existed. She shoved that memory as far back as she could, back in the past. It was time for her to start a new chapter in her life, if she could only figure out how to begin.

Chapter Twenty-Seven

"I hope this plan of yours works," Captain Stewart said, clasping his hands on the desk in front of him.

"I do, too. If it is Nettles's brother, he can help us get Nettles, or at least some information. How do you suggest we do that?" Josiah had foreseen several scenarios.

"We'll just hold him for questioning. Maybe he'll talk if he's afraid."

"That's what I would do. And it might even make Rafe Nettles come forward to protect his brother."

"Then I want you to stay near the fort for the time being in case he comes looking for you."

"Yes, sir, but..."

"You were planning to go somewhere?"

"Yes, it's that last bid I need to pick up from Turner."

"That can wait a few more days."

"Yes, sir. I'll stay busy around here." Josiah saluted and left the captain's office. He didn't have any work to do in his office, but he needed to take two of his uniforms to the laundresses for cleaning. He walked the short distance to his house and retrieved the clothes, then carried them to the laundry building behind the barracks, glancing around to see if any non-military people were near the fort. The sentries on duty would notice as well.

He busied himself around the post, then joined the other officers heading to the mess hall at noon. They had been briefed on the ploy to get Nettles in as well, so they were equally alert. After he ate, he walked outside and spotting the horses grazing in the nearby pasture, he went over to check on Prince. Josiah hadn't ridden him for a few days and felt guilty for neglecting the horse. Prince was on the far side of the field when Josiah approached, but noticed Josiah right away and came trotting over. Josiah stroked his head. "Hey boy. Sorry I haven't seen you lately. Did you miss me?"

Prince shook his head, and Josiah laughed. "You did too!"

Prince snuffed, sticking his nose over the fence so Josiah could pat him. "Look, Prince, if you see me with another horse, don't be offended. You're the only horse for me."

Prince neighed, his eyes darting to the side. Josiah looked over his shoulder and saw a sentry approaching with the man he expected, the man he assumed was Rafe Nettles's brother. He was leading the brown horse with the two-tone face. Just as Josiah expected, Lizzie had lost no time getting the news to Rafe.

"Sir, I believe this man is looking for you." The sentry saluted.

"Thank you. You may tell the others the horse is here," Josiah said, expecting the sentry to recognize his code. As the sentry walked away, Josiah faced the young man whose scraggly blond beard was thin and sporadic and extended his hand. "Lieutenant Josiah Hamilton. And what is your name, sir?"

"Will. Will Nettles." His eyes darted all around like a squirrel on a fence post. "I heard you wanna buy my horse."

So it was Rafe's brother, or at least, a relative. "I might. I thought he was a striking animal when you rode past me the other day. I've been wanting to get a closer look."

Will Nettles cocked his head. "Well, here he is. He's a good horse, worth a lot of money."

Josiah took the horse's reins and looked him over. "He's not a thoroughbred, but he looks healthy. Just needs some good grooming. I'll have our farrier check him out."

Will Nettles frowned. "How much will you give me for him?"

Four soldiers approached Nettle from the rear, and he spun around when he noticed them, right before they surrounded him.

Will's eyes filled with fear. "What's going on here?"

"I'm afraid we need to hold you for questioning, Mr. Nettles." Josiah nodded to the soldiers. "Please come along peacefully."

"But what did I do?" Nettles looked at though he might run, but the soldiers closed in.

"Perhaps you didn't do anything, but we have information that you might have aided others to steal government property." Josiah handed the reins to one of the soldiers. "Take this horse to the farrier, please." Josiah joined the other soldiers to lead the man inside.

Nettles paled and his shoulders drooped like a man condemned. His very demeanor told Josiah Will Nettles knew something, something they were about to find out.

The soldiers escorted Will into the fort where they were met by Captain Stewart. After taking Nettles into an empty room, Captain Stewart motioned for him to sit in the only chair.

"Mr. Nettles, we need to ask you some questions. I trust you're willing to cooperate with us." Captain Stewart faced Will with his arms crossed.

Nettles hung his head, shaking it. "I didn't do nothing."

"Perhaps not, but we believe you know who did. The fact is, someone or several people stole the lighthouse lens out of the lighthouse back in '62, during the war. How old are you, son?"

"Eighteen."

"When the item was stolen, you were only eleven years old. Am I correct?"

Nettles shrugged. "Guess so."

"So, you were only a child, and whoever stole the lens were adults. You're not responsible for what they did."

Nettles peered up at the captain, head tilted.

"However, I believe you know where it's hidden, and failure to tell us is a crime that could keep you in prison for a while."

Nettles' eyes widened with fear. "I can't be in jail. I have a wife and baby!"

Josiah's heart reached out to the young man, and he regretted having to take the fellow away from his young family.

Captain Stewart continued. "Then I suggest the sooner you tell us where the lens is, the sooner you can get back to your family."

Nettles head shook from side to side, and he fought back tears. "I just came here to sell my horse because we need the money." He shot Josiah a glare. "You tricked me."

"Would you have come in on your own?"

Nettles shook his head again, sighing. "I don't want to get nobody in trouble."

"I understand. But remember, you were a child when the lens was stolen. Are any of those who did it still in the area?"

Nettles cut his eyes to the wall. "Not all of them."

"Son, you need to tell us where the lens is—the sooner, the better."

Nettles picked at a hangnail, then chewed on it.

Josiah stepped forward. "Excuse me sir, may I?" He motioned to the prisoner.

Captain Steward affirmed with a nod.

"Will, we know you were on the side of the Confederates, so we were your enemies. However, the war is over. For good. Like it or not. Too many people have been hurt and killed on both sides." Josiah swept his arm around the room. "We've all lost something, friends or family, because of the war. But it's time to stop fighting so we can all live in peace, so *your* family can live in peace too. Help us take care of this one thing so we can all be done with it and leave the war behind us. Don't you want that for your family?"

Nettles studied Josiah, then nodded, blowing out a breath. "Yes." He glanced from Josiah to the captain. "What will happen to the others if I tell you where it is?"

"Right now, we're more concerned with getting the lens back."

"Will you promise me you won't arrest them if I tell you?"

"If you lead us to the lens and it's still there and nobody tries to fight us over it, we won't pursue the individuals who took it. However, it better be where you say it is."

"All right. I'll tell you." Nettles looked back and forth between them. "But if they know I told you, they might move it."

"Then let's hope they don't know. How were you planning to get home once you sold your horse?"

"My bro…I mean, a friend, was going to take me."

"Is he waiting for you?"

"Yes."

"Where?"

"Just north of the fort, on the road to Molino. He's probably wondering why I'm taking so long. He might not even be there anymore."

"We'll check and see, let him know you're all right. What's his name and what does he look like?"

Will Nettles gave a description of his brother Rafe.

"After we speak to him, you can take us to the lens."

"Today?"

"That's correct."

"Wait here. We'll be back to get you." Captain Stewart motioned to Josiah to come with him, and they left Will Nettles in the room with the soldiers.

"We need to get the brother right away and hold him. I'll send out a dispatch to get him now." Captain Stewart walked briskly to another officer and gave him instructions.

"I'll go too. I know what he looks like." Josiah rushed to get Prince and rode out with the other soldiers.

When they spotted Rafe Nettles, he saw them too and mounted his horse to escape, but the soldiers overtook him and blocked his getaway.

"Lieutenant Hamilton! What's the meaning of this?"

"Hello Rafe. We just need to talk with you."

"You could talk to me any time."

"All right. We'll talk later. But I need you to wait for me at the fort."

Rafe's eyes darkened, and his mouth formed a straight line. He tried to move his horse away, but the soldier nearest him grabbed the reins and led him, while the other soldiers closed in on all sides. They led him back to the fort and placed him in a separate section so he and Will wouldn't see each other.

Then they took Will out and saddled his horse, so he could lead the contingent of soldiers to the lens. The soldiers hemmed him in so he couldn't escape. "Where are we going, Mr. Nettles?" Josiah asked.

"Toward Molino."

After an hour's ride, Nettles took a seldom-traveled trail off the main road which led through a pine forest to a cabin and a dilapidated barn. No smoke came out of the chimney, and the place looked deserted. Josiah put his hand on his gun just in case they were riding into an ambush.

"Is anyone here?" he asked Nettles.

"No. Not anymore. Used to be my grandparents' place."

Nettles rode over to the barn. Josiah motioned to two of the soldiers. "Check out the house."

The other soldiers surrounded the barn as Nettles dismounted and walked to the door. Josiah dismounted as well, as did two other soldiers, who followed Nettles in. Inside, dust fluttered through the sunlight piercing the dark interior of the deserted building. The remnants of an old wagon sat in the corner, and behind it, a pile of boards and hay.

"It's over here." Nettles walked to the corner and pushed the wagon out of the way. Then he began moving some of the boards and brushing off the hay. Josiah waited, wondering how such a large lens could be hidden so well, but when sections of the brass and glass of the lens became visible, he breathed a sigh of relief. They had found it.

Chapter Twenty-Eight

"Sarah, I brought you some more work, if you're still interested in helping with the business," Father said, as he hung his hat on the hall tree. He carried the leather pouch Sarah recognized from the mill and placed it on the dining room table.

"Father, you know I'm interested, and I'll be happy to get to work on these." She opened the pouch and viewed the stack of papers inside.

"I can't see them very well, but I can tell they're a mess and need to be cleaned up, rewritten if not refigured."

"What did you say to Eben? What was his reaction?"

"Well, he protested at first, said he didn't like me not trusting him. He was particularly unhappy about hearing that you had seen errors."

"I'm sure that news didn't settle well with him."

"Well, you know how he feels about women working in the business. And I've always felt the same way. But I have to admit you have a good head for numbers, and we need someone who does besides me, with my poor eyesight."

Mother had walked into the room to greet Father and stood listening.

"Perhaps you and Eben could work together," she said to Sarah.

Sarah frowned. "With his attitude toward me, I doubt that would be possible."

"Now that might not be a bad idea, Sarah," Father said. "Once Eben gets over his objection to your working and sees what an asset you can be, you two might make a good team."

Sarah's stomach clenched. Why were they always trying to put her and Eben together? Couldn't they see how unlikely a pair they were? She certainly didn't need *his* help, but he did need hers.

"I'll get started on these right away," Sarah said.

"Not tonight. It's too late, and you have plenty of time to work on them tomorrow."

Sarah couldn't wait to begin working, but she'd waited this long already. "I suppose you're right. Besides, tomorrow, I'll have more light to see them better. They're too messy to see with these kerosene lamps."

"Fine. Tomorrow after breakfast, you can spread out on the dining room table," Father said.

Sarah tried to hide her disappointment about not going to Father's office to work. She loved sitting at his desk with the daylight through the window and the cozy, quiet atmosphere of his office. "Oh, I thought you'd want me to come to the office."

Father glanced at Mother. "I'll be working at my desk tomorrow, so I won't have a place for you to work."

Why did she get the feeling Father didn't want her there? He hadn't minded the last time. What had happened to change his attitude? Or was he still against her working outside the house? And from the look he gave Mother, she must know his reason as well. How strange that one moment he was praising her ability and the next, confining her to the house.

And what about Mother's attitude? She'd been sympathetic about Josiah and even participated in Bible reading, but she seemed to be hiding a secret. Was Sarah imagining things or was everyone hiding a secret from her?

~~~

"Are all the pieces accounted for?" Captain Stewart stood with his hands on his hips scrutinizing the lighthouse equipment they'd brought back on the wagon as carefully as they could.

"I'm not certain yet. I'll need to get it cleaned and put back together properly since they took it apart to remove it. But we did search the barn thoroughly to make sure nothing was left there."

"And Will Nettles? Did you let him go?"
~~~

"Yes, sir. Since he was too young at the time it was removed, I don't think he should be held accountable. Plus, he helped us recover it, so I let him return to his family. When you and I spoke about this previously, you agreed."

"You're right. I did, and I believe that was the right thing to do. However, what do you think we should do with our new prisoner, his brother? He's pretty unhappy right now."

"I'm sure he is. But he's one of the men who removed the lens in the first place which makes him guilty of stealing government property. Should he be charged with theft?"

"Perhaps. But at the time the lens was taken, the Confederates considered it to be *their* property."

"And since the war has been over, it's been federal property, and he's kept it hidden."

"You're right about that. We could charge him or not."

"I think we should at least hold him a while, whether days or months, I'm not sure."

"I'll send a letter to my commanding officer and see what his response is. But for now, we'll hold him. Do you think we should tell him that his brother helped us?"

Josiah rubbed his chin. "I'm not sure about that. I don't know what harm it could do."

"At the very least, he'd be angry."

"No doubt about that." Captain Stewart turned to leave. "Would you like to see the prisoner?"

Josiah nodded, but first spoke to the men working on the lens. "Be very careful, men. We need every part cleaned and intact when we put it back in the lighthouse."

He joined the captain's side as they walked toward the guardhouse where Rafe Nettles was being held. Upon seeing Josiah, Nettles sprang to his feet and rushed toward him. Two soldiers grabbed the prisoner's arms to hold him back. "Why am I here?" he shouted. "Where is my brother?" He struggled to get out of the soldiers' grasp.

"You're being held for questioning," Josiah said. "And your brother is on his way home."

Nettles frowned. "Home? You didn't buy his horse?"

"No, I didn't. He needed it more than I do."

The man appeared to be puzzled. "So what do you want to

question me about?"

"We believe you have some information about the lighthouse lens that was removed during the war."

"Why do you think that?"

"We have our sources."

Rafe Nettles crossed his arms. "Well, I ain't got nothin' to say."

"That's your choice. If you change your mind, let me know." Josiah motioned to the guard to let him out and started to leave.

"Hey! How long are you gonna leave me here?" Nettles yelled.

"Long enough," Josiah said.

As he stepped outside the door, Nettles said, "I'm not the one you need to be worryin' about."

Josiah glanced back at him, eyebrows raised. "And who might that be?"

Nettles grinned. "That's for me to know, and you to find out. And you'll find out soon enough."

Josiah strode outside, sucking in the fresh air. Who else was in on Nettles's plans? And why should Josiah be worried? The man must be referring to the lens that he didn't know had been recovered. What kind of warning was he giving?

Captain Stewart appeared at his side. "Do you have any idea who he might be talking about?"

"No idea." Josiah shook his head. "But it sounds like we should be on alert for any of his other accomplices."

"I agree. I'll step up the guard. So what is your next order of business?"

"I need to send a letter to the Corps of Engineers to let them know we found the lens. They'll probably send a lighthouse specialist to help reassemble it when we replace the other one."

"You go ahead and take care of that." The two walked toward their offices in the barracks. "You can go ahead and tell Mr. Ponder the lens has been recovered in case he wants to see it."

"You're right. He should know."

"So now that the lens has been recovered, you can devote yourself entirely to the building of the lighthouse and keepers' house. Have you picked up that last bid yet?"

"No. This lens business delayed my return to the Turner

company to get it. I'll take care of that tomorrow. When I finish the letter to the Corps, I'll ride over to Mr. Ponder's house and let him know about the lens."

"Fine. I'll let you know if the prisoner divulges any more information."

"Thank you, sir."

After Josiah wrote the letter, he dropped it off in the outgoing mail, then decided to walk to the Ponder house instead of fetching Prince, letting the horse rest since the morning's ride. Josiah needed the walk to clear his head. While he was relieved to have found the lens, Rafe Nettles' warning had unsettled him. He rummaged through his mind trying to think of anyone else he'd seen Nettles with, anyone else that had looked suspicious. Perhaps he was talking about one of the men who watched the bricks being unloaded. Josiah couldn't remember what any of them looked like, much less whether he'd seen any of them more than once. In fact, the only person he remembered seeing Rafe Nettles with was Lizzie, but she couldn't be the one he had referred to. She wouldn't have had anything to do with the removal of the lens. She wasn't in the area at the time and besides that, she was a Union sympathizer, not a Confederate.

He glanced over his shoulder as he left the post and headed toward Warrington, expecting to see someone lurking nearby. But he didn't see anyone suspicious. When he arrived at the Ponder house, Ponder answered his knock.

"Lieutenant. What brings you here?" He gestured for Josiah to enter. "Won't you come in?"

Josiah removed his cap and stepped inside. "I just wanted to let you know that the first order lens has been recovered."

"You don't say." Ponder arched his eyebrows. "Do you know who was responsible?"

"We have some suspects." Josiah scanned the room for sight of Lizzie.

"What kind of condition is it in?" Ponder picked up a pipe on a small table beside a chair and puffed on it. "Will we be able to use it or did the scoundrels ruin it?"

"It appears to be in fairly good condition. A lighthouse specialist from the Corps will come inspect it."

"Good. I'd like to see it myself."

"I figured you would, and that's why I came right over to let you know about it."

"Then I'll be over first thing in the morning."

"I won't be there because I need to go to Pensacola, but Captain Stewart will show you where we're keeping it."

"Fine, then. Thank you for coming to tell me."

Josiah nodded his response, then left the house, almost bumping into Lizzie just outside the door.

"Excuse me, Lizzie. I didn't see you there." He replaced his cap and tipped it in greeting.

"I heard you found that thing you were looking for, the thing that goes in the lighthouse."

She must have been listening to the conversation between him and her father. Who else knew? Will? Surely Will hadn't returned to the area since they'd recovered the lens. He'd hightailed it north when Josiah told him he was free to go.

"Yes, we did." She had no idea she had helped them find it by conveying the message about Will's horse, and he wasn't about to tell her.

"So who took it?" She eyed him curiously.

"We don't know for certain, but we have several suspects in custody." *Lord, forgive me for stretching the truth.*

Her eyes widened. "You do?"

"Yes. They won't be causing any more mischief for a while."

Lizzie's expression changed from curiosity to worry to anger.

"Do you know their names?"

"One of them is that Nettles fellow you know."

"He's in jail?" She gaped. "He stole the lighthouse thing?"

"He's being held because we think he knows about it. We're not sure about his part in the theft yet." Josiah affected compassion. "I'm sorry to upset you with that news."

Her eyes darkened angrily. "Why should that upset me? I told you I didn't know him that well."

"That's good, because I don't know how long he's going to be held." He looked overhead as dusk darkened the sky. "Well, I must be going. I'll see you soon."

As Josiah walked away, he knew Lizzie was watching him, perhaps even boring holes in his back with the anger he'd seen in her eyes. What would she do now that her source of information was put away? One thing for certain, she wouldn't need to "help" him anymore.

Chapter Twenty-Nine

Sarah arched her back and stretched when the grandfather clock chimed ten o'clock. Had she been sitting there two hours already? She glanced outside the window at the sunny day realizing the overcast sky earlier that morning had changed its mood without her notice. Ever since the breakfast dishes had been cleared away, she'd been sitting at the dining room table poring over the paperwork Father brought from the mill.

Mother had gone upstairs to work on her mending and Anna Grace was outside, leaving her alone with her work. Mother came down with some of Father's shirts in her hands. "How are you doing with all that work? Aren't you tired of it yet?"

Sarah tilted her head and pursed her lips. "Tired of the work? No, I find it challenging. Tired of sitting here, yes." She pushed away from the table and stood. "I need to stretch my legs, though."

"I don't understand why you enjoy that type of work. I wouldn't be able to make heads or tails of it." Mother scanned the stacks on the table. "But I suppose you got that from your father."

"Which appears to be a curse for a woman."

"Why, what do you mean?"

"Because all a woman is expected to do is stay home and take care of her husband and children. There doesn't seem to be a place for a woman who enjoys working outside the home, even an unmarried woman."

"Now Sarah, it's a blessing to be able to stay at home and take care of household matters and leave the work of earning a living to your husband."

"Perhaps if I had a husband, I'd feel differently." Sarah hated the cynicism she'd acquired recently.

"Sarah, you're still young enough to marry."

Did Mother have any idea how much she hurt from even the mention of marriage anymore?

"I suppose you're referring to Eben, aren't you?"

"He is a good man, Sarah, and you should appreciate the fact that he's interested in you."

"But why is he interested in me? He doesn't even know me or understand me. I think the only reason is because he wants to inherit the business someday."

"You sell him short. I just don't think you've given him a chance to know you."

"The only thing we have in common is our connection to the mill." She swept her arms across the table. "And Mother, I don't think he knows his arithmetic. I'm finding so many errors he made. It's a wonder Father's business hasn't suffered."

Mother stared at her, as if at a loss for an answer. "I need to go wash these shirts." She crossed the room to the back door.

"Mother, did you and Father know each other very well when you got married?"

Mother stopped and looked at Sarah. "Yes, we did, but we'd known each other a long time and felt more like brother and sister."

"So you've never had to explain yourself to him. He loves you just as you are, and you him. Isn't that the way it's supposed to be?"

A hint of sympathy softened Mother's eyes. "Not everyone has that kind of relationship, Sarah. Your father and I have been very blessed."

"Well, I thought I had that kind of relationship, but perhaps I was wrong." Sarah glanced away and bit her lip as the pain pricked her heart again.

When the door closed behind Mother, Sarah had an urge to escape the house as well. She crossed to the foyer, then out the front door to the veranda. Standing at the railing, she watched the ships moving in and out of the harbor. Life went on as if nothing had happened, at least for everyone else. She inhaled the sea breeze, invigorating her to go back inside and return to the work.

She settled back into her chair and reviewed her progress. One stack was finished, one still needed to be worked on, and one contained documents she had questions about, questions only her father could answer. Until she talked to him, she could go no further with them. Father had told her to stay home to work because he didn't have room for her in his office. But surely, he wouldn't mind if she took some over to review, get her questions answered, and his advice on how to handle them.

Yes, that's what she'd do. She'd only take up a little of his time, then come back home to finish working. She picked up the documents she needed help with and tucked them inside the leather binder. Then she checked her appearance in the mirror before grabbing her bonnet, gloves, and shawl. Just the opportunity to go to the office and discuss the business with Father renewed her interest in what she was doing. She hoped Father would understand the interruption.

She paused. What if he had an appointment like he'd had before? She remembered the aggravation he'd shown the last time she arrived while a private meeting was going on. Father didn't want his customer to be bothered by someone else's presence. Sarah pushed her concern aside. She'd just check to see if he had a guest before she barged in unannounced. There couldn't be any harm in that.

~~~

Josiah boarded the Navy steamer for Pensacola. There was no need to saddle up today, since he only had a few places to go in town, and he could walk to those easily. He was thankful to have taken one of the loads off his shoulders by recovering the lens the day before. Now, to wrap up the lumber issue. He moved to the front of the boat and faced the opposite shore of Santa Rosa Island, recalling the events of Saturday when he'd taken Lizzie sailing.

Could the day have gone much worse? Spending the day with Lizzie was miserable enough, but seeing Sarah was so unexpected. Her expression had been complete shock when she saw him. Obviously, she did not know he was in town, a little detail her father had most likely kept from her. The fact that she saw him with Lizzie was embarrassing, especially assuming Sarah had
~~~

drawn a conclusion about he and the keepers' daughter. But what difference did it make what she thought about what company he kept? The short distance between the boat and the beach might as well have been an ocean's width, so great was the separation between the two of them now.

A fellow soldier joined him at the railing. "I heard the lighthouse lens has been recovered."

Josiah startled out of his thoughts. "Yes, that's true."

"Guess you're happy about that."

Josiah nodded, reminded of how fast word traveled at the fort.

"The lighthouse keeper—bet he's happy too. Heard he's been complaining about the one they're using now."

"He was glad to hear the news."

"Did you get the people responsible for taking it?"

Josiah tired of the interrogation. "We have a couple of suspects. No one for certain yet. I believe many of them didn't come back after the war, for one reason or another."

The other man affirmed with a nod. "No doubt."

A flash of color on the other side of the boat caught Josiah's attention and he scanned the group of passengers. Was Lizzie on board the ship too? He continued to search but didn't see her. He must have been mistaken. Why would she be on board? Not that she couldn't be, but if she saw him, she'd probably attach herself to him like she always did, and he'd have the inconvenience of freeing himself from her. Just in case, he moved farther to the other side, trying to conceal himself among other soldiers.

When the boat docked at the wharf in downtown Pensacola, Josiah stayed with the other soldiers, casting glances over his shoulder to see if Lizzie was there when he disembarked. He breathed a sigh of relief when he didn't spot her, then headed toward Main Street. Hopefully, Mr. Turner would have the bid ready this time.

~~~

Sarah started out the door, then paused. Should she tell Mother where she was going? She looked out back and didn't see her anywhere. Not caring to take the time to hunt for her, she decided to tell Della instead. But no one was in the kitchen either. They
~~~

must be in the barn or the outhouse. Why did she have to tell anyone where she was going anyway? She was a grown woman, after all.

She went out the front door and down the steps, then walked to the street and crossed to the other side. It occurred to her that she'd never gone anywhere by herself before. Either she had been accompanied by her parents or had Anna Grace with her. Not having someone alongside was both daring and a bit frightening, like she was exposed and vulnerable. Courage, that's what she needed. She straightened her shoulders and focused ahead to assume the appearance of the confident person she wanted to be, ignoring everyone and the uncomfortable feelings that threatened her composure.

When she reached Father's office, she steeled herself for his response. As she pulled the heavy front door open, she was greeted by the heady smell of turpentine. She slipped inside. No noise was coming from Father's office and his door was open. Good. She wouldn't be interrupting a meeting. She peeked past a stack of turpentine barrels to get a glimpse of him. But when she looked in the office, Father wasn't at his desk or anywhere in the room. A smoldering fire in the fireplace was evidence of his earlier presence. Where was he? Probably either in the warehouse or on the docks. She'd wait for him. Meanwhile, she could use his desk, so she opened the folder and withdrew the papers, then settled into the chair.

~~~

Josiah took care of his other errands first, then headed toward the Turner offices. He spotted the warehouse up ahead as he turned the corner. A commotion caught his attention in the street leading onto the docks, and he turned to see a wagon whose wheel had fallen off, leaving the conveyance and its supplies in a precarious position. Josiah rushed over to help and several others joined him. He was tied up for the next half hour assisting the driver and wagon, delaying his visit to Mr. Turner.
~~~

Chapter Thirty

Sarah heard the creak of the front door and looked up from her work. "Father?"

She received no response, but listened intently, in case a visitor had come in. Still no sound. That was odd. She had heard the door open. Sarah stood and came around the desk, just as a familiar, pale blonde woman entered the office.

"You. What are you doing here?" She was Josiah's wife, the one she'd seen Saturday.

The woman smirked. "I'm here to make sure you leave my beau alone."

"Your beau? I'm afraid I don't understand." A crazed look held the woman's eyes captive.

She came toward Sarah, a scrawny finger pointing. "You know exactly what I mean. You think you can get Josiah back, but I won't let you have him!"

A quick look at the woman's hand revealed no wedding ring. She wasn't married to Josiah? Sarah's slight tinge of relief was quickly doused by the strange, menacing behavior of the woman.

"Look, um, I'm afraid I don't know your name." Sarah extended her hand in a calming motion.

"It's Lizzie, the future Mrs. Josiah Hamilton!"

Sarah gulped back the bile the woman's announcement inflicted on her stomach. She needed to get past the irrational woman and out the door. She glanced at the fireplace for a weapon. The other woman followed her gaze and ran to the fireplace, picking up an iron poker. She rushed toward Sarah with it, and

Sarah dodged out of the way. Lizzie came at her again, catching a lock of Sarah's hair and pulling her hair loose.

"Stop! I have no fight with you! I haven't seen Josiah in years!"

"Ha! You're lying. I saw you looking at him Saturday when we were in the boat, and he looked at you too."

"But…"

Lizzie swung the poker, knocking over a vase on the mantle. Pieces of china flew in all directions, and Sarah shielded her face with her hands.

Sarah saw her chance to escape and ran to the open door. Lizzie ran after her, poker held aloft. How could she stop this demented woman?

She glanced at the barrels outside the door and knocked them over, pushing them into the office and tripping Lizzie as it rolled toward the fireplace. Too late Sarah realized the danger and turned to run, just as the barrel exploded, knocking her down outside the office door. The last thing she saw were flames.

~~~

Josiah heard the explosion and jerked around to see flames coming out of the Turner building. Was Mr. Turner inside? He ran toward the building as others picked up the cry and ran after him. The door handle was hot when he tried to grab it, but he whipped out his handkerchief and pulled it open, releasing a blast of acrid smoke.

"Mr. Turner!" he yelled, holding the handkerchief over his nose as he entered the burning building. He could just make out the form of a person lying on the floor. Pulse pounding in his ears, he rushed over. Realized it was a woman, he scooped her up and carried her outside. His vision cleared and he saw who it was.

Sarah. His heart dropped. Was she alive? Was her father still inside?

He hurried to carry her a safe distance from the building and spotted Mr. Turner coming toward him. "Sir, you're safe! I was afraid you were inside."

Turner's eyes were fixed on his daughter. "What happened? Is she alive?"
~~~

"I don't know sir. I was coming to see you when something inside exploded. I thought you were inside and ran to get you out but found her on the floor inside the door."

"Dear God." Turner's eyes filled with tears. "Let's get her home."

~~~

Someone was wiping her face with a wet cloth. Sarah coughed, a nasty taste in her throat.

"Sarah. I'm here, Sarah."

Her eyes fluttered open at the familiar voice. "Josiah?" she muttered.

"Yes, Sarah, it's me."

"You're here?"

He was sitting beside the bed, holding her hand between his. Was this a dream? No, a nightmare. A crazed woman was trying to kill her.

She focused on his face. The sky blue eyes looked at her with such intensity, it radiated through her body. He gently rubbed the back of her hand with his thumb.

A tear ran down her face. "I thought you forgot me."

He shook his head. "Never. How could I forget the woman I love?"

"But…I never heard from you again."

"I tried, Sarah. I wrote you letters for a year, but you must not have gotten them."

Behind him, Mother and Father stood, watching. Mother held a handkerchief to her eyes. Sarah's mind began to clear, and she remembered. "There was a woman. Said her name was Lizzie and she was your betrothed. She tried to kill me to keep me away from you."

Josiah shook his head. "I'm so sorry. I was never betrothed to her. She was confused, and I'm afraid not sane."

"What happened to her?"

"She perished in the fire, unfortunately."

"Oh dear. It was my fault."

His eyebrows raised. "How could it have been your fault?"

"When she came at me with the fire poker, I shoved the
~~~

turpentine barrels at her to keep her away, and I guess they exploded."

"Shhh. It wasn't your fault. You were only defending yourself. She might have killed you."

"Can I see Sissie?" A little voice came from across the room.

Sarah tried to lift her head. "Anna Grace, come here."

Anna Grace ran to her side and reached across to hug her. "Are you going to die, Sarah?"

Sarah patted her little sister on the back. "No, Anna Grace. I'm fine." She glanced at Josiah who looked at the little girl. "I want you to meet a very special friend. This is Josiah. Josiah, this is my little sister, Anna Grace."

His eyes brightened and his smile spread. "It's very nice to meet you, Anna Grace."

Chapter Thirty-One

Josiah walked up the steps with a bouquet of flowers and handed them to Sarah, bending over to kiss her. “How’s my love?”

“Ready to get out of this chair.” She threw aside the quilt that had been over her lap in the rocking chair. “Can we go for a stroll?”

“Are you sure you feel well enough?”

She placed her hands on her hips. “I’m very sure.” She took his extended hand. “I’m not an invalid.”

He smiled and led her down to the yard where they walked over to the shore. She tucked her hands around his elbow, and they strolled the edge of the bay.

“Rafe Nettles, the man we’ve been holding, confessed everything.”

“Everything? He’s the one you suspected of stealing the lighthouse lens, isn’t he?”

“Yes, but he confessed to more. Apparently, Lizzie had roped him into doing things for her, like setting fires at lumber yards.”

“Why would she do that?”

“She wanted to keep me here, and in her convoluted thinking, believed the fires would delay my ability to secure the lumber for my assignments. Sad thing is, she did delay it. But what she didn’t intend was for me to end up with your father’s company as my last resort.”

“So when her accomplice was put in prison, she had to take matters in her own hands.”

“Yes, and I’m sure she would’ve set fire to your father’s office too, but she wanted to get rid of you herself first."

"Poor demented soul."

"Yes, it's a shame. And her father admitted she had a habit of setting fires, so he was suspicious right away. He just didn't know how she could go so far away to set the fires."

"And she didn't. Her friend did." Sarah paused to watch a string of pelicans soar over the bay. "But why did he do it? What was his incentive?"

"I'm not sure what kind of favors she promised him, but he said she expected to be rich once she married me and would pay him for his deeds."

"And to think I suspected Eben, Father's manager, of setting the fires. But his timely and mysterious disappearances were very questionable, especially since all the other lumber mills had fires and ours didn't."

"Did you ever find out where he'd been going?"

"Yes, a friend of one of the employees followed him. He'd been going to check on his mother. She's elderly and lives by herself about two hours away. He checked on her several times a week, so he'd work half a day, then leave to go see about her."

"That's commendable. But why didn't he want anyone to know?"

"He admitted to Father that he was afraid he'd be reprimanded for taking so much time away from his job for such personal affairs."

They'd walked to a place in the shore where a creek ran into the bay. "I guess we better turn back. Your parents will think I've stolen you."

"Would you like to?" She studied his strong chin with its special cleft.

"Absolutely. But now that I've gotten back on your father's good side, I don't want to mess it up again."

When they returned to the house, Mother and Father were standing on the porch waiting for them. "Are we in trouble?" Josiah said.

"I hope not, but stay by me, no matter what they say." She wasn't about to let him get away again.

"I intend to. Always."

They climbed the steps and Father said, "Y'all have a seat.

Virginia and I need to speak to the two of you."

Sarah and Josiah complied, sitting side by side in two of the rocking chairs. Mother and Father remained standing, facing them. Mother held something behind her back.

Father began. "I owe you both an apology. Josiah, you're a fine man, and I've seen what fine moral character you have in our business dealings. I'm still not happy about our differences in the war, but a man must follow his conscience."

Josiah nodded. "Thank you, sir."

"And Sarah, I underestimated your ability and I shouldn't have. You have a keen sense for numbers, and you should be allowed to use it. You have been a great help to me. Since Eben has proven how inefficient he is with figures, I'll need your help even more, unless you have other plans." He winked at her, then glanced at Mother, whose eyes were cast down as if she were embarrassed to look at them.

"Virginia, go ahead and tell them."

She pulled a pack of unopened letters tied with a ribbon from behind her pack. "Sarah, Josiah told you the truth. He did write you. But I knew Father's wishes to end your courtship, so I never told you about them, nor did I give them to you. But I just couldn't throw them away and thought some day many years from now, I'd give them to you so you could read them." She looked up at Sarah, eyes filled with tears. "I'm so sorry, Sarah. I know I betrayed you. I hope someday you can find it in your heart to forgive me."

Sarah's mouth was agape. How could Mother have done this, knowing how much she yearned to hear from Josiah? Yet, she knew in her heart that Mother had to stand with Father, even though she didn't want to. She reached for the letters and placed them in her lap, her eyes moist.

Josiah reached over and squeezed her hand. Then he stood, facing her parents. "Sir, I humbly request permission to marry your daughter."

Father and Mother exchanged glances, then Father spoke. "Permission granted."

Sarah had almost given up hope that she'd ever find love again. But true love waited, like a tiny ember waiting to be rekindled.

The End

Don't miss the other three books in the series:
Rebel Light
Revealing Light
Redeeming Light

About the Story

In a city as old as Pensacola, with history that goes back to the original landowners—the Pensacola tribe of Native Americans—pinpointing what happened in a specific year can be difficult. From the Spanish explorers who first recorded the name in 1677, through British control, then American possession, the city is rich in history, but documents are rare.

Of course, the biggest event that happened in Pensacola was the battle between the Confederates at Fort Barrancas and the Union-controlled Fort Pickens, on an island just across the bay. However, the city fell under Union control in 1862 when the Confederates left town to fight elsewhere. Florida was one of the first states to secede from the United States in 1861, but it was also one of the first states to be reinstated. However, the state governor requested that Union occupying troops during Reconstruction remain longer than required to keep the peace.

Pensacola was also one of the first cities to recover from the war because its location on the Gulf of Mexico as a deep-water port gave it an advantage for commerce. Only a short time after the war ended, the lumber business was thriving, with millions of trees exported until the turn of the century.

The original first order lens of the Pensacola lighthouse was indeed removed by Confederates before the Union gained control and was hidden somewhere in the area. In 1869, the lens was recovered and returned to its rightful place in the lighthouse. Although the actual records of the recovery weren't available, Rekindled Light is a work of fiction that presents a possibility of how it might have happened and where the lens might have been, based on similar stories from history. At the same time of the lens return, the new keepers' house was built. Both the lighthouse and the keepers' house are now open for tours.

The lighthouse is on the property of Naval Air Station Pensacola, just down the road from Fort Barrancas, where

Lieutenant Josiah Hamilton of our story was based.

The Turners lost two young sons to yellow fever. Indeed, Pensacola was ravaged by several epidemics of the disease, thought to be airborne, so commonly known as the "vapors." Since the disease usually occurred in cities near water, common belief was that the ships arriving in the harbor might carry the disease, and if anyone onboard was sick, the ship was quarantined. In 1905, the disease was discovered to originate in mosquitoes and is not contagious. That year, the city of Pensacola drained its swamps, and the disease no longer appeared.

Marilyn Turk
Historical fiction flavored with suspense and romance
Marilyn Turk's roots are in the coastal South. Calling herself a "literary archaeologist," she loves to discover stories hidden in history. She is the author of two World War II novels, and the Coastal Lights Legacy series set in 1800s Florida—Rebel Light, Revealing Light, Redeeming Light, and Rekindled Light—featuring lighthouse settings. Marilyn's novella, The Wrong Survivor, is in the Great Lakes Lighthouse Brides collection. She also writes for the Daily Guideposts Devotions book.
Website: @http://pathwayheart.com
Email: marilynturkwriter@yahoo.com

Made in the USA
Monee, IL
20 January 2020